THE GRIM RIPPER

ALSO BY JEANNE GLIDEWELL

A Lexie Starr Mystery Series

Leave No Stone Unturned

The Extinguished Guest

Haunted

With This Ring

Just Ducky

Cozy Camping

Marriage and Mayhem

The Spirit of the Season

A Ripple Effect Cozy Mystery Series

A Rip Roaring Good Time

Rip Tide

Ripped To Shreds

Rip Your Heart Out

Ripped Apart

Ripped Off

No Big Rip

The Grim Ripper

Rip Chord

Soul Survivor

THE GRIM RIPPER

A RIPPLE EFFECT COZY MYSTERY
BOOK 8

JEANNE GLIDEWELL

ePublishingWorks!
love what you read.

Book and cover design by eBook Prep
www.ebookprep.com

May 2023
ISBN: 978-1-64457-322-8

ePublishing Works!
644 Shrewsbury Commons Ave
Ste 249
Shrewsbury PA 17361
United States of America
www.epublishingworks.com
Phone: 866-846-5123

FROM THE DESK OF JEANNE GLIDEWELL

Dear Reader,

I'll be the first to admit the storyline of The Grim Ripper is a bit far-fetched. But then, the entire premise of the cozy mystery genre is inherently implausible. They are designed to be fast-paced, neither gory nor graphic, light-hearted, and humorous at times. They are not meant to be edge-of-your-seat gripping, factual accounts of a true-life homicide investigation. When an owner of a pastry shop, the president of the local quilters club, or a Siamese cat owned by the storyteller is solving murder cases right and left, there is automatically a sense of incredulity built right into the story. If you feel propelled to fact-check every aspect of this tale, you'll find a little truth mixed in with liberal amounts of imagination, exaggeration, and downright fabrication. My stories are meant to be entertaining. There's certainly not much in them you'd want to pass on as factual information because, trust me, there are people out there who will feel obligated to fact-check anything or everything you say.

I hope you enjoy this story, as believable or unbelievable as you may find it. Remember, it was written for readers to while away a day on the beach, a long flight, or a rainy afternoon. If you find The Grim Ripper entertaining, please tell a friend and post a review on Amazon, Barnes & Noble, GoodReads, etc. If not, please email me through my publisher, and I will personally refund you the cost of the book. In other words, satisfaction is guaranteed or your money back.

Happy reading,

Jeanne Glidewell

Dedicated to my many friends who are currently working in the medical field and to those readers also employed in this most honorable profession. I would be dead several times over if not for the remarkable skills, compassion, and dedication of a fantastic team of professionals including, but not limited to, physicians, nurses, technicians, radiologists, anesthesiologists, pathologists, surgeons, ambulance drivers, EMTs, and phlebotomists. I owe the last seventeen years of my life to a transplant surgeon with "magical hands," as the anesthesiologist during that surgery described Dr. Murillo, and a twelve-year-old organ donor and his family. It's a debt I'll never be able to repay. But I can honor them in small ways like this and will continue to be grateful for the rest of my time on Earth.

ACKNOWLEDGMENTS

I would like to thank my editor, Hannah Phillips, for her exceptional editing skills, and my proofreaders, Sarah Goodman, of Olathe, Kansas, Sheila Davis of Fairway, Kansas, and Cindy Travis, of Mission, Kansas, for their much-appreciated advice, time and efforts. I am forever indebted to these remarkable ladies.

I'd also like to thank Brian Paules, Anna Paules, and the rest of the eBook Prep and ePublishing Works team. They have been supportive, patient, professional and encouraging while allowing me to be me, and for that I am eternally grateful.

CHARACTER LIST

Rapella Ripple——Rapella is a seventy-two-year-old full-time RVer who has a bad habit of sticking her nose where it doesn't belong. Her impulsiveness often puts her own life at risk, but she's determined to bring justice for murder victims, whom she has an uncanny habit of coming across in her travels around the country.

Clyde "Rip" Ripple——Rip, also seventy-two, is Rapella's patient husband and finds himself a patient at the STAT Cardiac Clinic where he has a cardiac stent implanted. When his surgeon dies suddenly just after the procedure, he feels compelled to help Rapella investigate Dr. Moretti's suspicious death.

Dr. Marco Moretti——Dr. Moretti is a cardiac surgeon and is found unresponsive in the clinic's parking lot immediately after performing the stent placement procedure on Rip Ripple. His death was unexpected and a shock to his colleagues.

Frankie Moretti——Frankie is Dr. Marco Moretti's new wife who's floored by her husband's sudden death. She was oblivious to Marco's philandering.

Pratyush Patel——Patel is a cardiovascular technologist at the cath lab and he's stunned by the sudden death of his friend and mentor. He's the one who informs the Ripples of the surgeon's demise.

Dr. Mitch Murphy——Dr. Murphy is an anesthesiologist at the lab and has just begun dating the cardiac ward floor nurse, Maggie Brown. He was the anesthesiologist during Rip's procedure and one of the last people to see Dr. Moretti alive.

Jolene Sarcoxie——A brunette-haired, blue-eyed registered nurse, or RN, Jolene had just recently become Dr. Moretti's operating room nurse, replacing Candace Kobialka, who is bitter about the demotion she doesn't feel she deserved.

Dr. Kellan "Blaze" O'Ryan, a.k.a. Kelly——Dr. O'Ryan is a red-headed Irish cardiologist who takes over as Rip's personal physician after Dr. Moretti's death. O'Ryan was second in line for the director position that was filled, and now vacated by, Dr. Moretti.

Olivia O'Ryan——Olivia is Dr. O'Ryan's wife of fifteen years. The two are expecting a son to join their family in three months, a welcome addition to their current brood of twin daughters.

Candace Kobialka——Candace is a slim, statuesque cardiac ward floor nurse who had dated the victim before he married Frankie. She had a hard time accepting the fact Dr. Moretti dumped her for another woman in his private life and swapped her for another operating room nurse in his professional life.

Maggie Brown——Maggie is a cardiac care floor nurse who had recently begun dating Dr. Murphy, the anesthesiologist. She and Rapella form a close bond following Rip's stay in the ward as her post-operative patient.

Charmaine Boyd——Charmaine is a forensic nurse who is able to obtain a portion of the autopsy report due to her position in the medical examiner's office.

Monica Corry——Monica is Dr. O'Ryan's office nurse at STAT Cardiac Clinic. She and Charmaine look as if they could be sisters, with their blonde hair and hazel eyes.

Eva Clemens——Eva is Dr. O'Ryan's operating room nurse. She's the oldest nurse at the STAT Cardiac Clinic and had worked there since the lab first opened its doors.

Henrietta Stringer——Henrietta is an older white-haired volunteer who decided to donate her time and efforts to the STAT Cardiac Clinic after her husband had a pacemaker insertion surgery there.

ONE

I was putting three skinless, boneless chicken thighs in the oven when I looked out the window and saw my husband, Clyde Ripple, better known as Rip. He was slashing at the ground with a handheld weed whacker that resembled a small scythe. He looked like a man possessed. We'd sold off nearly everything we owned over a decade ago to become full-time RVers. I'd asked him then why he was packing the lawn tool in one of the undercarriage compartments of our thirty-foot travel trailer to haul around the country. Part of the reasoning behind our decision to become full-time RVers was not having a yard to maintain. He'd replied, "It just seems like something that might come in handy someday on our travels." Ten years later, it appeared to have finally come in handy. Rip was using it to assault a figment of his imagination.

I opened up the trailer door and asked, "What in the world are you doing, Rip?"

"I was getting ready to light the grill so I could charbroil the corn on the cob and zucchini when I noticed a snake right by my foot."

Visions of my husband being bit by a timber rattler flitted through my mind. We were in Rochester, Minnesota, for a visit to the Mayo Clinic and I knew the venomous snakes could be found in the southeastern region of the state. I must have thought the snake was about to burst into flames because I grabbed the fire extinguisher we carried in the RV and rushed outside.

"Where is it?" I shouted, glancing around frantically. "I can't see it."

Rip used the sharp tip of the weed whacker to move some grass out of the way and expose what looked like pieces of a gooey jigsaw puzzle. From growing up in a rural area of south Texas, I recognized the mutilated mess as a common garter snake.

"That poor little thing couldn't have harmed you if it tried, Rip," I said.

"I know *that's* right!" Rip sounded inordinately proud of the bravery, skill, and brute strength it took to maim a pencil-thin, harmless snake, no more than eighteen inches long. "You know what they say, don't you, Rapella? The only good snake is——"

"——a dead snake," I finished his sentence while rolling my eyes at him.

"Yes." Rip nodded. "A dead one that is diced into a hundred pieces so there's no chance of it coming back to life is even better."

Rip was wearing an old black and gray L.A. Raiders jersey and black sweatpants. Covering his nearly bald head was a dark blue ball cap. I studied him as he stood over the mangled snake with a scythe in one hand and a bottle of lighter fluid in the other. Sarcastically, I asked, "Well, aren't you the Grim Ripper?"

I laughed, but Rip just looked at me as if I'd suddenly begun speaking in Mandarin Chinese. Rather than bothering to explain my quip, I shook my head and turned my back to him. As I walked toward the trailer, I said, "The chicken will be ready at six."

We sat at the RV's booth-styled table forty-five minutes later, dining on heart-healthy baked chicken, corn on the cob, grilled squash, and unsweetened ice tea. As I refilled our glasses, we discussed Rip's upcoming cardiac appointment at the Mayo Clinic. Several years ago Rip had experienced a "cardiac event" similar to a mild heart attack while we were on an Alaskan cruise, which resulted in him having a triple bypass in Seattle, Washington. Dr. Murillo, the cardiac surgeon who performed the operation, saved Rip's life. It was not an occasion we ever wanted to repeat.

A week ago we were visiting my brother Billy in Mora, Minnesota, when Rip suddenly experienced chest pains very similar to the ones he'd had on the cruise ship. A Mora ambulance had transported Rip to the Welia Health Center, where it was determined he needed an angioplasty procedure to widen the obstructed artery. That diagnosis forced us to cut our visit with Billy short, pack up our travel trailer, and head to an RV park near the Mayo Clinic, which was only two and a half hours from Mora.

Rip was put through a battery of cardio tests: nuclear stress test, electrocardiogram, coronary angiogram, and a MRI of his heart. Finally, they hooked him up to a Holter device for twenty-four hours to remotely monitor his cardiac health. The doctor described the Holter as "an ambulatory electrocardiography device." Rip described it as "an uncomfortable pain in the ass."

After all of the testing was complete, the team of cardiologists at the Mayo Clinic referred Rip to an independent cardiac catheterization lab, commonly referred to as a cath lab, called STAT Cardio Clinic. The STAT Clinic was only seven blocks from the Mayo Clinic campus, and even closer to the RV park we were staying in for a month. An appointment was made for Rip, and a week later a stent would be surgically inserted into an aortic artery.

We were feeling at ease and convinced that the procedure would be a success. The stent placement procedure he required now seemed like a minimally invasive surgery in comparison to the triple bypass he'd had in Seattle.

Little did we know at the time that Rip's cardiac surgeon would suffer an untimely and highly suspicious demise in the parking lot of the clinic immediately following Rip's operation. When the police department ruled the physician's passing as death by natural causes, Rip was skeptical. As the retired sheriff of Aransas County, Texas, his gut told him the circumstances demanded further investigation.

In my wildest dreams, I could never have imagined the day would come when my husband, not me, would insist we stick our noses where they don't belong to uncover the truth behind a possible murder.

———

"I hope Billy wasn't upset we had to leave so suddenly," Rip said, between bites of the grilled squash spears. Billy's husband Bryce had picked the zucchini out of their garden in the newly added solar-vented greenhouse they'd built on the south side of their brick home. Along with the squash, he'd loaded us up with cucumbers, tomatoes, green peppers, sweet corn, and radishes before we'd headed out, all from their first winter crop in the greenhouse. It'd been a labor of love for both men.

"I'm sure both Billy and Bryce understood the importance of getting your cardiac procedure taken care of as soon as possible," I said to Rip, who nodded without looking up from his plate. "After all, Bryce was a registered nurse at Welia Health Center for thirty years before he retired a few years back. Besides, even though neither man would ever say so out loud, I'm sure we were starting to smell like ahi tuna that'd been lying on the back porch for the entire ten days we were in Mora."

"Yeah, you're probably right. I was wondering if we weren't

overstaying our welcome when Bryce said he was heading out to the garden to pick a basketful of produce for us to take with us when we left. 'Soon' seemed to be the unspoken word at the end of that sentence." Rip laughed at his recollection. "And speaking of 'soon,' those last two tomatoes he gave us need to be eaten in the near future. How about making BLTs for lunch tomorrow?"

"Fine," I began, "if you'll settle for BTs. Bryce said the lettuce in their greenhouse was done for the season. I do have a pack of bacon in the freezer though that I picked up at the Smokey Mountain Market and Sundries store in Gatlinburg before we left Tennessee."

"Actually, a BT sounds even better!" Rip had replied around a mouthful of chicken. "I never could see any value of adding lettuce to a perfectly good bacon and tomato sandwich. Lettuce is also like adding blades of grass to a juicy hamburger."

"Hence the reason behind your upcoming stent procedure."

When Rip failed to rise to the bait I had dangled so invitingly in front of him, I decided there was nothing to be gained by goading him to eat better. There was no sense in arguing about something that was already in our rear-view mirror. "Visiting the Great Smokey Mountains National Park was fun, wasn't it?" I asked instead of pursuing the "healthy eating" conversation. "I'm glad you thought of going there. It had been on my bucket list a long time."

"Yes. I enjoyed it too. However, I didn't enjoy the several times while in those mountains I felt my chest tighten up as though I was being crushed between a giant rock and a Mack truck."

"What?" I exclaimed, aghast at his remark. I'm sure I resembled Popeye with my eyes practically bulging out of their sockets. My mouth was hanging open, as well. "Why didn't you ever mention those episodes to me? I would've canceled the visit to Minnesota and flown you straight to Seattle to see Dr. Murillo."

"That's exactly why I didn't tell you. I figured the pressure I was feeling was due to the high elevation and nothing to be concerned about. Besides, I didn't want you to cancel our visit with Billy and Bryce. I knew how much you wanted to spend some time with your baby brother."

"Of course I wanted to see Billy. And Bryce, too," I admitted. "But I didn't want to see them so badly that the visit couldn't have waited until after you'd been evaluated by Dr. Murillo. We could've easily rescheduled the trip to Minnesota for afterward. Putting the visit off would've been the smartest decision we could've made. Why would you risk your life like that, honey?"

"I was just thinking about you and didn't want to disappoint you."

"Damn it, Rip!" My anger was spilling over like a cup of coffee left too long in the microwave. Even though I knew Rip had not shared his cardiac scares with me out of love and compassion, I wanted to slap the cob of corn, also grown by Bryce, right out of his hands. Even though he was, at best, two feet away from me, I nearly shouted at Rip. "Don't you know how much I need you, Rip? How lost I'd be without you? I do appreciate how thoughtful it was of you to be thinking about me and not wanting me to be disappointed, but——"

"You're wel——"

Just as he'd interrupted me, I cut Rip off before he could continue and was adamant with my commands. "Don't *ever* think about me again! From now on, I *want* to be disappointed! In fact, I insist on you disappointing me!"

Rip cocked an eye at me. "No problem, my dear. Disappointing women *is* what I do best."

"Smart ass," I responded with a brief chuckle. "I know that came out wrong, but you know what I meant."

"I do," he relented. "And I'm sorry. I promise it won't happen again."

I wasn't convinced it wouldn't happen again, but at least I'd made my point clear. Rip would be livid if I felt ill and didn't tell him about it. His own reluctance to tell me about the chest tightness he'd experienced on several occasions while in Tennessee could have proven to be a fatal error in judgment. I never wanted my husband to die on account of not wanting me to have to reschedule my plans. After all, one of the advantages of being full-time RVers was that we could travel anywhere in North America we wanted to, whenever we wanted to, and didn't have to be beholden to anyone.

Since leaving our hometown of Rockport, Texas, behind, a year after Rip had retired as the sheriff of Aransas County, we'd been traveling the world in the "Chartreuse Caboose." It was the nickname I'd given our travel trailer after painting it that color, along with a few sunflowers for added zest. Our daughter Regina referred to our RV as an "eyesore," and it took a few years for Rip to get past his humiliation at being seen towing the bright trailer down the highway. He'd once remarked, "At least your paint job has made us much safer on the road." When I'd asked for clarification, he'd explained, "The trailer is so *loud* now that other drivers ought to be able to see *and hear* us coming from a mile away."

Currently, as I gathered up the dinner plates to wash in the undersized kitchen sink, I thanked my lucky stars that Rip's reluctance to tell me about his chest pains while in the Smokey Mountains had not ended in tragedy. We had paid for a month's stay at the Autumn Woods RV Park, a nice resort in Rochester within minutes of the Mayo Clinic and STAT cath lab. They had laundry facilities, good-sized full hookup pull-thru sites, and internet service. As nice as the park was, I hoped a month would be all the time required to stay there.

We had plans to head to California once Rip was cleared to travel by the cardiology team at the clinic. Seeing the giant trees in the Redwood National Forest was another item on my bucket list I was anxious to cross off, and I prayed Rip was up for the adventure by the time our rent was due again.

"Are you ready for your procedure?" I asked Rip as we pulled into the parking lot of the STAT Cardiac Clinic two days later. It was twelve-fifteen in the afternoon and his angioplasty was scheduled for one-thirty. Dr. Marco Moretti, the surgeon performing Rip's procedure, had told him he'd be his last patient of the day. When Rip ignored my question, I asked it again. "Are you ready for this?"

"Do I have a choice?"

"No."

"Then I guess I'm ready." Rip sounded as though he'd rather be bungee jumping off the Royal Gorge Bridge in Cañon City, Colorado, than having the cardiac procedure to widen a blocked artery to his heart with a balloon. "Can we stop at McDonald's afterward? Knowing there's a Big Mac in my future will help tremendously."

"Big Macs are probably part of the reason for your procedure today, Rip. I don't want to burst your bubble, but I'm afraid your lunch will more likely consist of Jell-O and a bowl of beef broth."

"What?" Rip exclaimed. "Have you no mercy?"

"Don't blame me," I said. "It's your surgeon who will determine your menu while you're here."

"Has Dr. Moretti no mercy?" His rhetorical question was followed by a dramatic groan.

"Sorry, honey, but you know the doctor told you they'd be keeping you overnight so they can monitor you for complications. That's why I packed you an overnight bag. If all goes well, you will be released tomorrow."

"Oh, God, just kill me now." Rip groaned again, even louder this time.

I wouldn't go so far as to say Rip's remark was prophetic, but someone did die that day. Fortunately, it wasn't my husband.

TWO

"Do I have a choice?" Rip repeated when Dr. Marco Moretti asked him the same question I had just asked him in the parking lot.

"Of course you do," the cardiac surgeon responded. "It is totally your decision on whether or not you like living or would rather your artery clog up like a toilet in a cheap rental house, stopping your heart mid-beat. Personally, I'd choose living. Life has been good to me and I'd like to keep enjoying it for as long as humanly possible."

"Well, when you put it like that," Rip mumbled. He had the decency to look ashamed at his attempt at levity. Dr. Moretti clearly did not think of cardiac health as a laughing matter. And neither did I, for that matter.

Just then, an incredibly handsome young man in blue scrubs walked into Rip's room. He was about my height of five-foot-eight. Stitched into the fabric of his top was "Dr. Mitch Murphy, Anesthesiologist."

"Howdy folks!" He said in greeting. He nodded at me and turned to Rip. "So you must be Clyde Ripple."

"Yes," Rip replied. "But please call me Rip."

Even though Clyde was Rip's given name, he preferred to be called by the nickname he'd been given as a young boy. The name Clyde reminded him of the cranky grandfather he'd been named for who hadn't given him the time of day when Rip was a child.

"All right," the anesthesiologist said. "Rip, I'm going to be assisting Dr. Moretti today in your procedure. We're going to be giving you general anesthesia because of the delicate nature of this stent placement."

"Is this a risky procedure?" I asked, alarmed by his description of Rip's procedure as being of a delicate nature.

"Well, it could be." Dr. Moretti answered my query in lieu of Dr. Murphy. "Stent placement is not inherently dangerous, but this stent is to be placed in an artery right next to the heart. I don't want Rip moving while I'm placing it. There's very little room for error, I'm afraid."

"I see." I didn't see anything but an image of me as a grieving widow flash before my eyes. I *did* look remarkably trim and fashionable dressed in all black, but still…

Dr. Murphy obviously sensed my uneasiness. He stared directly into my eyes as he tried to comfort me. "Mrs. Ripple, I can assure you that you couldn't be in any better hands. Dr. Moretti was just promoted. He now leads the entire cardiology department here at the clinic, and he didn't receive that honor for no reason. He's the absolute best when it comes to cardiac health and surgery. He's like the human version of *Drano*. If Dr. Moretti can't unclog your husband's artery, nobody can."

"Thank you." I was feeling totally positive until his last remark, but realized our only option at this stage was to put our trust in Dr. Moretti and his surgical team's hands. And at the same time, we'd continue to put our faith in God's hands, as well.

"I'll be fine, sweetheart," Rip told me softly before turning his attention to the surgeon. "Can you tell me what is involved in this procedure?"

The surgeon then looked directly at Rip as he explained what he was going to do. "I'm going to make a small slit in your left wrist and thread a catheter through the blood vessel all the way up to the heart until it reaches the restricted area."

"Why are you going through the wrist and not the groin?" I asked, recalling my cousin Larry having had a stent placed via the groin area about ten years ago. Rip turned to look at me as though I'd just asked the doctor to hack off his nuts with a machete.

"I'm just curious," I told my anxious husband. "I wasn't actually suggesting he go in through your groin."

Dr. Moretti chuckled and winked at Rip. He then concentrated on me. "Using the wrist instead of the groin reduces the recovery time, Mrs. Ripple. It's much easier on the patient. Trust me, Rip will be back in the saddle much quicker this way."

I wasn't sure what the doctor meant by "back in the saddle", but if it meant what I thought it meant, I should've recommended this procedure a long time ago. I must've had a dreamy expression on my face because the surgeon asked, "Mrs. Ripple? Did you hear me?"

"Oh, yes. I heard you." No doubt my face was now crimson from the blood rushing to it. "So, what happens after the catheter reaches the restricted area?"

"A small balloon at the tip of the catheter inflates and deploys a tiny, mesh metal tube. This stent holds the artery open, restoring blood flow to the heart. This particular artery is currently ninety-five percent blocked. Without a stent it would soon be totally occluded, known as chronic total occlusion, or CTO, at which point placing a stent can be quite challenging. It's a fortunate thing we caught it before it reached that stage."

"I guess the chest pain he was experiencing was an auspicious warning," I said.

The cardiologist nodded, and stepped aside as Dr. Murphy stepped forward to address his involvement in the procedure. "Okay, Rip. In a few minutes, a certified registered nurse named Jolene Sarcoxie will come in and put an IV in your right arm from which the intravenous medications will be infused. I will then insert a breathing tube in your throat once you are out and then monitor your vital functions and manage your breathing throughout the procedure. With Dr. Moretti as your surgeon, Jolene Sarcoxie as the operating room nurse, and me as your anesthesiologist, you will be in very capable hands. Do you have any questions?"

Rip shook his head so slightly it seemed more of a twitch than a negative response. I don't know if either doctor was aware, but I knew my husband well enough to know he was still musing about being back in the saddle soon and hadn't taken in a single word the cardiologist or anesthesiologist had said since. When Rip failed to give a satisfactory answer, I said, "No, we both understand exactly what this procedure involves and how general anesthesia works."

I suppose I shouldn't have automatically spoken for my husband as many wives are in the habit of doing, because he did have another question. I'm sure I blushed again when he asked, "So, Doc, are you saying that after this procedure I won't need those little blue pills any longer?"

Both physicians laughed, and Dr. Moretti replied, "I wish I could promise you that, Rip, but I can't. You're fortunate though. Before 1998, there was no magic cure for erectile dysfunction."

Now my husband was blushing. ED was a very personal issue that Rip, like most men, didn't want to openly discuss as though it was nothing more than an ingrown toenail. Thankfully, a pretty brunette with shockingly blue eyes walked through the door of Rip's private room just then and introduced herself as Jolene, the operating room nurse. Rip and I greeted her before Rip said, "Guess I'm ready to go whenever you are, Doc."

"Okie-dokie, Rip." Dr. Moretti nodded. "Give your wife a kiss and let's get this show on the road."

I kissed Rip on the lips and whispered, "Good luck, honey. I'll be right here beside you when you wake up."

"You better be, sweetheart, or I don't even *want* to wake up."

His loving remark warmed my heart. It also made it skip a beat. I was glad I wasn't hooked up to one of the clinic's EKG monitors. I truly would be lost without my husband of nearly fifty-two years. I said a quick prayer as I walked back to the waiting room.

I was wearing out the tile, pacing in circles around the small waiting room. I was the only person in the room so I could've selected any channel on the wall-mounted television that I pleased. I was so engrossed in my thoughts I barely noticed the show that was airing. A man and woman, both naked, appeared to be running amok in the woods with their private parts blurred out. The pair looked like they were about to freeze solid. The G-rated nudity failed to pique my interest. I did, however, momentarily wonder if there was a reasonably sane point to the show.

The surgeon had told me the procedure shouldn't take much longer than an hour. As the clock slowly ticked closer and closer to the two-hour mark, I became increasingly agitated. When Dr. Moretti walked into the waiting room a few minutes later and gave me a thumbs-up gesture, a tear escaped my eye and rolled down my cheek. I took the first full breath I'd taken since I'd kissed Rip before he was wheeled back to the operating room.

The surgeon seemed to be short of breath and more lethargic than he'd been when I'd seen him a couple of hours earlier. He actually stumbled slightly as he approached me. I prayed it wasn't a sign of him having just performed a stressful operation on my husband. "Are you all right, Dr. Moretti?"

"Yes, just a bit tired and nauseated all of a sudden as if something I ate didn't sit right with me. I'm sure it's nothing and I'll be back to normal shortly."

"I hope so. I'm sorry you're having an upset stomach. And Rip? Did his procedure go well?"

"Everything went as expected, Mrs. Ripple. You'll be able to see Rip in the recovery room shortly. Once he's fully awake, he'll be moved to a private room on the second floor so we can monitor him overnight. At this point, it looks as though he'll be ready to be released tomorrow, barring any unexpected complications: bleeding, heart attack, stroke, or death. All are extremely rare."

I thanked the doctor profusely even though I found his assurances anything but reassuring. I'd have been much happier not knowing about the unexpected complications, no matter how low the odds of any of them occurring. Ignorance is indeed bliss at moments like this. I knew he sensed my trepidation when he smiled and said, "No worries, Ma'am. Rip's going to be just fine."

As I thanked him one more time, the doctor's face appeared flush and he wiped his forehead with the back of his hand as if he'd broken out in a sweat. I found it odd because, like any medical facility, it was cold enough in the building to store a recently butchered hog. I was concerned, but told myself that the surgeon had just confessed he was a bit fatigued and having a bit of a tummy ache. *He doesn't seem too concerned about it so I shouldn't either*, I told myself. Dr. Moretti looked to be in his early forties and extremely fit. He'd mentioned running marathons and being a vegetarian at Rip's first visit with him. *Perhaps he's been working harder than usual and the extra workload is beginning to wear him down.*

I was awash with relief that the surgeon had affirmed Rip was going to be just fine. Looking back, I wish I could've assured Dr.

Moretti he was going to be just fine too. If I had, however, I would've been dead wrong.

After Dr. Moretti exited the waiting room, I commenced pacing again. I was still on edge and too anxious to sit and watch a couple of naked adults trying to survive an entirely unnecessary ordeal on the boob tube, which in this case was a very fitting term for the television.

I spent five minutes with Rip in the recovery room but he was so out of it he didn't even know I was there. The room was crowded and busy and I didn't want to be in the way, so I went back to the waiting room. Fortunately, it only took an additional forty-five minutes for Rip to be moved into a private room in the post-surgery observation ward on the second floor of the facility. He was still groggy when I walked into his room. "How do you feel, honey?"

"Why would I want a banana peel or honey?" He asked in reply. "Maybe I'll have a piece of pizza later. Okay?"

I just nodded, knowing full well pizza was not likely to show up on his supper tray. He'd clearly misheard my query. He never wore his expensive hearing aids and it didn't help that his brain was still a bit like mashed potatoes from the effects of the anesthesia he'd been given.

I pulled a chair up to his bed and clasped his hand. "Just rest, dear, and I'll be right here if you need anything."

Twice I adjusted his pillow and once, at his request, I scanned through the TV channels until I found a station airing a *Bonanza* marathon. He promptly fell back to sleep and I was forced to watch an episode of the old western series rather than a show I actually enjoyed. I knew if he awakened to an old *Golden Girls* rerun, he'd immediately ask me to turn the channel back to *Bonanza*.

When he woke again an hour later, he complained about being hungry, I explained they probably didn't want him eating anything for a while. "I'm sure they'll bring you a dinner tray later on."

"They better," he grumbled. "Nothing's crossed my lips since ten o'clock last night."

A breathing tube's crossed your lips, I wanted to say, but instead, I asked, "How about some ice chips?"

"You're offering ice chips to a starving man?" Rip asked. "What kind of wife are you?"

The twinkle in his eyes and twitch of his lips let me know he was teasing me and the squeeze of my hand in his told me he loved me. I leaned over and kissed his forehead. "I'll give you some ice chips now, but promise you a juicy steak once you get home. **A** steak, mind you, as in one. After that we're going to have to return to a heart-healthy diet. I don't want you to have to go through this stent-placement procedure again and again."

"Again and again? I wasn't planning on making a habit of it."

"I know you weren't. But neither were you planning to go through the one you just went through. You were lucky that's *all* you had to have done. If not for a stroke of good fortune, you might've checked out on me while we were in the Smoky Mountains. And if not for another stroke of good fortune, you might actually have suffered a stroke. Do you recall how unpleasant the last six years of your Aunt Jackie's life were? I guarantee you, if she'd had her druthers, she would've chosen the first option of checking out when she'd first had the stroke."

"Point taken," Rip consented. "And you're right. Aunt Jackie actually told me she wished she was dead on several occasions. How about I forego the juicy steak and settle on a nicely grilled filet of sole?"

"That's my boy!" I said with a laugh. "I was just joking about the steak, to begin with."

"You, my dear, would make a pitiful comedian."

Just then a staff member we hadn't met before walked into Rip's room. His name tag read, "Pratyush Patel, Cardiovascular Technologist." He looked pale and on edge. His eyes were red and watery as though he'd been crying. His voice broke as he introduced himself. "I am here on Dr. Moretti's behalf."

"Where is Dr. Moretti?" I asked. "When will he be in to see my husband?"

"He won't be, I'm sorry to say."

"What do you mean by, 'I'm sorry to say,' Dr. Patel?"

"It's Mr. Patel, ma'am," he began before stopping to blow his nose. It sounded like the horns of two angry cab drivers vying for a parking spot. "I'm a medical professional, but not a doctor. And to answer your question, Dr. Moretti has…"

Patel, clearly emotional, stopped speaking and reached for his hankie again. I waited impatiently for him to finish honking his horn and compose himself. I then prompted him with, "Go ahead."

"I hate to have to tell you this, but Dr. Moretti passed away about twenty minutes ago. I had just finished my shift when Terrence Smith, the president of the board of directors, called to tell me the news and ask if I could cover for Marco. Marco was not only my boss and my mentor, he was also one of my closest friends. And now he's gone. I feel like I've lost a brother."

"Seriously?" Rip asked. The expression on his face was one of complete disbelief. He looked as though the cardiovascular technologist had placed a platter of barbecue ribs in front of him only to snatch it back up and sprint out of the room. I knew he didn't suspect Mr. Patel of lying to him, or trying to pull his leg, but he just couldn't wrap his head around the idea that the man who had likely just saved his life had lost his own shortly thereafter. "What in the world happened to him?"

"Ironically, it appears as if it was myocardial infarction."

When both Rip and I stared at Pratyush as though he'd

responded to Rip's question in his native language of Hindi, he explained. "Myocardial infarction is otherwise known as a heart attack. A nurse named Jolene Sarcoxie, who had worked beside Dr. Moretti during your procedure, Mr. Ripple, had just ended her shift when she found Dr. Moretti unresponsive in the clinic's parking lot. He was lying right next to his Mercedes. Jolene performed CPR on him until Dr. O'Ryan, another one of the four cardiologists at STAT, arrived on the scene. Blaze took a turn at performing CPR, but eventually had to pronounce Dr. Moretti dead. I suppose it's fortunate it happened before he got behind the wheel and out in traffic." Pratyush shook his head as if he were still in disbelief about the death of his friend and colleague.

"Did he have a pre-existing heart problem?" I asked.

"Not that anyone knew about," the cardiovascular technologist replied. "But all too often the first sign of a heart condition is a massive myocar——oh, I'm sorry——a fatal heart attack."

He must think we are mentally impaired, too freaking old to remember anything for more than ten seconds, or didn't catch his clarification the first time, I thought. We'd heard the term "myocardial infarction" several times before during Rip's previous medical appointments. If we looked dazed and confused to Pratyush Patel, it was just because we *were* dazed and confused about the news he'd just shared with us and we were having trouble accepting the fact Dr. Moretti was dead. Snuffed out like a candle in his prime, it seemed. A cardiologist dying of heart failure seemed dreadfully ironic to me. It was uncanny in the same way it'd be if Jennifer M. Granholm, the US Secretary of Energy, had her lights turned off for failing to pay her electric bill.

It became apparent to me that Rip was unconvinced a cardiac issue had befallen the cardiac surgeon when he said, "I can't believe this has happened! How can it be true? I find it difficult to believe Dr. Moretti just performed a successful procedure on me, only to die of a heart attack in the parking lot a short time later. The surgeon appeared to be the epitome of health."

"It's hard for me to believe too, Mr. Ripple," Mr. Patel responded. "But I can attest to the fact that performing a delicate stent placement like the one you just underwent can be stressful for the surgeon performing the procedure. And, as you know, stress can induce myocardial infarction. Appearances aren't always what they 'appear' to be, you know."

"Of course. But he was a cardio——"

"Trust me, Mr. Ripple," Mr. Patel said. "Even heart surgeons can have heart problems. Do dentists not have occasional cavities? Do psychiatrists never suffer from depression? Besides, what else could it have been?"

"A whole lot of things," I cut in as Rip nodded in agreement. Whether he was in agreement with me or the cardiovascular tech-nologist was unclear. "I just conversed with Dr. Moretti an hour ago and he seemed as fit as a fig tree. In fact, he was…"

I stopped suddenly, as I thought back and recalled being concerned for the man in the waiting room after the surgeon had seemed listless, slightly off-balance, and as though he'd experienced facial flushing due to a sudden hot flash. He'd claimed to be nauseous and had been sweating as though he'd just learned his fifteen-year-old mistress was expecting their child. Just assuring me that my husband's operation had gone smoothly had seemed to take more energy than Dr. Moretti had possessed. I'd chalked it up to a heavy workload. Now I wondered if something more serious had been at play.

"What is it, Rapella?" Rip asked.

"On second thought," I began, looking from Rip to Mr. Patel, and back again, "the doctor did seem to be affected by some kind of medical issue when he came to talk to me right after your surgery was over. In my excitement to see you after you were released from the recovery room, Rip, I'd forgotten about it."

I went on to elaborate on what I'd witnessed about Dr. Moretti to Rip and Pratyush Patel. Patel had assisted Dr. Moretti during Rip's procedure, along with Jolene Sarcoxie, the nurse who'd been the first to administer CPR on the late surgeon in the parking lot.

"That's odd. Marco seemed fine throughout the procedure, and afterward, when he left the operating room to get a bottle of water out of the doctors' lounge," Mr. Patel said. After a moment of deep thought, he added, "I'm sure an autopsy will be performed, though, and that should confirm the cause of death."

"Of course," Rip replied. "And I wouldn't be totally shocked if it proved Dr. Moretti's death wasn't due to myocardial infarction after all."

THREE

I sat with Rip while he picked at the food on his dinner tray. Surprisingly, he didn't complain about the lime Jell-O, beef broth, or orange sherbet. He drank the coffee and only two swallows of broth. He polished off the sherbet, and said, "It soothes my sore throat. I feel like someone scrubbed my tonsils with steel wool."

"You haven't had tonsils since you were six years old," I reminded him. "Your throat is sore due to the breathing tube the anesthesiologist put down your throat during surgery."

"I knew there was something about that Mick Morris I didn't like."

The doctor's name was actually Mitch Murphy. I was shocked Rip got as close as he did and decided not to rag him about his inability to remember names. I would've been less surprised if Rip had called the man John Smith. I knew Rip was trying to be funny so I laughed at his remark. "Next time tell the medical staff you've decided to pass on the anesthesia because you don't want to have to deal with a sore throat afterward."

"Good idea, dear. Remind me, won't you?"

"I'm hoping there's not a next time, Rip." I patted his shoulder and removed the dinner tray from his table. It was obvious he'd eaten all he planned to. "I'm praying the new medication Dr. Moretti prescribed for you, along with a stricter diet and the new exercise program he mentioned, will prevent you from having to have any more stents inserted. Do you think we'll have any trouble getting a prescription filled that was prescribed by a deceased doctor?"

Rip picked up his remote and switched the television channel to the evening news. He always maintained that he liked to be up-to-date on what was going on in the world. I had a tendency to think he just liked to have new and different things to grumble about, as there never seemed to be anything positive or uplifting on the news. He was hard of hearing, but I'd spoken as loudly as I dared without waking up a patient in an adjacent room.

"So what do you think, Rip?"

"About what?"

"I asked you if you thought we'd have difficulty filling the prescription Dr. Moretti gave you, being he's dead now."

"I'm sorry, dear," he replied. "I guess I tuned you out after you mentioned a stricter diet and a new exercise program."

"I realize you aren't looking forward to the lifestyle changes, but it's become abundantly clear they are necessary to keep you alive. Unless you have an overwhelming death wish you haven't shared with me, you're going to have to follow the doctor's orders. I will be eating healthier and going on daily walks, as well, so you won't be the only one making adjustments."

"I guess misery *does* like company," Rip muttered. "Even if the company is an unrelenting taskmaster determined to make me suffer."

"Would you rather I didn't give a rat's ass if you died?" I responded angrily.

When Rip heard the icy tone of my voice and noticed the

disgusted look on my face, his attitude softened. He picked up my hand, which was resting on his hip, and kissed the top of it before saying, "I'm just kidding, honey. I really do appreciate all the care and compassion you show me. I promise I will follow the doctor's orders and try not to complain about it too much. And in regards to your earlier question, I don't anticipate any trouble filling the prescription Dr. Moretti gave me, particularly if the pharmacy here hasn't been notified of the cardiologist's death yet."

"And if they have?"

"Then we'll just get it filled at Walgreens. I noticed there's one just a couple of blocks from the park we're staying in. Relax, honey. Don't worry about a potential problem that can easily be rectified."

"You're right. I've just been so worked up all day that——" I was interrupted when the nurse walked into the room.

"Clyde Ripple?" She introduced herself as Maggie Brown and Rip told her to call him Rip as opposed to Mr. Ripple, or Clyde. Her last name fit her appearance perfectly. Maggie had a tanned, lithe body and short brown hair as curly as that of a young Shirley Temple. She was just as cute as the former child actress as well. Her light brown eyes reminded me of biscuits just beginning to turn color in the oven. She carried a clipboard in one hand and a pen in the other. Maggie proceeded to ask Rip a dozen questions, such as, "Are you having any pain in your chest?", "Are you experiencing any difficulty with breathing?" and "Did you not finish your meal because you didn't want to get full before a cheeseburger and a plateful of French fries magically appeared on your tray?"

I loved this nurse already. I knew immediately Maggie Brown and I were destined to become fast friends, despite our vast age difference.

When Rip looked down, refusing to reply to her sarcastic question, the nurse laughed and asked, "Seriously, Rip, are you finished with your meal?"

"Yes. Thank you. I choked down all I could muster."

"Good," Maggie said after chuckling again. "That's all we could ask of you."

"Will Rip be visited by Mr. Patel again tonight?" I asked after I finished giggling at the nurse's response.

"No. We will monitor his vitals overnight and Mr. Patel will stop by in the morning. After that, his follow-up care will be handled by one of the other surgeons on the staff here named Blaze O'Ryan."

"Blaze?" I recalled Mr. Patel referring to Dr. O'Ryan as Blaze earlier when he informed us of Dr. Moretti's death. He'd been the individual who'd taken over for Jolene Sarcoxie performing CPR on Dr. Moretti in the parking lot.

"Yes," Maggie responded. "His actual name is Kellan, but I believe the nickname of Blaze was based on his bright red hair. When the sun shines on him, he looks like someone needs to use a fire extinguisher to put out the flames on his head."

I smiled at her analogy and waited for her to continue.

"If all looks well tomorrow morning, Mr. Patel will order Rip's release papers and let you drive him home. There's to be no driving by Rip for at least forty-eight hours."

"Are you folks *trying* to give me a heart attack?" Rip asked with a mock expression of horror. "Isn't letting my wife drive my truck going just a little too far?"

"By then, you'll be wanting to go home so badly, you'd let Jeffrey Dahmer drive you there." The young nurse smiled and added, "Our meals might suck here, but at least you and Rapella aren't on the menu."

"Okay, okay," Rip said. "Thanks for the image I won't be able to get out of my head all night. I promise I'll let Rapella drive me home, Margaret. I'm just so accustomed to driving Miss Crazy wherever she needs to go, not the other way around. And, by the way, I'm already looking forward to being at home."

I didn't correct Rip on Maggie's name and was surprised when she didn't either. I'd find out later he'd been spot on. It was accidental, to be sure, but nonetheless, Rip was absolutely on the mark. Maggie's given name *was* Margaret even though she'd been called Maggie since the day she was born.

Maggie checked Rip's blood pressure. She looked at the monitor and nodded. "Cool beans. A reading of 139 over 88 should be your ticket out of here tomorrow morning. 'Should be' being the operative words, Rip. If you're aiming for a *golden* ticket, try for a perfect 120 over 70 when Patel checks your blood pressure in the morning. All right?"

"You really shouldn't expect a perfect blood pressure reading after informing me my wife was going to drive me home after I'm released. But, at this point, any reading that gets me sprung from here tomorrow morning is fine with me."

"And me too, Rip," the nurse agreed. "It's always so much easier to recuperate in your own home."

"It sure is," Rip agreed with a smile. "And the meals are more palatable too."

Maggie whacked Rip on the thigh with her clipboard, and asked, "Do you need anything or have any questions before I leave?"

"No, Megan," Rip replied. "But thank you."

I groaned and apologized to the nurse. "He's still a little loopy from the anesthesia."

"No problem," she said. "I've been called worse."

Stay tuned. I can almost promise you will be again, I wanted to warn her. "I'm sure you have," I said with a chuckle instead. I would write "Maggie" on the underside of Rip's right hand with an ink pen before I left for the evening to help remind him of her name.

As Maggie turned to leave, Rip stopped her. "Oh, I do have one question."

"Yes?" She prompted him.

"Can I order biscuits and gravy with a side of bacon for

40

breakfast?"

I shook my head in disgust. I hoped Maggie thought my husband was being facetious, even though I knew he was seriously hopeful. *Keeping Rip alive is going to be the death of me,* I thought.

"Of course," Maggie replied with a straight face. "You can order anything you want, Rip." When her patient's face lit up like a solar flare, she added, "However, getting what you order is a whole different bowl of watery oatmeal."

The nurse winked at me, stuck her tongue out at Rip, and sashayed out the door singing in an off-key soprano, "Oh, what a beautiful morning. Oh, what a horrible meal. I have a terrible feeling, everything's going downhill."

I could tell Maggie's jovial attitude was forced, but didn't want to inquire about it. Rip couldn't help being amused by her comical rendition of the infamous Rodgers and Hammerstein tune, while I was laughing so hard my eyes began to water.

I felt duty-bound to sit with Rip that evening until visiting hours were over. The chair I was sitting in was hard and uncomfortable and my mind was numb from watching *Bonanza* reruns. Even Rip dozed off in the middle of an episode, which was filmed in 1962. I was beginning to think the clock would never strike eight. It was like watching a tray full of water in a freezer turn into ice cubes.

Maggie entered Rip's room about an hour later. "Your biscuits and gravy have arrived!"

At her words, Rip's head swiveled like a barn owl who'd just heard a mouse squeak. His smile faded as he watched her place his evening snack on his tray: a small container of applesauce and a package containing two graham crackers. He looked up at her grinning face and said, "You and my wife should do a joint stand-up routine at the local comedy club."

"Sorry, Rip. I couldn't resist." Maggie appeared to feel remorseful for kidding Rip. She placed a second pack of crackers on his plate. "Here you go, you big baby. I thought you might still be hungry after eating so little of your dinner. Don't tell anyone I'm giving you preferential treatment."

She and I were snickering at her remarks. Rip? Not so much. Despite the fact he'd acted annoyed at the evening snacks she'd given him, he gobbled them down like a hungry fox feasting on a pocket gopher.

Rip fell asleep shortly after Maggie exited his room. She'd checked all of his vital signs and seemed satisfied with the results. She chuckled when she turned Rip's hand over to check his pulse and saw her name written on his palm. The last thing she'd done before leaving was turn off the lights over his bed and behind his head, leaving only the one in the bathroom illuminated. It was apparent she wanted him to get some rest so I refrained from trying to carry on a conversation with her patient. Soon Rip was snoring like a hibernating grizzly bear. I was left with nothing to amuse myself other than watching Little Joe Cartwright convince his older brother Hoss to try and fly off a cliff with a pair of poorly constructed, feather-covered wings strapped to his back. I drifted off to sleep before Hoss worked up the nerve for his attempt at flight. I could only assume he crashed and burned as a result. Obviously, he didn't crash badly enough to be killed as Hoss was present in the remainder of the 431 total episodes.

When I was awakened by Nurse Maggie entering the room to check Rip's vitals again, I was surprised to see I'd been asleep in the recliner for almost an hour. My neck was stiff and my stomach was growling. It was then I remembered I hadn't had a bite to eat all day. I didn't want to eat in front of Rip so I planned to stop and grab something on the way home to take and consume in the Caboose. I'd enjoy supper while in my pajamas and watching something silly on television that I was never able to watch when Rip was there. I'm not sure what or who had assigned him the job of controlling the remote, but after over fifty years of watching cop shows and "shoot 'em up bang-bangs," I'd just accepted the fact that watching humorous sitcoms was going to be a very rare treat. Since this was an opportunity that only came along once in a blue moon, I didn't want to waste it. I could already imagine bingeing on old *King of Queens* or *Big Bang Theory* reruns.

"So what do you plan on doing tonight, Mrs. Ripple?" Maggie asked. "Are you going to do something fun while you have me watching over this big lunk of yours?"

"Big lunk is right, Maggie, and please call me Rapella, dear," I replied, before truthfully answering her inquiry. "I'm just going to use this opportunity to catch up on a few things I haven't had a chance to do lately. I'm also going to do some serious thinking about what might've caused Dr. Moretti to die so suddenly and unexpectedly."

"Really?" The nurse asked. She looked as if she'd swallowed the cotton ball she'd used to swab the site where a phlebotomist had just taken a vial of Rip's blood for lab work. Being on a blood thinner, Rip bled like the dye in a cheap washcloth.

"Yes," I replied. "Neither of us is convinced his death was due to natural causes. Are you?"

"Um, well, not really, but the autopsy should confirm it one way or the other."

"It *should*," I said, emphasizing the last word. "But if it doesn't, we might look into it ourselves."

"Rapella, honey," Rip said, still a bit groggy from having been awakened from a deep sleep to have his vitals checked. "That's not something we want to make public knowledge."

"I won't say anything, Rip," Maggie said. "I promise. If it was anything but natural causes, I want the truth to come out."

"As do we." I briefly explained how Rip and I had been involved in numerous murder investigations and successfully gotten to the truth behind each and every one of them.

"And Rapella nearly got us killed in nearly every case too," Rip chipped in.

"And yet here we are," I said to Maggie, for Rip's benefit. "Still alive and kicking."

"That's incredible," Maggie said. "I'm very impressed and so happy for you."

Her expression read differently. It indicated she'd be happier if we *had* been eliminated in one of those murder cases we'd insanely butted into. I was baffled by the look on her face but chalked it up to exhaustion from working a lengthy shift. "I'm sure you are looking forward to skedaddling out of the clinic tonight. You look worn out, Maggie."

"Trust me, I am. My shift is over in a few minutes and I have the next two days off."

"How wonderful for you, Maggie. I know you nurses put in long days."

"Twelve-hour shifts," she clarified in response.

Maggie had appeared pale and on edge all day as if she'd been burning both ends of the candle for several days in a row and was now running strictly on nervous energy. Her occasional attempts to be spirited and good-humored were admirable and might've had Rip fooled, but I knew she was barely holding it together. "Well, then maybe you can get caught up on a few things, too, like relaxing and resting up on your days off."

"I wish. Mostly I'll be busy getting ready for the Scentsy party I'm hosting tomorrow night."

"The what party?" Rip asked. The look on his face implied he thought she'd said she was planning on throwing a "swingers" orgy.

"Scentsy," she replied simply, and at least two octaves louder, as though Rip's confusion was based on his hearing loss issues. "At the party I'm throwing, people can buy these warmer things that melt scented wax cubes. I'm hosting it for a friend of mine who is a consultant for the company."

"We already have something that will melt wax cubes. It's called a stove," Rip said.

Her explanation of "Scentsy" had made perfect sense to me, but to Rip it was like explaining the big bang theory to a third grader; not the show I enjoyed so much, but the actual thing.

I'd read that the big bang theory suggests that almost fourteen billion years ago the universe began with all of its energy jammed into a single point. That point eventually exploded and created matter which slowly created the billions of galaxies in our universe. *That theory might well be true, but it sounds preposterous even to* me, *much less a third grader,* I thought. *And I'm sure the idea of paying for a warmer to melt wax in one's home sounds just as ludicrous to Rip.*

When Rip stared blankly at the nurse, I said, "I've wanted one of those for the Chartreuse Caboose for a while now. It would be nice to enhance the aroma of the trailer."

"You've wanted one of those things for 'a while now,' Rapella?" Rip sounded cynical. "If you want to make the trailer smell, couldn't you accomplish that by leaving some of the leftover shrimp out on the counter from the seafood salad you made a couple of days ago? That would definitely 'enhance the aroma.'"

"Not that kind of smell, Rip!" I'm sure I sounded perturbed. "The melting wax emits a pleasant scent such as jasmine or evergreen."

"If you want to smell evergreen, why don't you sleep outside in a tent tonight? There are a lot of pine trees in Rochester. In fact, there's a blue spruce right behind the trailer."

I sighed and Maggie smiled at me. Ignoring Rip's remarks, she asked, "Have you really thought about getting a Scentsy warmer?"

No, not really, I could've replied. *I was just trying to prevent Rip from saying something stupid again.* Instead I nodded my head to be polite.

"Why don't you come to my Scentsy party tomorrow night, Rapella?" Maggie implored. "You'll recognize a couple of the nurses there; Jolene Sarcoxie and Candace Kobialka both work here. Jolene assisted Dr. Moretti during Rip's surgery and Candace will be his night nurse. She's due to come in and introduce herself any minute. The party begins at 7:00 and should last about two hours. There will be refreshments and door prizes. My address is 1522 Sixteenth Avenue, Unit B. You turn right on Sixteenth Avenue right before you go under Interstate 52."

Rather than make a commitment to attend, I asked, "Do you have any Cowboys warmers? Rip is a big Dallas Cowboys fan."

"We used to. Now we just have a Cowboys replacement dish for ten bucks that might work with another warmer."

"Yes, I can see where it might. Thank you for the invitation, Maggie." I smiled, but made sure it was a noncommittal grin. "I'll see what tomorrow brings."

"I hope you can come," Maggie said. "And, Rip, I hope you have a restful night."

I nodded. Rip glanced at the palm of his hand and replied, "Thank you for taking care of me all afternoon, Maggie."

After the nurse left his room, I was surprised to hear Rip say, "You should go to the party, dear. I still have no clue what a Scentsy is, but it sounds like fun and you shouldn't have to just sit around and watch me rest in front of the television all evening tomorrow while I'm recuperating."

"How is that different than any other evening?" I didn't mean to sound like a shrew, but Rip's expression indicated I'd hurt his feelings. "I'm sorry, sweetheart. I didn't mean that the way it sounded. Maggie's party just doesn't sound like anything I'd be interested in attending, but I'll think about it."

Just as I finished responding to Rip's suggestion, the night nurse, Candace Kobialka, strolled into the room, pushing her rolling cart ahead of her. A nurse at the Cardiac Center in Seattle where Rip had undergone the triple bypass operation had referred to her cart as a COW, or Computer On Wheels. Candace referred to hers as her MATE. "As in 'most aggravating thing ever,'" she explained.

The raven-haired nurse, who was tall and thin, reminded me of Popeye's significant other, Olive Oyl. Her luminous eyes were mesmerizing, and it was hard for me to take my own cornflower-blue eyes off her bright green ones, which brought to mind the color of the emerald tree boa constrictor found in the South American rainforests. We'd seen one of the colorful snakes in the Nocturnal House exhibit at the Wildlife Encounter Zoo at Ober Mountain in Gatlinburg, Tennessee, during our visit to the Smoky Mountains. After introducing myself to the night nurse, I said, "You have the most beautiful eyes, Candace."

Candace thanked me and sat a plastic container of lemon Jell-O on Rip's tray as an additional evening snack. "Here's a little something to soothe your throat, Mr. Ripple."

"Call me Rip, dear. Can I talk you out of a container of sherbet? Any flavor is fine. It helps my sore throat so much more than Jell-O."

"Of course, Rip," Candace said. "I'll bring you some next time I get this way. You can eat the Jell-O in the meantime."

"Thanks! I might have to pass on the Jell-O, but I do appreciate you bringing me some sherbet," Rip responded.

Candace nodded and checked his vitals. She then walked into the restroom and returned to his side with a wet washcloth. I had to laugh out loud when she scrubbed "Maggie" off the palm of his hand, and wrote "Candace" in its place with her ballpoint pen.

After chuckling, Rip said, "Evidently, my reputation precedes me."

"Was it that obvious?" Candance asked with a grin. "I'm just trying to relieve you of any undue stress."

"Thank you," Rip and I said in unison.

"You're welcome. Do either of you have any questions before I continue on with my rounds?"

She appeared dumbstruck when Rip asked, "So are you going to get one of those smelly things tomorrow?"

I quickly had to clarify what Rip was talking about. Candace laughed and said, "Of course! I'll have to buy a Scentsy, or at least some wax cubes."

"You'll *have* to?" Rip asked.

The nurse winked at me before replying, "Ask your wife. There's an unspoken expectation to purchase something——even if it's the cheapest item available——when you attend a party like that. I like to refer to it as Tupperware Obligation Protocol, or TOP. Am I wrong, Mrs. Ripple?"

"Call me Rapella, and no, you are not wrong, Candace!" We both laughed. I felt an instant kinship with Candace, just as I had with Maggie. Her made-up acronyms were an example of a playoff personality that I found endearing. "Otherwise you feel as though you are just taking advantage of the door prizes, free refreshments——"

"——and the booze," Candace finished for me. "I'm lucky I have tomorrow off. Chantell Williams will be your night nurse tomorrow if you don't get released in the morning."

"Maggie didn't mention anything about alcohol," I said before Rip could say something stupid about getting sprung from the clinic come hell or high water.

"With Maggie, booze is a given. She always serves lots of wine and mixed drinks. Her mango margaritas are absolutely the best. They are truly to die for. And, after all, it's all about the adult beverages, not whatever the hostess is peddling. In fact, that's why I'm bringing a platter of paszteciki that my Polish mother-in-law makes; anything to absorb some of the alcohol before we all have to drive home."

"What is paszteciki?" I asked.

"It's a traditional Polish pastry filled with minced meat," Candace explained. "They are often served at Christmas and Polish weddings."

"Meat?" Rip asked. The pastries didn't sound all that appealing to me, but one look at Rip and I knew he was salivating at the mere thought of a plate full of meat-filled pastries. He glared at Candace and said, "You're killing me, Nurse Ratched!"

"My last name's Kobialka, not Ratched," Candace corrected my mocking husband. Clearly offended by his exclamation, she added, "And I'm trying to take care of you, not kill you."

Rip's teasing reference to a cold, heartless nurse in *One Flew Over the Cuckoo's Nest*, a movie released in 1975, or about two decades prior to Candace's birth, went over the nurse's head like a bowl of lemon Jell-O heaved in her direction. After her description of the treat she was taking to the Scentsy party the idea of pitching the Jell-O probably *had* crossed Rip's mind.

"He was kidding you, dear," I told her so she wouldn't be upset by his remark.

Nurse Candace left the room, with a little less joy than she'd pretended to have when she'd entered it a few minutes earlier. Like Maggie, I didn't think she was in as joyful a mood as she was acting like she was. I had to wonder if either, or both, of the nurses were putting on a front so as not to fall apart in front of their patients. They were coworkers of Dr. Moretti, and his sudden loss had to have been a shock to their systems. When Candace exited the room, her demeanor seemed much more authentic.

"I think you hurt her feelings, Rip," I admonished him as the door closed behind Candace.

"I didn't intend to," he said, even though I never thought he'd intentionally offended her. "I will explain my smart remark next time she comes in to check on me or to bring me some sherbet."

"And apologize?"

"Yes. And apologize," Rip promised. He then grinned at me and asked, "Does the Scentsy party sound more appealing to you now that you know there'll be mango margaritas there that are to die for?"

"Well, I wouldn't want to be rude and…"

"You definitely should not be rude." We both laughed at his remark.

"Well, honey, it's almost eight. I better get out of here before they come and kick me out. I wish I could stay here with you all night, but it's just not allowed."

"Sure you do," Rip said with a chuckle. "And I wish they'd let me take a couple of laps around the building before gnawing on a plate of sushi. You're a terrible liar, dear, but I love you for hanging around all evening to keep me company. I just hope you don't end up with a backache from that uncomfortable-looking chair you've been sitting on."

I could've told him that the backache ship had sailed two hours earlier, but I didn't want him to feel guilty. Nor did I mention I was so hungry that his uneaten lemon Jell-O was starting to look appealing to me. "It's not too bad. Besides, I'd rather be here with you than home by myself in the trailer."

"You wouldn't be by yourself, Rapella. Speaking of which, give Dolly my love once she gets over being pissed off at having her dinner served several hours late."

"Oh goodness," I said, having forgotten about Dolly. "Her Majesty is probably royally ticked off that her supper is so overdue."

"No doubt." Rip laughed. Dolly, our tubby tabby, had him wrapped around her little gray and white paws. "You better have a good excuse to give her when you get home."

"I do have a good excuse," I replied. "It's you! I'll be blaming *you* for why her supper is late. I don't want her mad at me. She already prefers you to me a hundred times over."

"Well, of course," he said, "I *am* the cat's meow, you know."

We engaged in lighthearted bantering for a couple of minutes more before Candace Kobialka walked back in to remind me that visiting hours were over. She set a plastic container of raspberry sherbet in front of Rip. He thanked her and after he explained his Nurse Ratched quip to her, she snatched the TV remote out of Rip's hand and turned off the television. After he grunted in displeasure, she explained to him it was time for him to get some quality sleep. As she exited the room, she winked at me and quipped, "That's what Nurse Ratched would've done, isn't it?"

After she'd left, I said, "Call me later on if you're awake and let me know how you're feeling. If I don't hear from you, I'll assume you're sleeping soundly."

I kissed him and told him I loved him before I exited his room. As I was closing his door, I heard his customary response. "Love you more!"

Still thinking about our beloved fur baby, I decided to stop at Walgreens to get Rip's new prescription filled, and while there, pick up a can of their most expensive cat food. You get what you pay for, right? If it cost more than twice what I thought any cat food ever should, then it must be twice as yummy was my reasoning. Dolly deserved a special treat for having spent all day by herself in the Caboose. She never got the memo telling her cats were supposed to be independent and aloof. Unaware she should prefer to be left alone in peace, she didn't handle solitude very well as a rule. And, after all, there isn't much we all wouldn't do for our pets, is there?

As I stepped outside the clinic, I realized it had sleeted since I'd been outside earlier in the day. I nearly skated all the way across the slick concrete entranceway to the curb. As I rubbed my hands together, my stomach rumbled so loudly a man waiting for his wife to pull their car up in the pickup lane looked around as if searching for the threatening creature that had just growled at him. I looked around too so he wouldn't know my belly was the source of the freaky sound. I hadn't mentioned to Rip I was starving and hospital food sounded about as appetizing to me as Rip's salt-free beef broth had looked earlier.

I decided Dolly would have to wait a few minutes more. As soon as the nervous man's wife had him seated safely inside their Volvo, I phoned in a pickup order at the seafood restaurant two blocks from the hotel. It was directly across the street from the Walgreens I needed to go to. For some reason the idea of eating a couple of garlicky Cheddar Bay biscuits had been floating around in my head for hours. And now I found myself craving a mango margarita, as well. One that was "to die for" sounded even better. Perhaps the Chartreuse Caboose truly was in dire need of something to make it smell like jasmine or evergreen instead of used kitty litter and pork rinds from the open bag on the table beside Rip's recliner. Note to self: *Pitch rest of the pork rinds and unopened bag of Lay's chips into the campground's dumpster before Rip arrives home. Or, better yet, pitch the pork rinds and snack on the potato chips while watching sitcom reruns late into the evening.*

"Good morning," Dr. Pratyush Patel greeted Rip and I as he entered Rip's hospital room the next morning.

"Good morning," Rip and I responded in kind.

Rip had been in the process of trying to choke down a bowl of the watery "god-awful" oatmeal Maggie had promised him along with a side of tasteless cantaloupe and musk melon. He failed miserably. The fruit looked like a full week could pass and it still wouldn't have ripened, but he managed to get it down. "When you have to cut melon with a steak knife, it's not fit to serve to patients for breakfast," Rip had lamented just before the cardiovascular technologist had walked into the room.

Rip and I both turned our full attention on Mr. Patel, anxious to see if Rip was going to be cleared to go home. Or, as Rip had put it, "be released on his own recognizance." I was glad to see he had a smile. It was a sad smile, to be clear, and didn't extend to his red-rimmed eyes. The sorrowful gentleman asked, "How are we feeling today, folks?"

We? I thought. *Rip seems to feel fine, Mr. Patel, but I'm still a bit hung over.* Exhausted and so hungry when I'd returned to the travel trailer the previous evening, I could've eaten the expensive high-falutin' cat food I'd spooned into Dolly's bowl. I'd proceeded to eat a full order of kung pao noodles with chicken and too many Cheddar Bay biscuits. I later polished off nearly an entire bag of Lay's potato chips. I blamed the food for my current headache and nausea even though I'd washed all the comfort food down with an oversized tequila sunrise. With no one else in the Caboose, save for Dolly, to question my decisions, I'd refilled the quart canning jar I customarily used for my daily allotted cocktail three times, polishing off the half-full bottle of *Jose Cuervo*. In return, Dolly had expected me to refill her food bowl the same number of times, and I'd obliged her, because as Rip had said, "misery loves company." Gluttony, I discovered, loved company too, even if the company is only your cat. The two of us had nary a care by the time we passed out; I was splayed out on the couch, and Dolly curled up in Rip's recliner. A horrific hangover greeted me when I'd awoken that morning. Trying not to groan, I listened as Rip responded to Mr. Patel's inquiry about how "we" were feeling.

"I'm feeling good as new, Doc, and I am ready to go home."

"Why don't we leave that decision up to me, Rip?" Patel replied. "And I'm a cardiovascular technologist, not a physician. You can call me Pratyush."

Yeah, right, I thought. I could only imagine how badly he would butcher the man's name if he'd even get close to it in the first place. I could barely spit out "Pratyush Patel" without mangling it. Rip would turn the man's full name into a word salad if he ever even attempted to use it. *Now that the "Doc" option had been eliminated, my guess is he'll call Pratyush "son" like he does every other man who is sixty or younger.*

Patel examined Rip thoroughly before declaring him eligible for release. He promised the nurse would arrive shortly with his discharge instructions and release papers.

"Any news on what caused Dr. Moretti's death?" I asked him.

"No," he replied softly. "Other than an autopsy was performed on his body last night and the authorities are awaiting the results."

"I hope the results explain how a man who seemed as healthy as a racehorse could perform a stent placement procedure so excellently on my husband and then drop dead in the parking lot less than an hour later." When I saw tears well up in Patel's eyes I wished I had worded my remark a bit more sensitively.

But was that even possible? I wondered. *Perhaps I could've said "expired in the parking lot?" No. That sounds like the man was a parking meter rather than a world-renowned cardiac surgeon. "Took his last breath in the parking lot?" That is entirely too dramatic. "Went to a better place?" Personally, I'd choose* Red Lobster *as a better place. "Gave up the ghost?" Nope! Too much of a silly cliché. "Kicked the bucket in the parking lot?" Absolutely not! There is just no tactful way to put it,* I decided.

"Marco's passing was a complete shock to all of us who knew him and worked with him," Mr. Patel said with a slow shake of his head.

Marco's passing? Well, okay, maybe there is a more tactful way of putting it, I thought. In my defense, it's easy for one's brain to turn into the consistency of cottage cheese when they're in a state of disbelief. And, I might add, as hung over as a teenage girl the morning after her senior prom.

I carefully pulled the Chevy truck up to the curb in front of the cardiac clinic to pick up Rip who'd been wheeled outside in a wheelchair by a stout, white-haired woman named Henrietta Stringer. I recognized her as the volunteer who'd come into Rip's room earlier to remove his breakfast tray. Henrietta was about my age and acted as though she loved every minute she spent helping out at the clinic. I admired her joyful personality and her keen sense of humor. As she'd picked up Rip's tray, with his empty coffee cup and uneaten bowl of runny oatmeal on it, she'd said, "We have a pool going. We're betting on what day a patient might actually finish their bowl of this nasty-looking oatmeal. I'm thinking your nurse must've gotten caught in an isolated rain shower on her way to your room with it. And, just in case you're curious, I stand to win a bundle if it happens next Thursday."

When Henrietta had come to collect him thirty minutes later in the wheelchair she was pushing, Rip had told her he was fully capable of walking. Henrietta had responded, "And I'm fully capable of doing my job by wheeling you down to the curb as I am required to do. We don't want me being fired from my backbreaking, non-paying job, now do we? Nor do we want you falling over dead of a heart attack on your way out of the building. If we allowed that to happen, instead of being a paying customer, you'd just become a liability. And, potentially, even the subject of a malpractice lawsuit. Unfortunately, letting you die on my watch is not listed on my job description."

"Understood," Rip said with a laugh. "I will try to postpone falling over dead until I'm on the way back to the RV park."

"Thank you," Henrietta said. "I'm sure that'd be very much appreciated by the staff here. The paperwork required when they lose a patient before they can get them out of the clinic is a bitch."

We were all chortling by the time we had Rip buckled into the passenger seat. Rip and I stopped laughing abruptly when Henrietta added, "And I reckon I ought to know since my husband of nearly fifty years passed away here six months ago, shortly after his procedure."

"Oh, no," I replied, suddenly serious as a heart attack. Pardon the pun. "What happened?"

"They said it was a rare blood clot that formed at the site of the pacemaker they'd just implanted in his chest."

"Oh, heavens!" I was now fretful the same type of tragedy could befall *my* husband too. "I'm so sorry for your loss, Henrietta. That had to be completely shocking!"

"Yes," she said. "It was certainly unexpected. But I'm moving forward, even volunteering my time here where I feel closer to my Stanley."

I hugged the volunteer and told her I admired her resilience and altruistic nature. As I was getting settled in behind the steering wheel, Henrietta's melancholy appeared to dissipate and her sense of humor returned.

"Drive crazy, Rapella!" Henrietta hollered as she turned to wheel the now empty wheelchair back into the clinic.

"I always do!" I yelled back, happy to see her in better spirits again.

"Oh, boy," I heard Rip mutter as I peeled out so I could split the gap between a white Mazda that had just pulled away from the curb, and a blue van that was headed in our direction.

I glanced back and saw Henrietta bent over the back of the wheelchair from laughing so hard.

FOUR

"Refill?" Maggie asked me that evening as she made the rounds from one party guest to the next.

"No, thank you," I replied. "I learned my lesson last night."

I'd been nursing the mango margarita for half an hour already and thought I could make what little remained in the glass last throughout the evening. It was as delicious as Candace had assured me, but I wasn't keen on inviting another hangover the following day. While I sipped on my drink, I listened in on a conversation the nurses were engaged in. I quickly lost interest in their gossip about an elderly cardiac patient with a lisp and a tramp stamp.

It was then I noticed a pregnant woman sitting next to the refreshments table who, like me, wasn't interacting much with the other party guests. Her platinum blonde hair hung below her belt line and the color of her roots reminded me of the bluish-black tongue of a Chow Chow my brother Rusty adopted when we were in primary school. The contrast between her light hair and dark two-inches-long roots was startling.

As the nurses were discussing new safety protocol the cath lab was implementing, I walked over and introduced myself to the expectant blonde.

"Hi Rapella," she responded. "It's nice to meet you. My name is Olivia O'Ryan. My husband is a cardiac surgeon at the STAT Clinic where most of these ladies at Maggie's party work as nurses. I noticed you were looking at my dark roots. I decided to let my hair revert to its natural color after I'd heard that hair dye was not safe for a baby during gestation."

"I'd heard that too, Olivia, but I think they've since determined it's a very minimal risk, and even then only during the first twelve weeks of pregnancy. But I'm glad to hear you take safety precautions like that seriously."

"Yes," she replied. "You can't be too safe when it involves a baby's health; minimal risk or not, I'd rather err on the side of caution. I see you aren't part of the nurses' clique, either."

"The hostess was my husband's day nurse following a stent placement procedure, and Candace was his nurse that evening. As for the rest, I'm not familiar with them. So I take it you're not a nurse either, but do you work outside the home in some other capacity?"

"No. I'm just a stay-at-home mom."

"That's an honorable job, Olivia," I assured her. "There's no 'just' about it."

"Thank you. Before I got pregnant with my first two kids, who are two-year-old twin girls, I worked a full-time job for years in a storage facility. Now I feel like most employed ladies look down on me because I'm no longer a member of the workforce, or 'not gainfully employed' as the nurse named Jolene described me. I don't particularly care what they think, but I'll admit, being nothing more than a mom and housewife is getting to me. Sometimes I just want to have a conversation that doesn't involve Elsa, Bluey, or the Paw Patrol, and do something more exciting than sniffing a kid's bottom to see if their diaper needs to be changed.

Other than getting a manicure at the mall every Thursday morning, I rarely see the outside of our house. That's why I jumped at the chance to come to this Scentsy party."

"I don't know how you even get away long enough to get your nails done."

"My younger sister works at a bookstore and has Thursdays off. I drop the kids off at her apartment at nine and usually pick them up by ten-thirty, so it's a short reprieve, but I'll take any bit of 'me time' I can get." Olivia smiled, revealing such a perfect set of straight, white teeth they made my manmade dentures look crooked.

"I don't blame you, sweetie. I enjoy every second of 'me time' I can get too."

"You have young children at home?" She asked, clearly taken aback.

"No. I have a hardheaded husband at home." When Olivia stared at me oddly, I added, "The same one for over fifty years now."

"Enough said," she replied with an unladylike snort. "I don't know which is worse."

"Listen, Olivia. Being a mother and homemaker is an honorable profession and a full-time job without trying to work outside the home."

"There's a zillion and one women out there who do both."

"That's true, Olivia. Perhaps once all your children are in school you can go back to working full-time. Your former job at a storage facility sounds interesting, though." *Yikes!* I thought. *That line of work sounds so uninspiring I'd probably be tempted to saw away on my wrists with the jagged side of a padlock key after just one eight-hour shift.*

"I don't know about interesting, but it certainly was stressful. If I decide to rejoin the workforce, I think I'd try to land a job less nerve-racking." Olivia brushed her hair away from her face as she spoke. Her nearly white hair had a tendency to fall forward and cover her right eye.

I couldn't imagine how a job working at a storage facility could be nerve-racking, but I didn't question her assessment. "I could never quite understand why people would fill a storage unit with a bunch of stuff they never use and then pay a monthly fee to keep it there. Some friends of ours stored their excess stuff for years, such as bicycles they hadn't ridden in decades and a set of old golf clubs he'd picked up for twenty bucks at a garage sale in case he ever decided to take up the sport. He didn't."

Olivia's deadpan expression never wavered as I continued. "They even paid to store a rusty propane bottle that didn't fit the grill, or anything else they owned. After they both were dead, their children loaded the entire contents of the storage unit onto a flatbed truck and hauled it all straight to the dump. Seemed to me like such a waste of time, effort, and money."

Olivia continued to stare at me silently, as if her thoughts were miles away from where we sat. I felt like my lips had been flapping but no sound was coming out. I was afraid she'd found my remarks offensive so quickly switched gears. "So how far along are you, Olivia?"

"Six months."

"And are you expecting a boy or a girl?" I had gained her full attention now.

"A boy." She replied. "As far as I know, none of these other ladies at the party have any kids, which is probably why they can't relate to me very well."

"I'm sure you're right." I felt bad that Olivia appeared to feel left out. *Obviously, she's a friend of Maggie's,* I thought. *I'd think the hostess would make more of an effort to include Olivia in the group. Not that I mind conversing with her while the others at the party chatted amongst themselves.* "I'll bet your husband is excited by the idea he's going to have a son this time around."

"He's definitely excited about the idea," she replied. "I just hope he's still as delighted after the boy is born."

I got the feeling Dr. O'Ryan had reservations about having another child. *I doubt it's the idea of having another mouth to feed*, I thought. *He surely makes a great living as a heart surgeon. Maybe Olivia is afraid he won't spend as much time bonding with their new son as she wants him to.*

"Why wouldn't he be thrilled to death after your son is born?" I asked, only to find out my suspicion was correct.

"I have done ninety percent of the child-raising when it comes to our girls." Olivia looked even more exhausted when she said, "I have no reason to believe that will change just because we're having a boy this time."

"Maybe you'll be pleasantly surprised, Olivia," I said, trying to cheer her up. Could a workaholic who didn't have, or wouldn't make, time to spend with his first two children change? Would he find time to spend parenting after his third child came along? I doubted it, but didn't want to sound negative.

"I truly hope so," she replied. Olivia licked her lips as though her mouth was uncomfortably dry.

"Me too, honey," I said as I patted her hand. "I know you can't have any of Maggie's mango margarita mix right now but I'd be happy to go round you up something else to drink if you'd like."

"Thanks, Rapella, but I'm fine. When I was pregnant with the twins, I craved peanut butter on celery sticks and strawberry ice cream. This time around I can't get enough olives or sweet gherkins. I've already about polished off all the pickles and Greek Kalamatas on Maggie's relish tray."

"You are entitled to hog all of the refreshments," I replied. "And I didn't mean that the way it sounded, Olivia. I, for one, can understand how overpowering pregnancy cravings can be. A hundred years ago, when I was pregnant with my daughter Regina, I'd make Rip get up in the middle of the night and drive to the gas station to buy me Slim Jims. Under normal circumstances, I couldn't stand the thought of eating the greasy meat sticks. But while I was pregnant, the craving for them was intense."

"Tell me about it." Olivia looked down at her hands, which were trembling as if she was chilled. "So far I haven't made Kelly get up in the middle of the night and drive to the gas station, but I can't promise your anecdote isn't a preview of coming attractions."

"Are you cold, dear?" I asked after laughing at her response. I wasn't surprised she chose to call her husband Kelly, rather than Blaze, as everyone at the cath lab referred to him. I thought her nickname for her partner was endearing. "Would you like something like a blanket or coat to drape over you?"

"No, but thank you, Rapellla. I won't be staying long. After I pick out a new warmer, I'll probably head home. By now the twins will have my husband's head spinning. Kelly's not used to having to watch over them all by himself."

"Maybe it's good practice for him then."

With a smile that could light up the darkest room, Olivia's entire appearance changed following my last comment. I grinned at her in return. I told her how beautiful I found her smile to be and she placed her right hand on my left hand and patted it warmly. "Thank you again. I appreciate the compliment, your compassion, and most importantly, the company. I was beginning to feel like a leper sitting over here by myself."

I squeezed Olivia's hand as a sign of solidarity and we continued to exchange small talk about a number of topics.

Soon, the nurses' gabfest ended and Maggie made introductions for those of us who weren't in the "clique," as Olivia had called their group.

Other than Olivia, me, and an old high school buddy of Maggie's named Holly Fisher, everyone in attendance was employed as a nurse at the STAT Clinic. As I'd explained to Olivia, I'd already met Jolene Sarcoxie when she'd inserted an IV into Rip's artery prior to surgery. A bit queasy from observing this pre-surgical necessity, I'd headed to the waiting room soon after. I'd become better acquainted with Rip's tall, green-eyed night nurse, Candace Kobialka, and of course, the hostess Maggie Brown, who took care of Rip in the cardiac ward the day of his procedure.

The remaining ladies were introduced as Charmaine Boyd, Monica Corry, and Eva Clemens. Eva appeared to be nearing retirement age. I was entranced by her beautiful white hair and contrasting dark gray eyes. The other two were in their mid-thirties, blonde and attractive with hazel eyes. Charmaine and Monica were so similar in appearance they could've been sisters.

A late arrival named Carolyn Hobbs joined the group just then. Carolyn was adorable. She was a near identical doppelganger of Meg Ryan when the actress starred in *Sleepless in Seattle*.

Carolyn explained to the group she'd been delayed by a stubborn blaze in an abandoned warehouse in south Rochester. "Clearly an act of arson," she'd said. Carolyn lived in an apartment across the hall from Maggie, who told us her humble neighbor had the distinction of being the first female fire captain in Olmstead County. After everyone greeted her, I told Carolyn she was quite an inspiration, especially to young women just entering the workforce. "Not just for the courage it takes to run into burning buildings, but also for the commitment it took for you to smash through glass ceilings to get to that point."

Carolyn appeared to be in her late thirties or early forties. At three to four decades older than anyone else in the room, other than Eva Clemens, I was beginning to feel like Grandma Moses propped up in the corner of the room with a cane in one hand and a margarita in the other. Or, better yet, Charlotte Rae in her role as housemother in the *Facts of Life* sitcom which aired in the 1980s. Like those girls in the New York boarding school, these young ladies giggled and carried on like they were at a slumber party instead of a Scentsy party. The more they downed the adult beverages, the sillier they became.

I was about to use the excuse I needed to get back to the RV park to check on my husband, when Charmaine said, "Did you all hear about the results of the autopsy they performed on Dr. Moretti?"

"I heard it was inconclusive," Monica said.

"That's odd," Eva said, "I heard homicide was suspected."

"How could that be?" Olivia spoke up for the first time. "Didn't he have a heart attack?"

"I heard there was no sign of cardiac issues," Maggie said.

"Bull hockey!" Jolene exclaimed. "I was the one who performed CPR on him. It was clearly a heart attack."

"Ladies! Ladies!" Charmaine had spoken in a louder-than-normal voice to quiet the hubbub her original question had invoked. "I got the autopsy results straight from the horse's mouth. Dr. Steed to be exact and I apologize for the pun."

"Did you assist Dr. Steed in the autopsy?" Jolene asked with a wry grin. The skeptical look on her face indicated she thought Charmaine could've altered the results. Charmaine remained impassive, as though Jolene was merely a cheap vase from Target on the end table.

"No, Jolene, I did not. I haven't quite reached that level of expertise yet. But Dr. Steed's findings are verbalized and taped as he performs an autopsy. A recording of the actual examination can be useful in the future," she explained. Charmaine cleared her throat and began to speak again, her gaze fixed on me as I'm sure the nurses in attendance were aware of her job status. "I'm currently working as a forensic nurse in the medical examiner's office."

"That sounds like it'd be a gruesome, but interesting position," I said.

"Yes to both," Charmaine replied.

"So what'd Dr. Steed say?" I asked after I let her bask in her glory for an appropriate amount of time.

My interest was now so thoroughly piqued, you couldn't have removed me from that party with the Jaws of Life. In fact, the fire alarm could go off with Carolyn Hobbs leaping to her feet to fight it, and the only way I'd leave the room is draped over the broad shoulders of a large firefighter like a bag of dirty laundry.

I would remain for the rest of the party and take home the door prize I won: an ornate metal trivet to place my new warmer on. I'd relent and polish off another margarita, and even abide by what Candace referred to as the Tupperware Obligation Protocol and order a "Land of Liberty" warmer. The adorable Scentsy was a replica of a small travel trailer painted in a red, white, and blue American flag motif. How fitting for a couple of full-time RVers to display on the only remaining six inches of counter space available in the Caboose. I'd felt compelled to order the warmer to have something to place on the stand I'd won in the drawing. Purchasing a warmer meant I also felt compelled to order three packs of scented wax cubes: Aloe Water and Cucumber, Coastal Sunset, and Coco (nuts) for Coconuts. Intrigued by the name "Angel: Experiment 624," I eventually decided to add a package of those cubes to my order as well. Rip was out of luck when it came to the Dallas Cowboys replacement dish. It was not compatible with the warmer I'd chosen. Had it been, I would've concocted another reason not to buy it anyway. I had refused to be a Cowboys fan ever since Jerry Jones had forced Jimmy Johnson into stepping down from his role as head coach. Jones had quickly replaced him with Barry Switzer in 1994 after Johnson had led the Cowboys to back-to-back championships in 1992 and 1993. Even if I have no other impressive credentials, I *am* a first-class grudge holder!

After Maggie refilled everyone's glass with a fresh mango margarita, Charmaine reiterated what the medical examiner had stated during the autopsy. "Dr. Steed explained the autopsy revealed nothing of significance. No specific macroscopic or micro-scopic findings were detected in the body and no signs of cardiac damage either. A tox screen was run, of course, even though no toxic chemicals were suspected. The toxicology report typically takes weeks to be received by the medical examiner's office. Four to six weeks is the norm."

"Good grief!" Monica exclaimed. "Why does it take so long?"

Charmaine had studied well, which was evident as she responded to Monica's inquiry. "The final report is compiled of results from multiple tests, and some take days, weeks, or even months to get through the procedure of being confirmed and investigated by toxicologists and pathologists. They have to identify and quantify potential toxins and interpret the findings. It's a real process, let me tell you. When death by natural causes is suspected, the results are rarely expedited. Not to mention there's nearly always a significant backlog at the toxicology labs. And when a mass casualty occurs, that backlog can grow expeditiously. People just don't have the decency to take that into account when they decide to kick the bucket in large numbers."

After we all chuckled politely at her gallows humor, Charmaine continued. "Seriously, though, it may take well over a month before ——"

"Basically," Monica interrupted, having obviously grown impa-tient, "other than what may or may not show up on the toxicology report, I was right. The autopsy was inconclusive."

"And I was right too," Maggie added. "There were no signs of cardiac issues."

"Yes," Charmaine sighed. "I suppose you both were right, but not entirely. Dr. Steed suspects the root cause of Moretti's death was anaphylactic shock, but he can't be certain. According to Dr. Steed, serum tryptase levels could not be determined."

"How about signs of an asthma attack?" Jolene asked. "Did Dr. Steed check to see if Marco had experienced an asthmatic episode? For instance, was mucous plugging and/or hyper-inflated lungs detected in the body? What about petechial hemorrhages or pharyngeal edema?"

The nurses were now talking about Dr. Moretti as if he was a medical experiment rather than a much-loved human being who had died tragically. I found it rather distasteful, even more so than Charmaine's quip about inconsiderate people dying in masses. Maggie's neighbor, Holly, asked what I too was wondering. "Did Dr. Moretti even *have* a history of asthma?"

"Well, not that I know of," Jolene replied defensively. "But that doesn't mean he *wasn't* asthmatic, or have other pulmonary problems."

"The medical examiner didn't mention any of that," Charmaine replied diplomatically.

Just then Olivia stood up and said she needed to be going. She explained that her organs were being kicked like they were tires on a used car the baby was considering purchasing. Olivia concluded by saying, "I feel a little nauseous." I had to wonder if the twenty-three olives and sixteen pickles I'd watched her eat had anything to do with her tummy troubles.

After everyone told the expectant mother goodbye, Charmaine continued speaking. "Most likely, Dr. Moretti's health history showed no asthma diagnosis. I got the impression his diagnosis of potential anaphylactic shock was based more on witness reports from those who were around him shortly before he passed."

"Like me," I said. Charmaine's last remark had been my cue to get involved in the conversation. "He came and spoke to me at the conclusion of my husband's stent placement procedure and I noticed he was fatigued, sweaty, and short of breath. He even told me he felt nauseated as though something he'd eaten hadn't agreed with him. One thing I forgot to mention was that his pupils looked extremely small for a fairly brightly-lit room."

"That's called pinpoint pupils," Jolene said. "Also known as myosis."

I thanked her for the clarification even though I didn't really need to know the technical name for small pupils. I felt as though she was either talking down to me or trying to impress the other nurses in the room with her knowledge. "Well, other than the *myosis* Dr. Moretti exhibited, I reported all of that to the cardiovascular technologist when he came into Rip's room to check on him and inform us about Dr. Moretti's death."

"Are you talking about Pratyush Patel?" Maggie asked. Her tone sounded skeptical.

"Yes," I replied. "Why?"

"I was just wondering."

I let it drop, but was curious about the vibe she'd given off. It was as though she didn't like, or didn't trust the man. Apparently, my curiosity was evident on my face. Candace stepped up to explain and tease her co-worker in the process.

"Maggie has an axe to grind with Pratyush. They dated for six months before he broke it off with her to date a lady who volunteers in the pediatric ward at the Mayo Clinic. Maggie hasn't forgiven him or gotten over it yet."

"I have so gotten over that jerk!" Maggie declared. "I wasn't going to say anything, but I've been out on four or five dates with Mitch."

"Murphy?" Eva asked. Her jaw dropped open, and it obviously wasn't just to stuff the deviled egg she was holding into her mouth. "Mitch Murphy?"

"As in Dr. Murphy, the anesthesiologist?" I broke in. "He took care of Rip during his surgery. The last surgery Dr. Moretti performed before his death, I might add."

"Yes, that's him," Maggie admitted shyly.

"I can't say I blame you. He's as handsome as a movie star." To the amusement of all of the young women in the room, I added, "I may be in my seventies and have been married to the same man for over fifty years, but that doesn't mean I don't appreciate a hunk when I see one. You chose well, Maggie!"

"Uh, thanks," she replied shyly.

"You go, girl!" I raised my hand and Maggie somewhat reluctantly slapped it in a high-five manner. *Do the younger generations still do that?* I wondered. *Or am I merely showing my age?*

"He is pretty handsome," Maggie agreed. For Candace's sake, no doubt, she added, "Much better looking than Pratyush."

"Dr. Murphy reminds me of Peter O'Toole," I said to ease the tension that was developing between the two ladies.

"Reminds you of who?" I was surprised when nearly every young lady in the room asked the question in stereo.

"You girls have never heard of Peter O'Toole?" I asked in dismay.

"I have," Eva replied, waving her hand. "He was one of my mother's favorite movie stars."

"I've heard of him too," Carolyn said. "But I don't think I've seen any of his movies."

The rest of the collective faces were blank. I felt the age difference between me and the younger nurses in the room glowing like a miner's lamp on my forehead. "You're surely familiar with the movie *Goodbye, Mr. Chips*?" Eva nodded. When no one else responded, I said, "No? How about another film O'Toole starred in called *What's New Pussycat*?"

Again, no one but Eva and Carolyn showed any signs of recognization. "Seriously? Surely you've all heard of *Lawrence of Arabia*."

Monica raised her hand like she was my student in a grade school classroom. "I've heard of that one! Didn't it have something to do with a horse?"

"Um, well, there *were* horses in the film." I leaned back and selected a stuffed Greek olive off the appetizer plate being passed around. I was surprised Olivia hadn't already snagged it from the tray. I didn't necessarily like olives, but I'd needed something to plug up my pie hole before I made an even bigger spectacle of myself. I could feel myself becoming more and more of a relic. I could feel my wrinkles getting wrinklier and new age spots forming on top of my current age spots. I sat there surrounded by a bunch of young ladies who weren't even born yet when Ronald Reagan was President and told Mikhail Gorbachev to tear down the Berlin Wall. How could I possibly carry on a relatable conversation with any of them besides Eva? I'd be lucky if the gaggle of nurses didn't opt to carry me down the stairs to my car, in fear I might fall and break a hip on my way out.

At that point, I thought it best to just sit back and take in the chat fest silently. My resolve lasted a full fifteen seconds. After Eva scanned the room, apparently to make certain Olivia had indeed departed, she mentioned the fact that Dr. Blaze O'Ryan had always been jealous of Dr. Moretti. I felt compelled to ask, "Why was he jealous? Weren't they both heart surgeons?"

"Yes," Eva began, "but Dr. Moretti was chosen as director of the clinic, a position Dr. O'Ryan felt *he* had earned due to his tenure at the clinic. With six more years of employment at STAT and, before that, a decade as a cardiac surgeon at the nearby Mayo Clinic, he felt he should've been selected as head of the department. I was kind of shocked by the clinic's choice myself. I thought O'Ryan had it in the bag."

Everyone seemed to be in agreement with Eva's assessment. Several responded with, "So did I."

"Wasn't he the cardiologist who took over performing CPR on Dr. Moretti for you, Jolene?" I asked, still not convinced that foul play hadn't played a part in the surgeon's death.

"Yes," Jolene replied. I got the impression she felt the same way.

"But it was a pathetic attempt to revive him. He may have done a total of five chest compressions before he stopped and said, 'Waste of time. The dude's a goner.'"

There was a collective gasp in the room. Monica was the first to regain her ability to speak. "Dr. O'Ryan actually said those exact words?"

"Yep!" Jolene nodded and repeated the doctor's remarks. "'Waste of time. The dude's a goner.' And he said those words with absolutely no inflection in his voice, as if he was merely confirming the sky was blue. It pissed me off so much I wanted to strangle him with his own stethoscope."

Eva spoke next. "As his operating room nurse, I feel obliged to defend Dr. O'Ryan. Jolene, you said yourself that Marco truly was as blue as the sky and past reviving at that point."

Jolene nodded. "True, but I still thought it was a totally unfeeling thing to say, and I told him so."

"Good for you!" Charmaine said as Eva merely shook her head in response. "What exactly did you say to him?"

"Well, I don't recall exactly, but in so many words, I told him I found his attitude cold, callous, and calculating."

Beginning her response with the phrase "in so many words" told me that Jolene could have actually said anything from, "You're a heartless prick that should be reported to the chief of staff" to "that sounded a wee bit dispassionate, sir." But I didn't comment on Jolene's ambiguous response. Besides, all of the nurses, except for Eva, were now giving Jolene props for her directness with the clearly unpopular physician. They were proud she'd had the courage to stand up to the self-indulgent man and I had no desire to take that away from her. I could tell she was uncomfortable with the attention, and she proved it when she next spoke.

"Enough about me!" Jolene insisted. "Candace, didn't you date Dr. Moretti for a number of months before you caught him cheating with Frankie, the woman he ended up marrying about a year ago?"

"Well, um, yeah, but, I, um," Candace stammered. She appeared even more uncomfortable than Jolene just had, and seemed unable to put a full sentence together.

Jolene cut her no slack and pressed on. Her demeanor had turned from teasing to antagonistic. "And didn't you tell me at the time of the breakup that Marco would pay for cheating on you the way he had? It's got to feel extremely satisfying to you that karma has struck. Doesn't it?"

Candace's face turned crimson, even redder than the goblet of wine she held in her right hand. "No, of course not! You know damn well I didn't mean what I said. I was just hurt at the time. I was very happy to see Marco and Frankie get married. They were perfect for each other."

"That's not what you said back then!" Jolene was now in full attack mode. "In fact, Candace, I recall you saying you wanted to give them a set of knives for their wedding in hopes they'd use them to carve each other up like pineapple chunks in a fruit salad. You told me Frankie was a gold digger and only interested in Marco's money. She wanted to be the trophy wife of an esteemed cardiac surgeon, you said, so she could flaunt it in front of her friends."

"That was a long time ago, Jolene! I've moved on since then and you should too!" Candace's voice had risen as she responded to her imperious co-worker. She was now beyond incensed and raced out of the apartment, slamming the door behind her. With an evil smirk, Jolene mumbled, "good riddance" before chugalugging the last of her drink.

"Let's get back to this wonderful collection of Scentsy products." Maggie, the ever-gracious host jumped up out of her chair with a box of the warmers in her arms. In an obvious attempt to change the topic, and lower the current smoldering temperature in the room, she said, "I better go after Candace while you all listen to Holly as she talks about the Scentsy Company and shows us some of the new products they've recently released. There are several of them that are just fabulous and I'm sure you'll agree."

The quiet, mild-mannered neighbor, who I now realized was the consultant Maggie had mentioned when she first invited me to attend her party, suddenly changed into an assertive salesman who could've hawked every clunker on a used car lot given the opportunity. It didn't hurt Holly's cause any that all of the Scentsy warmers were as cute as they were clever.

Maggie returned to her apartment a few minutes later, sans Candace. With a shrug as a response to Eva's question on whether or not Candace was returning to the party, everyone chose to let the matter drop and carry on as though the contentious confrontation they'd just witnessed had never occurred. It sure raised a few questions in my mind, however. I would need to make some notations in my notebook as soon as I returned to the Caboose. I was starting to realize that more than a few of the victim's colleagues might have a personal reason to want to do away with Dr. Moretti.

As it turned out, I was extremely glad I'd decided to attend Maggie's party. I could hardly wait to repeat to Rip all of the juicy gossip and autopsy details I'd heard at the party I'd originally been reluctant to attend.

And, later on, if and when Rip decided he wanted to pursue the surgeon's death further on his own——with my help, of course ——I would already be armed with multiple suspects who had viable motives to want the esteemed doctor dead.

FIVE

"Any news on what caused Dr. Moretti's death?" Rip asked Dr. Blaze O'Ryan at his follow-up appointment at the STAT Cardiac Clinic a few days later. With Dr. Moretti's passing, Rip had become a patient of Dr. O'Ryan's, and all of his follow-up care would be handled by the cardiologist who we'd soon learn had a personality that was as fiery as his hair. The surgeon's mop of crimson hair really did remind me of a red oleander bush in full bloom that had been set ablaze.

"Nah." Dr. O'Ryan shook his head. His obvious lack of empathy was alarming. "I'm sure it was just a case of natural causes. Maybe he ate something he was allergic to. I know he was deathly allergic to peanuts, which show up in so many food items these days. "

"Really?" Rip asked.

"Uh-huh." The doctor's tone was so cold that if I'd stuck my tongue against his two-syllable response, it would've stuck to it as though it were a frozen flagpole. I'd met his wife, Olivia, at Maggie's Scentsy party and couldn't imagine the warm, friendly woman being married to this surly doctor.

I had joined Rip at his appointment as I always did. I served as his ears and was more apt to ask important questions than he was. I spoke now to the surgeon. "I heard the medical examiner, Dr. Steed, I believe his name is, said he thought it was a potential case of anaphylactic shock, which would go along with your theory Dr. Moretti had an allergic reaction. Wouldn't it?"

"Yep."

O'Ryan was either a man of few words or entirely indifferent to the untimely fate of his colleague. I decided a different tactic was in order.

"Have you heard who's going to be in charge of the clinic now that Dr. Moretti's gone?"

The doctor's head spun so fast to look at me that, if he'd been wearing a hairpiece it would've been flung across the room. "Why do you ask? Have *you* heard something?"

"Well, no," I replied, troubled by the instant change in his demeanor. "I just knew Dr. Moretti used to hold the director's position, and figured they'd have to select someone to replace him now that he's deceased."

"Yes, they will." Dr. O'Ryan placed the stethoscope Jolene had wanted to use as a murder weapon up against Rip's chest, no longer interested in anything I had to say. I barely heard him mumble, "Better be me after all I've done to earn that position."

"Excuse me?" I hoped he'd elaborate on his utterance, but he clammed up, refusing to respond or even acknowledge I'd spoken. Looking directly at Rip he said, "Everything sounds fine. Don't forget to keep checking your blood pressure. As I'm sure you know, a normal reading is 120/80. A systolic, or first number, reading of 140 or higher, and/or a diastolic, the second number, reading of 90 or higher, is considered to be hypertension. If those elevated readings are consistent, the hypertension needs to be treated with medication, as yours is. Take your blood pressure medicine as prescribed, and let me know if your readings are consistently higher than 130/85. All right?"

"Yes, sir," Rip said. "Rapella makes sure I check it at least four times a day."

"Good. Continue to do so." Dr. O'Ryan looked straight into Rip's eyes as he spoke. "You are free to go now. Tell Colleen at the check-out desk I want to see you back again in one week."

"That was almost uncomfortable, wasn't it Rip?" I asked my husband as we walked down the hallway toward the check-out desk.

"It wasn't too bad," Rip replied. "My wrist is still sore, of course, but other than——"

"I'm not talking about you, Rip," I said, interrupting his response. "I was referring to Dr. O'Ryan's total disregard for the death of Dr. Moretti, a colleague he's worked closely with for a number of years. How could a loss like that not have a significant effect on Dr. O'Ryan? He couldn't have been any less concerned had it been the pothos plant in his office that had died."

"Have you been in Dr. O'Ryan's office?" Rip asked.

"Of course not!"

"Then how do you know he has a pothos plant in there?"

"Oh, good Lord." Sometimes carrying on a conversation with Rip took more patience than I possessed. "I have no idea what the man has in his office. I was just using the pothos plant as an example."

"If you're talking about what O'Ryan said about how much he'd done to earn the head position at STAT Clinic, then yes, that *was* a bit uncomfortable. He sounded bitter."

"You heard that? I could just barely make it out." I was initially astonished. But after I thought about it for a few moments, I became more angry than surprised. "How in the world could you hear his faint whisper when you can't hear me holler at you to take the trash out?"

"Could it be because I'm not always in the mood to jump up and carry the trash up to the RV park's dumpster?" Rip laughed to let me know he was kidding. But it was too late. I had already walloped him with my shoulder bag. It was a clear case of what I always accused Rip of having——selective hearing. "Seriously, honey. The doctor was leaning over me when he said it, no more than a foot from my head. I couldn't help but hear him."

"Yeah, I guess that's true. I was sitting across the room from you two at the time. So, what do you make of it? Do you think it's at all conceivable that Dr. O'Ryan had something to do with Dr. Moretti's death?"

"Anything's possible," he replied. "But it sounds like they're still classifying it a death by natural causes."

"Do you believe that to be true?"

"Not entirely. But as much as I'd like for them to delve a little further into it, there's not much we can do if they decide not to."

I beg to differ with you, I thought.

"While we're here at the hospital, I want to stop by the nurses' desk on the second floor and see if Maggie is working today," I told Rip after the receptionist handed him an appointment card for the following week and we'd stepped away from the checkout desk. "I want to thank her for inviting me to her Scentsy party."

"Why don't you go ahead?" Rip asked. "I'll wait for you in the truck."

"Okay, fine. I won't be long." I was actually delighted Rip was not going to accompany me to visit with the nurse. I wanted to open an access portal, so to speak, so I'd be able to use it to speak with Maggie, Candace, Jolene, or any other of the nurses, should we decide to do a little investigating into Dr. Moretti's death on our own. I didn't want to be forced to explain to Rip what I was doing while in the company of any of the potential suspects. As I parted ways with Rip, I said, "And don't be stopping to buy a candy bar from the vending machine on your way out!"

"Spoilsport," he replied as he walked away from me.

———

I found Maggie at the nurses' desk in the post-operative cardiac ward where all of the patients stayed while they were under observation following heart surgery of any kind. The clinic primarily performed stent placements, catheter ablation, balloon septosomy, and other basic cardiac procedures such as these. While pacing around in the waiting room during Rip's operation, I'd spoken to a woman whose husband was having a pacemaker implanted. We'd chatted for a bit to pass the time. The woman told me that more critical surgeries, like aorta valve replacements and heart transplants, were performed by the cardiac team at the nearby Mayo Clinic. When the surgeons at Mayo got to a point they wanted, or needed, a less stressful job, they often came to STAT to apply for a position on their cardiac staff. "The work here comes with a smaller salary and less benefits, but it also comes with a reduced amount of pressure and fewer hours," the lady had said.

Maggie was entering data into the rolling computer she pushed from one patient's room to another all day long when I walked up to the desk. She looked up and recognized me immediately. She nearly tripped over her cart as she rushed up to envelope me in a hug. "Oh, Rapella, it is so nice to see you again."

"The feeling is mutual," I replied warmly.

"I hope you didn't come here to pick up your Scentsy order, because it's not due to be delivered for several days."

"Oh, no. I'm in no hurry for that." At my response, Maggie appeared a little deflated, so I added, "Not that I'm not anxious to get it. The warmer I ordered is just the most adorable thing I've ever seen and will be the perfect addition to our travel trailer."

Maggie smiled. "The Chartreuse Caboose?"

"Yes. Good memory."

"I would love to see a travel trailer painted chartreuse with sunflowers all over it."

"Not exactly *all* over it, but there are a number of them to be sure," I explained, not wanting her to get the idea our home on wheels was gaudy. Or, an eyesore as my daughter described the trailer. "I will have to invite you over one day for a drink."

"I'd love that," she replied. "I'll bring a pitcher of my mango margaritas that you enjoyed so much."

"That'd be awesome, Maggie! I never thought I could find an alcoholic beverage that could compete with my daily tequila sunrises, but your margaritas are every bit as tasty. When's your next day off?"

"I'm off on Tuesday. Write down your address, or how to locate your trailer, and I'll stop by that day. Would that be okay with you?"

"It's absolutely okay," I replied. "If you can find the Autumn Woods RV Park, I can assure you you'll have no trouble spotting the Caboose. What time?"

"Whenever it's convenient for you is fine by me. I have something I want to run by you anyway so that would be an ideal time to do so."

As I scribbled the address of the RV park and our site number on a post-it note I found on the desk next to us, I said, "How about three o'clock Tuesday afternoon? That's when Rip and I usually indulge in the once-a-day cocktails our primary doctor allows us."

"That'd be fine. I look forward to it."

"I look forward to it as well, Maggie. Just out of curiosity, what's the nature of what you want to run past me?" I asked casually. As you should know by now, patience is *not* one of my virtues.

"I can't really chat right now because I have to go check on my patient in room 206. The alarm is going off on his infusion pump again. Another occlusion, no doubt," the nurse said, rolling her eyes. "The IV is in his elbow and I keep telling the old fogey not to bend his arm, but he does it anyway."

"We old fogies almost never follow instructions well," I replied.

When we both stopped chuckling, she assured me, "You're not an old fogey, Rapella. You remind me of Jamie Lee Curtis. You could be her twin."

"Really?" I asked, hoping it wasn't just insincere flattery. "My granddaughter told me the exact same thing. And that's a comparison I take as a high compliment coming from either one of you."

"It's true. You have the same hair color and cute hairstyle, blue eyes, and slender build as the actress. You're a very youthful seventy-two-year-old, Rapella, and a whole lot of fun to be around."

"Thank you, dear. That means a lot coming from a young lady who really knows how to throw a party. Speaking of which, do you know if Candace and Jolene are speaking to each other again?"

"I don't know, but probably not. Candace reports for duty here on the post-surgery ward at seven tonight, and Jolene now works as an anesthesiologist nurse alongside Mitch during heart surgeries, so they rarely see each other," Maggie explained. "As soon as Dr. Moretti's position is filled, she'll likely go back to being an operating room nurse. We only have three surgeons on the staff currently so she's the odd man out, or girl in this case. Although I did hear the position will be open to anyone who applies for it.

And, frankly, I hope Candace gets her old job back. The way she was replaced by Jolene was terribly unfair."

"Hmm," I mused. "Well, then, I'll keep my fingers crossed for Candace. I didn't exactly warm up to Jolene at your party."

"She *can* be a little overbearing."

"A *little?*" I asked. "That may be in the running for understatement of the year. So it sounds like during work hours, Jolene is working with Dr. Murphy, who's the same doctor that you're playing with *after* work hours. That could get a little dicey, couldn't it?"

"Maybe, but I hope not," Maggie replied. "I've no doubt that if Jolene was to develop an interest in Mitch, she'd have no qualms about trying to steal him from me. But I don't think Mitch is particularly enamored with her 'it's all about me' attitude, either."

"Good, because Jolene couldn't begin to measure up to the beautiful and very special woman he's already dating."

"Thank you, Rapella." Maggie beamed at me in appreciation. "Now I really need to get back to work, but we'll discuss something that's been bothering me about Dr. Moretti's death when I come over on Tuesday."

After sharing another hug, I left Maggie to get back to her job. After all, there was an old fogey waiting on her to turn off the alarm on his IV pump so he could bend his arm again after she exited his room.

As I walked to the parking lot where Rip was waiting for me in the truck, I had to wonder what it was about Dr. Moretti's death that had Maggie troubled. *Does she believe the natural causes that killed the surgeon were not so natural after all? Like Rip and I suspect, does Maggie also believe there was more to his death than meets the eye?* I could hardly wait to converse with the floor nurse on Tuesday. If I had thought waiting for the visiting hours to be over at the cardiac cath lab was like watching a tray of water in a freezer turn into ice cubes, then waiting for three o'clock on Tuesday afternoon to arrive was going to be like watching a glacier melt.

"How was Maggie doing?" Rip asked when I joined him in the truck.

"She looked as if she was getting along all right." I was impressed Rip had gotten Maggie's name right ever since I'd written it on his hand while he was in the hospital.

Maybe that's the trick, I thought. *I need to start writing everything I want for him to remember on one of his hands, as if he were a human memo pad.*

"That's good. She's a sweet girl," Rip said.

"I agree. She is definitely a great nurse and an even better person. I was surprised when she said there was something about Dr. Moretti's death that was bothering her."

"Did she elaborate at all on that sentiment?" Rip asked.

"No. She was on the clock and had to get back to work. But we made arrangements for her to stop by on her day off, which is this Tuesday. Maggie's going to bring over a pitcher of her delicious mango margaritas and we're going to discuss whatever it is that's on her mind."

"You'll enjoy that, I'm sure; both the conversation and the margaritas. They *are* to die for, after all," Rip said with a smile.

"Yes. I definitely will enjoy both. Since she'll be here during our normal cocktail hour, you'll be able to participate in the discussion, as well. It will be interesting to see the situation from her perspective."

"Yes, it will be."

"Do you know what else she told me?" I asked rhetorically, because unless he'd recently acquired psychic powers and failed to mention it to me, there was no way he could know the answer.

"What else did she tell you?" Rip wore a bemused expression. I knew he was tickled to see me so animated.

"She said that I was a very youthful seventy-two-year-old and a lot of fun. She even told me I reminded her of Jamie Lee Curtis, just as Tiffany had said when we were in Albuquerque for her birthday."

"She weren't lying neither, cupcake. You are everything Maggie said you was and more."

It was such a sweet response I decided not to correct his atrocious grammar. "And she said she'd love to see the Chartreuse Caboose, too. I don't think she can quite picture a chartreuse travel trailer with sunflowers painted on it."

"And who could?" he asked. "I know it didn't turn out anything like what I'd expected when you first told me you were going to paint it."

"Was it better or worse than you thought it'd be?"

Rip effectively took the fifth by ignoring my question and changing the conversation to an entirely different subject. "How would you feel about going out for supper tonight? I noticed a restaurant on Broadway Avenue called Salad Brothers Café and Deli, and I thought that sounded healthy and appealing. I know you like salad bars and I'm going to have to start liking lettuce too, whether I like it or not."

"That sounds absolutely wonderful," I agreed. "There's a lot more to salad bars than just lettuce, you know. "

"I know. I'll have to start liking carrots and radishes a little more too, I guess."

"You're so bad, Rip," I teased. "I think you'll find a lot of things you like if this place offers a decent variety of stuff on their salad bar."

"I suppose."

"I wasn't really in the mood to cook tonight anyway, so I'd appreciate a break from the kitchen."

And that, believe it or not, is how I ended up in the Mayo Clinic's emergency room an hour later. Hives as big as silver dollars and nearly dying from oxygen deprivation notwithstanding, it was a stroke of good fortune. What we learned there would set Rip and me on a path to get to the truth behind Dr. Moretti's death. I couldn't predict whether or not it was the right path, but at least it was a place to start.

SIX

"I'm going to order a Cobb salad," Rip said as he spread his dinner napkin across his lap. "What sounds good to you?"

"I haven't had shrimp in forever, so I think I'll try the grilled shrimp salad with feta cheese and cherry tomatoes. The man in the orange shirt sitting over there by the door has a Rueben sandwich on his plate that looks delicious, but the shrimp salad would be a much healthier choice."

Ironically, it was the healthier choice that nearly killed me.

"What's wrong, Rapella?" Rip asked me as he helped me to the truck. He was carrying my purse which undoubtedly weighed more than the maximum amount he was supposed to lift after his stent placement. "Should I take you to the emergency ward?"

"I don't know. I'm having difficulty catching my breath."

"That answers my question. I'm driving you straight to the Mayo Clinic. I heard their ER has an excellent reputation."

"Okay," I squeezed out, but just barely. As I struggled to

breathe, I noticed welts forming on my arms. I recognized them as hives. *Am I having an allergic reaction to something I ate?* I wondered. I'd never experienced anything like this before and was unaware of any allergies I had, other than codeine.

We pulled up to the curb outside the emergency room entrance no longer than five minutes later. I felt as if a Burmese python had wrapped itself around my neck and was squeezing tighter and tighter with each breath I struggled to inhale. A staff member appeared instantly with a wheelchair. Once inside the building, two nurses descended upon us. I indicated I couldn't breathe and one of the nurses quickly strapped an oxygen mask to my face, which only marginally helped. The second nurse rolled me through a large red door and down the hallway to a room. A white-haired physician, who looked well past retirement age, appeared almost immediately while the nurse was inserting an IV in my arm and hanging a bottle of fluid from a hook above the infusion pump. Whatever flowed into my vein had an instant effect and I could breathe again. Once the panicky feeling eased up, I read the front of the bag and realized they'd given me epinephrine, the same medication in epi-pens, which made perfect sense.

While visiting Lexie Starr and Stone Van Patten at the Alexandria Inn in Rockdale, Missouri, over the holidays, I'd seen a young lady experiencing the same symptoms as I had. An EMT gave her an injection via an epi-pen and her breathing had improved rapidly too. In her case, she'd inadvertently ingested crab meat and her shellfish allergy had immediately flared up and rendered her unable to breathe.

Oh my! I just ate shrimp! I realized. *Could I have developed an allergy to shellfish too? I know it's a very common allergy and I've heard you can develop an allergy to a certain substance at any point in your lifetime.*

It was determined that a new shellfish allergy was exactly what had preempted my sudden case of hives and the swelling of my windpipe.

"You are lucky to be alive," the physician told me. "Another couple of minutes and you might not have been so fortunate."

I glanced over at Rip, who had visibly paled. He'd always told me that I was not allowed to predecease him. "I want to go first," he'd always say. "I would be lost without you, but you would be able to get by just fine without me. Women are tougher than men when it comes to that type of thing."

"I would be lost without you too," I would always reply, even though I wholeheartedly agreed that women were tougher than men in nearly every possible way except physically. And there were even a few exceptions to men having more physical strength than women. Have you ever seen a young woman lift a car off her trapped child? Okay, I've never actually witnessed that scenario either, but I've heard it's happened.

I thanked the doctor for saving my life, and asked, "Did you know Dr. Marco Moretti, the director of the STAT Cardiac Clinic?"

"Of course," the doctor responded. "He was a legend in the medical profession. What happened to him was such a shame."

"Do you know exactly what *did* happen to him?" Rip took the words right out of my mouth.

"Yes. He died." The doctor appeared perplexed as he gave his simplistic response.

"We knew that he passed," I said. "Rip was curious if you knew if the official cause of death has been determined."

"Not that I know of," the doctor began, "but I wouldn't be surprised if he accidentally ingested something with peanut in it again."

"Again?" I asked, recalling Dr. O'Ryan mentioning Moretti's severe peanut allergy at Rip's appointment.

"Yes." The doctor went on to explain. "He was attending a meeting here at Mayo when he ate a cereal bar he didn't realize contained peanuts and ended up in the emergency room. I was the physician on duty at the time. There are folks like Dr. Moretti who are so deathly allergic to nuts that the smallest bit of peanut residue can put them out of commission. It is the most common food allergy among children and the second-most common allergy in adults. Shellfish is one of the most frequent types of allergy people acquire later in life, like you clearly did."

I'm not sure if he was violating the Hippocratic Oath he'd taken by discussing another patient's health records with us, but it wasn't like we were going to rat him out. I suppose when one approaches eighty years of age, they really don't give a flying fig about things like that. He must've been thinking the same thing as I was because when I asked him if the cardiac surgeon had experienced a life-threatening reaction during his ER visit like I had, he replied, "We'd better just concentrate on you for now."

What we'd learned about the late surgeon wasn't terribly significant, but it did give us hope that his death had been accidental. Or so we thought until the ER doctor said, "What would be surprising about a peanut taking Moretti out is that he was always so careful after that visit to the emergency room to not eat anything that contained nuts. He painstakingly scrutinized all of the ingredients listed on every single package he or his wife, Frankie, purchased at the store. He also told me that without exception, he never ate anything if he was unsure of its contents."

"I totally understand. You can be certain I'll never eat another shrimp."

"Or any other kind of shellfish, just to be safe," Rip added.

"I agree." I loved seafood but after the doctor had informed me my allergic accident was nearly fatal, I wasn't taking any chances. I thought back to the night I'd picked up dinner at Red Lobster and took it back to the trailer to eat while Rip was staying overnight at the cath lab. *Had I unsuspectingly ordered shellfish instead of chicken and been alone when the anaphylactic shock occurred, I might not be sitting here today. Dolly had been great company, but it's not like she could've hopped off the couch and called 9-1-1 when she noticed I was strug-gling to breathe. Nor could Dolly have rendered CPR if I'd become nonre-sponsive. More likely she'd have checked to see if there was any leftover food in my mouth she could help herself to. I shuddered at the thought.* "Absolutely no shellfish will ever cross these lips again from here on out."

"Excellent," the doctor said. "Just don't forget that accidents can happen, like one did to Dr. Moretti. In the same vein as peanuts, shellfish can sometimes be found in dishes you'd never expect to find them in. I'd advise you to purchase an epi-pen to carry in your purse every time you leave the house."

I could've told him our house was actually a thirty-foot travel trailer but knew he had more important things to do than sit around and listen to me babble. Rip had another question, however. I could tell my brush with death had scared him spitless. "Are epi-pens available here in the hospital's pharmacy? I'd like to get one before we leave the premises."

"Yes, I'm nearly certain the pharmacy carries them," the doctor replied. "If they don't, we might be able to find an extra one here in the supply cabinet."

"Okay, thanks," Rip said. "We'll stop and get one before we leave."

"But only if you can't find one in the supply cabinet," I added, not being one to look a gift horse in the mouth. I'd heard epi-pens were expensive and so naturally I preferred a free one. "We are on a fixed income, you know."

"Of course." The doctor pondered my remark for a moment. "Let me go see if I can find one to give you, but keep it to yourself if I do. It'll save you about seven-hundred dollars."

"Seven-hundred dollars for an epi-pen?" I gasped. For a second I thought I wasn't going to be able to catch my breath again. Even Rip looked as though his entire life had just passed before his eyes in less than three seconds. "That's plum crazy! No wonder so many people can't afford health care anymore. Dying is so much cheaper."

"Not really," the doctor said with a chuckle. "Have you paid for a funeral lately? My wife died a couple of years ago and I'm still making payments to Manfranz & Pine Funeral Home. Why do you think I'm still working at eighty years old?"

I knew the physician was being facetious about still making payments, but it answered my question about why he was still working. Clearly, he felt it was better than rattling around in his home all alone. No doubt the home was full of memories of a happy life with his late wife.

"I'm so sorry about the loss of your wife. But, I do get your point," I conceded. "I'd rather pay for an epi-pen than die with that seven-hundred dollars folded up in my pocket."

"Yep," the elderly doctor agreed. "It's a sign of the times. The price of everything has gone out of sight. You should thank the good Lord that neither of you are an insulin-dependent diabetic. I paid more for a tank of gas this morning than I did for my first car. It was a used piece of crap, but it got me to and from med school for a number of years."

"I know the feeling," Rip said, as the doctor exited the room. When the ER physician returned with a white bag containing two unused epi-pens, Rip was sincerely grateful. "Thank you, sir. We are both very appreciative."

"Yes," I piped in. "Thank you so very much. This will save us more than my first two cars cost put together."

The doctor nodded and said, "My pleasure. Mum's the word."

I assured him we'd never tell anyone the source of the life-saving devices and Rip nodded back in a manner that assured the doctor a gang of young thugs could not beat the epi-pens' true origin out of him.

We thanked the physician once again and waited for a nurse to bring me my discharge papers. As we exited the building, I clutched the white bag to my chest as though it contained the Hope Diamond rather than fourteen hundred dollars worth of epi-pens. After all, both were equally out of reach in our budget.

It was late by the time we returned to the RV park. The look Dolly gave us when we entered the trailer made it clear she'd come to the conclusion she was now an orphan. If I'd left my iPad on, she'd probably already have posted an ad on *Indeed*, advertising two openings for new servants to tend to her every need and desire.

Once Her Majesty was taken care of, I asked Rip, "Do you think it's likely that Dr. Moretti accidentally ate something with peanuts in it? It could explain his mysterious passing."

"I think it's feasible. I'm not sure how likely it is, but it's certainly within the realm of possibilities."

"Do you think the medical examiner checked Dr. Moretti's stomach contents during the autopsy of his body?"

"I don't know but I would certainly think so." Rip absentmindedly stroked the fur on Dolly's neck as he responded. Her purring reminded me of the humming sound an old chest freezer we owned used to make. By that stage, the seal around the lid had dried up so badly it was nearly nonexistent. The old appliance finally conked out while we were on vacation. We returned to a house that smelled as if it contained a dozen decomposing raccoons.

"Have you got any idea how we can find out more about the autopsy report?"

"Not really," Rip replied. "But coming up with schemes and scams is more in your wheelhouse than mine."

"Thank you."

When Rip's eyebrows arched in response, I realized his comment had not been meant as an accolade. But at that point, I didn't care. I needed to concentrate on an idea to find out autopsy information that wasn't normally meant for public scrutiny. I was convinced Charmaine had shared all she knew about the autopsy results with us at the Scentsy party. I decided to sleep on it and see if anything came to mind by morning.

I awoke suddenly at three o'clock the next morning, an idea brewing in my mind. The daughter of our good friend, Lexie Starr, was the official medical examiner of Buchanan County in Missouri. Wendy Van Patten was a good friend of ours, as well. If I could persuade Lexie to persuade Wendy to help us, maybe Wendy could pull some strings and persuade Dr. Steed to fax her a copy of Dr. Moretti's autopsy report. Granted, that was a lot of "persuading" and could potentially cost Wendy her job and Lexie her loving relationship with her daughter, as well as destroy our friendship with Wendy and her husband, Andy.

Would it be worth it? I wondered. *No, definitely not.* I flopped from side to side like a neon tetra that had jumped out of an aquarium as I considered the risks and rewards of approaching Lexie and Wendy. Exhausted, I finally climbed out of bed at six. I started the coffee maker and fed Dolly her breakfast while I continued to chew over the situation.

By the time Rip got up at seven-fifteen, I had decided it couldn't hurt to run the situation past Lexie and see how she reacted to my dilemma. Just before Christmas, I had helped Lexie get to the truth behind the death of her friend who lived next door to the Alexandria Inn. Maybe I could entice her to return the favor.

As it turned out, it didn't take much persuading or enticing to get Lexie Starr on board. I waited until nine to call her, knowing she'd be busy cooking breakfast for her bed and breakfast guests if I called earlier. I could hear the rattling of dishes as we spoke. She said the Alexandria Inn had been especially busy the last few weeks and she was currently cleaning up after a breakfast she'd prepared for their eight overnight guests. She described the French toast, eggs, and bacon as "disappearing faster than a sixteen-year-old boy when he hears his girlfriend's father open up the front door at the end of a date." It sounded very much like a dream Rip had reported having two nights ago. He said it was more like a nightmare because the spread of breakfast foods went up in a cloud of smoke the moment he walked up to the buffet table with his plate. I could feel his pain. I used to have a recurring nightmare about my teeth falling out for no discernible reason. Once I'd had all my teeth pulled to be fitted for dentures, I never had the dream again.

I should not have been surprised that Lexie was instantly intrigued by the story of the cardiologist's mysterious death. I think she gets some kind of enigmatic and unexplainable pleasure out of probing into murder cases. Even as that last thought crossed my mind, I could visualize the black pot on my stove calling the tea kettle colorful names.

SEVEN

L exie called me back an hour later. She had spoken with her daughter and had good news for me. "Wendy said she'd see what she could do."

"That's awesome, Lexie!" I exclaimed. "Thank you so much!"

"I did kind of have to fib to Wendy though." Lexie sounded upset with herself for deceiving her only child.

"It's for a good cause," I said to ease Lexie's remorse.

"And I also had to throw Rip under the bus."

"No worries," I assured her. "He's been there before. I've thrown him under the bus so many times, he probably thinks of it as his second home."

Lexie's chuckle told me she was feeling better about the situation already.

"What did you tell Wendy?" I asked.

"I was kind of vague, but my story had something to do with Rip wanting to look into a case that had something to do with his doctor's death. And because the surgeon had something to do with saving Rip's life, Rip thought he owed something to Dr. Moretti."

"I think 'vague' might be an understatement." *It sounds like her story to Wendy had too many "something to do with's" to be believable, but Wendy always did have a soft spot for Rip.*

"I couldn't risk giving any detailed information."

"No, I suppose not. Actually, I'm surprised she agreed to do it for us. Wendy has a reputation of going strictly by the books."

"That's true," Lexie agreed. "And that's why I threw Rip under the bus and made it sound as if it was his idea and for his benefit. No offense, Rapella."

"None taken," I said. *Well, maybe a little, but if that's what it took to potentially get a copy of Dr. Moretti's autopsy report, the sting of being a bit offended was worth it.* "I would've done the same thing if our positions were reversed."

"Good. Those two, along with Stone, have always been on the same page when it comes to you and me getting involved in murder cases, so I decided it was our best bet to make her think she was doing Rip a favor."

"Absolutely! Even though Wendy would actually be doing it for both of us, it was technically Rip who instigated the personal investigation this time around."

"That's an unexpected twist," Lexie said. "But I understand. It was basically Stone's idea that we get involved in investigating the truth behind what happened to his nephew Andy's best friend at Wendy and Andy's wedding."

"Yes, I remember that now. And thank goodness you did too."

"Exactly!" she said in concurrence. "I'll let you know when I hear something. Wendy said it would likely take a few days."

"Of course. Thank you so much, my friend."

"My pleasure, Rapella. I owed you one anyway!"

Rip was asleep in his recliner when my phone rang three days later. I saw it was Lexie calling, so I hurried outside and closed the trailer door behind me. I didn't want the phone to disturb Rip, because he was still recuperating from the stent procedure and supposed to be taking it easy. I think he felt completely healed but, being a man, and all, he was naturally compelled to milk the situation for all it was worth.

I also wanted my conversation with Lexie to be just between her and me. I wasn't in the mood to do any explaining, justifying, or fabricating after I ended the call. I didn't know how Rip would feel about being thrown under the bus by Lexie. He expected me to do so on occasion, but Lexie had Stone, her own husband for that kind of thing.

"Hello?" I said habitually into the phone.

"Hey, Rapella. It's Lexie. Have you heard anything about the doctor's tox screen results?"

"Nope. As far as I know, they haven't come back yet, but I heard it can take weeks. Was Wendy able to find out anything about the autopsy?" I asked with excitement evident in my voice.

"She couldn't get an official copy of the autopsy report," Lexie said. "Too much red tape to go through, she told me. But she did get the clerk in the medical examiner's office to give her some of the information off the report. Since Wendy is a medical examiner herself, the clerk probably thought it was official business and her duty to assist."

"That's what I'd hope would happen. What information was Wendy able to glean from the clerk?" I asked.

"Dr. Steed found no peanut residue in Dr. Moretti's stomach contents."

"Dang it," I said, disappointed at the news.

"But…" Lexie drug it out for as long as she could to elevate my anticipation level, a page she'd taken directly from my own book.

"But what?" I asked with a laugh. "Don't torture me and make me wait."

"Why not?" she asked with a giggle. "You do it to me all the time."

"Come on, buddy, you're killing me," I replied with a groan.

"All right, all right," she began, "I'll cut you some slack. The medical examiner did find a substance called 'lupin' in your doctor's system."

"What's lupin? Is it a toxin?"

"No."

"If it's not toxic, why is the discovery of lupin significant?" I asked.

"Wendy explained to me that because lupin and peanuts both belong to the legume family, there is cross-reactivity. As much as forty-two percent of people with a peanut allergy will also have a reaction to lupin."

"Wow!" I exclaimed. "So you're telling me it's possible that Dr. Moretti had a fatal allergic reaction to this lupin in his system?"

"Yes," Lexie replied. "And Wendy also said that some people with a peanut allergy don't realize they are also allergic to lupin, so don't look for it on food labels."

"That makes sense. But Dr. Moretti is a very intelligent physician. My guess is that he not only knew about the significant chance of being allergic to both, but that he was tested for it during one of those skin-prick allergy tests. According to the ER physician, Dr. Moretti was hyper-alert to what was in everything he ate, and I'd bet he checked the labels for both peanuts and lupin."

"Yes, the clerk made a similar remark, but she said the autopsy report indicated there were a few small particles of lupin in his stomach contents that had originally been in the form of lupin beans. The dust-like substance hadn't totally broken down yet." Lexie paused to let the importance of what she'd said sink in. When she sensed it was not only not sinking in, it was floating like a bloated fish carcass in my brain, she elaborated. "Dr. Steed noted that it appeared as if the late doctor had ingested something containing ground lupin directly following his last surgery."

"Which would've been the stent procedure he performed on Rip," I broke in.

"Sadly, yes," Lexie responded. I could tell she'd Googled the name of the substance before calling me, as she went on. "Lupin beans may be eaten whole, boiled or dry and are a common snack in Europe and Asia, but can also be found here in America. The beans can be ground into flour or bran and used to add fiber, texture, and protein in food manufacturing. Lupin is gluten-free and may often be found in gluten-free products as a substitute for wheat."

"You know what?" The importance of the discovery had finally sunk in and a sense of relief washed over me like a rogue tidal wave on the beach. "I'll bet Dr. Moretti had celiac disease."

"That's exactly what I was thinking." Lexie was silent for a few seconds before continuing. "It's very possible he ate something that didn't come out of a package and didn't have an ingredient label on it for him to scrutinize. Perhaps whoever made it for him was aware of his peanut allergy and the fact he couldn't tolerate gluten so he or she substituted ground lupin for flour, having no knowledge of the lupin-peanut cross-reactivity. You and I had no idea about it until recently, so there's a good chance others wouldn't either; even nurses who weren't in the allergy and immunology field."

"Yes, I think you are definitely on to something. I can't thank you and Wendy enough for your help," I said.

"I was more than happy to assist," Lexie said. "And as I said before, I owed you one. Like I told you, Wendy was under the impression she was doing a favor for Rip, so she was glad to help too. And it's not that she wouldn't be just as delighted to do you a favor. It's just that she has a tendency to think you and I are foolish to put ourselves at risk to try and solve murder cases we have no business being involved in. And that is a direct quote."

"I figured as much," I replied dryly. "And a popular opinion, it seems."

"Yes, unfortunately, it's pretty much a unanimous opinion amongst the people we hold most dear. Rat bast——"

We were both laughing too hard for her to finish her last remark.

"There's just one other thing about the autopsy report that Wendy was able to garner from her conversation with the medical examiner's office clerk."

"What's that?" I asked.

"Dr. Steed noted that other than the lupin bean residue, there was nothing else in Dr. Moretti's stomach, as though he hadn't had a bite to eat for quite a few hours. The medical examiner put in his report that Moretti hadn't ingested much of anything since the previous day. You'd think a physician would realize that breakfast is the more important meal of the day. And then to skip lunch too is kind of strange."

"And you'd think Dr. Moretti would've needed a little sustenance to sustain enough energy to get through a full day's workload. Rip was his final patient of the day. He'd already performed several other surgeries prior to Rip's stent placement procedure." I briefly mulled over the new information, not sure if it would prove to be of any consequence or not. I had basically closed the lid on the case when I learned he'd ingested lupin, a substance he likely had a severe allergy to. I decided I could consider the implications later, and asked Lexie about her three-month-old grandson, Chet.

We chatted for another ten minutes about the baby and other personal matters before bidding each other adieu. "Give Stone and the kids my love."

"I will," Lexie replied. "You do the same with Rip. And, just F.Y.I., Wendy made me promise not to tell anyone that she passed on information about Dr. Moretti's autopsy report because it could potentially cost her the job of medical examiner. She said she'd deny being involved with your investigation to her last breath. We don't want to put her in a bad position."

"No, of course not," I said. "I would never tell a soul we got any information from Wendy. Except for Rip, who will totally understand the need for secrecy in the matter."

"The first thing we should do is report the information you got from Wendy to the Rochester Police Department," Rip insisted when I relayed the information a few minutes later. I stared at him in disbelief. "It might have an important effect on their course of action in the investigation."

"No, Rip!" I exclaimed. "Has the salami slid off your saltine? The very idea is unthinkable! Telling the local police department what we heard from Wendy is the *last* thing we should do. We can't jeopardize her job. She's worked hard to get to where she's at in her career and we sure as heck aren't going to be the cause of it all crashing down on top of her. I would slice my own wrists before I'd do something that'd hurt Wendy."

Rip stared at me as though my eyes had turned fluorescent red and smoke and fire had shot out of my mouth as I'd spoken. I felt obligated to elaborate on my stance. "For that matter, I would not only slice my own wrists, I'd also slice *yours* before I'd let you do such a thing. What kind of thanks would that be to Wendy for agreeing to help us?"

"Okay, okay. I can see you are serious about this situation, but it sounded to me as if she only agreed to help me, not you," he replied in the smuggest tone I'd ever heard. It was technically true, but irritated me all the same. It didn't, however, irritate me half as much as Rip's next comment. "And if she did it as a favor to me, shouldn't what we do with that information be up to me as well?"

"In a normal situation, yes, it should be. But in this situation, absolutely not! Chances are the surgeon's death was an accident, in that he mistakenly ingested whatever had the lupin in it. There's no sense getting Wendy in trouble over a death that more than likely was accidental to begin with."

"What if the ingestion of the lupin, or whatever killed the surgeon, was *not* accidental, but rather intentional?"

"Even then, it's not worth getting Wendy in trouble, Rip," I said. "She adores you and potentially getting her in deep doo-doo is simply not an option."

"I suppose you're right," Rip agreed. "I really don't want to hurt Wendy, or her career, any more than you do. But the emergency room doctor had said Dr. Moretti was extremely careful about what he ingested. Maybe we can find out more about what he ate and how he came about eating it on our own without having to involve Wendy."

"That's exactly what we're going to do. Chances are the detectives have full access to the autopsy report anyway and know even more about what's in it than we do."

"Yeah, you're right," Rip consented. "I hadn't given it enough thought. I just can't help thinking someone could've spiked whatever he ate with lupin. It could've been something that didn't normally contain the substance, so as not to alert the surgeon to the possibility of an allergic reaction."

"Let's start by seeing if we can ascertain where the food Moretti consumed came from. That information will go a long ways toward figuring out if the ingestion of the food was inadvertent or otherwise."

"Agreed." Rip nodded. "And how do you plan to do that?"

"What do you mean by 'how do I plan to do that?'" I asked. "Am I going to have to do this all on my own? Lexie's done all she can for us at this point, as has Wendy."

"I realize that. I'll help you, Rapella," Rip assured me. "But this kind of information-seeking scheme is your forté, not mine.

Besides, I'm still recovering from my stent placement procedure. In fact, I could use a snack when you get a chance to fix me something."

"All right." I wasn't going to argue, even though I knew he was not beyond milking the situation. Rip had not only given me permission to stick my nose into a potential murder investigation that neither of us had any authority or right to be involved in, but he'd also agreed to assist me in my quest to get to the bottom of Marco Moretti's death. If I ran my mouth too much, all of that could potentially disappear into thin air. "Let me heat up some bean and bacon soup while I give some thought on how I might be able to attain more information on what Moretti ingested before his death."

"Okay. Soup sounds good."

"I'll get right on it." I knew anything with bacon in it sounded good to Rip. I didn't want to burst his bubble by telling him the amount of bacon in bean and bacon soup was so minuscule, the name of the soup was almost a misnomer. I was certain that the top echelon of the *Campbell Soup Company* was aware that "bean and bacon soup" sounded infinitely more appealing than simply "bean soup" ever could.

"Thanks." Rip looked at his watch. It was two-thirty in the afternoon. "While you're at it, why don't you fix our afternoon cocktails a bit earlier than usual? I could use a strong Crown and Coke right about now."

He'd taken the thought right out of my mind. I had a sudden hankering for a stiff drink as well. I had a niggling notion in the back of my mind that getting the information I needed would not come as smoothly as I hoped. But, then, when had it ever come without unforeseen pitfalls that embarrassed me, injured me, or nearly got me and/or someone I loved killed? Why should this case be any different?

EIGHT

An early morning phone call woke me up the next day. I looked at the screen on my phone and saw Maggie's name. *What perfect timing,* I thought. *Well, other than the fact it is six-fifteen and your call woke me from a dead sleep.*

"I wanted to catch you before I have to report for my seven o'clock shift," I heard Maggie say as I hurried to get out of bed and to the living room before my talking woke Rip up.

"The Scentsy order came in yesterday afternoon and I thought you could either pick it up at my place, or stop by the STAT clinic today, whichever is easier for you. I know you were anxious to get it and might not want to wait until I stop by on Tuesday."

"Well——"

My hesitation was due to not being fully alert yet, not indecision. I didn't have the heart to tell Maggie that I could wait until the week after never to get the Scentsy stuff I'd ordered and not be particularly distressed about it.

"Oh, no, honey," I said. "You don't need to worry about when I get my order. I'm not in any kind of..." I stopped talking abruptly when I recalled that I needed to delve into what Dr. Moretti had eaten directly before his death and whether or not he had celiac disease. Jolene had caused a ruckus at the Scentsy party when she confronted Candace Kobialka about dating the late cardiologist for a few months before Moretti dumped her for the woman who would become his wife. *Maybe I can use this opportunity to my advantage*, I thought. "Hey, Maggie, do you know if Candace is on duty today?"

"She'll replace me at seven this evening as the night nurse on this floor. Why do you ask?" Maggie's tone sounded skeptical. I wasn't sure if it was wise to clue her in on the fact Rip and I were now ready to get more involved in investigating Dr. Moretti's death on our own. The authorities seemed content to rule his death as being by natural causes, but we weren't. We'd decided I should do some snooping around on my own with as much assistance from Rip as he was able to provide while he was recuperating from his stent placement surgery. Without actually saying so, Rip made it clear he didn't expect to have much involvement in the actual investigation other than useful suggestions and plenty of moral support. So, in other words, the same amount of involvement he'd had in most of the cases we'd previously involved ourselves in.

"You're going to have a long enough day as it is without messing with me. But I think Rip would totally love the meat pastries that Candace brought to your Scentsy party and I wanted to see if I could get a copy of the recipe from her or her mother-in-law if Candace doesn't have it."

"Candace doesn't cook, but I'm sure she wouldn't mind asking Katarzyna to e-mail you the recipe for paszteciki," Maggie said. "Her mother-in-law goes by Kat, by the way."

"Katarzyna Kobialka? No wonder she prefers to be called Kat."

"Exactly," Maggie replied with a laugh. "Do you want me to ask Candace when she comes in tonight?"

"Better yet," I said. "I've got a lot on my plate today but I really am anxious to get my new warmer. How about if I stop by around seven this evening and speak to Candace myself? I can get my order from you then too, and cross both tasks off my list at the same time."

"That sounds perfect," Maggie replied. "I'll be so busy all day anyway because we are short a floor nurse today and the rest of us will have to pick up the slack. I find it hard to believe Chantell Williams has Covid-19 for the third time in six months. I know her husband, Justin, is celebrating his fiftieth birthday today too, which makes it even more doubtful. But since I used that same excuse in December, there's not much I can say about it. I spent my seven days of 'quarantine' on a beach in Grand Turk. Reading a cozy mystery with my toes in the sand while sucking down Mai Tai's all week——for medicinal purposes, of course——sure seemed to be just the therapy and medication I needed."

I had to chuckle at the orneriness in her voice and wonder if Maggie was just pulling my leg. I thanked her and rang off so she could get back to work. I could hear an IV machine alarm beeping in the background and realized another "old fogey" had probably bent his arm after being instructed not to.

"Before I hang up, can I ask you a question, Maggie?"

"Of course you can, Rapella."

"What was all that animosity about between Jolene and Candace at your party the other night? Do you think Candace could've played a part in Dr. Moretti's death, out of spite, jealousy, or just pure bitterness from having been dumped by the doctor?"

"That's one of the things I want to discuss with you on Tuesday. I don't have time to go into it right now."

"Oh, okay." I was disappointed but tried not to let it show in my voice. "Then I'll let you go for now and we'll talk about it then."

It sounded to me like Maggie *did* believe Candace might've had something to do with the sudden death of the good doctor. *Was it just a gut feeling?* I wondered. *Or is there something more concrete that justifies her suspicions? I guess I'll have to be patient and wait until Tuesday to find out. It's Sunday, seven a.m. right now. I just have to get through fifty-six agonizingly slow hours until Maggie joins Rip and me for our chitchat as we enjoy her mango margaritas.*

I was looking forward to stopping by the hospital at seven that evening and hoped I could use this visit to find out more about what Dr. Moretti ate before he collapsed in the clinic's parking lot. If Candace had dated Dr. Moretti, even for a short amount of time, she surely knew about his peanut allergy. Could she have slipped lupin into whatever he ate following Rip's stent procedure? If so, she wasn't likely to admit it. At the very least, she might have some insight into her former boyfriend's sudden demise, or could perhaps lead me to someone who did. Candace might even slip up and expose a motive or clue that implicated her in his death. One could only hope.

As the bells were tolling nineteen times at the St. Francis of Assisi Catholic Church a few blocks away from the STAT Cardio Clinic that evening, I was walking through the front door of the cath lab. I was on my way to pick up my Scentsy order from Maggie and strike up a conversation with Candace Kobialka.

"Good evening, sweetie," I greeted Maggie as I approached the nurse. She looked flustered as she was busily typing something into her rolling computer. "I was afraid I might've gotten here too late and was going to miss you."

Her responding laugh was more melancholy than mirth. "Just because they quit paying me at seven doesn't mean I ever get out of here before eight. And that's on a good day! It usually takes me at least thirty minutes to bring the night nurse up to speed on all of the patients, something I've yet to get done tonight."

"I know you must be exhausted and I won't keep you. Has Candace arrived yet?"

"Yes. I saw her in the break room a few minutes ago." As she spoke, she pointed down the opposing hallway. "Why don't you go ask her about the paszteciki recipe while I finish up entering the necessary data into this computer? I'll leave your Scentsy order right here on this desk if I don't see you before I leave."

"That'd be great, Maggie," I said as I gave her a quick hug. "Thanks so much, dear."

"My pleasure. Oh, and please tell Candace I'll be ready to bring her up to speed on the patients in about fifteen minutes."

"Will do, honey." I was glad she'd mentioned the name of the Polish pastry because it had slipped my mind and getting the recipe for paszteciki was my excuse to approach Candace. I strolled down the hallway in the direction Maggie had pointed. As I passed room 213, which had the name George Godfrey written above "Fall Risk" on the small chalkboard beside the door, I heard a loud and long rumbling sound emanating from inside. *Mr. Godfrey must be on a full diet*, I thought with amusement. *You don't get gas like that from broth and gelatin.*

Soon I came across a door with "Staff Only" on it and assumed I'd found the break room. I opened the door and walked inside as though I'd been on the clinic's payroll for a dozen years. I was surprised to find shelves of supplies such as towels, bedding, latex gloves, bottles of disinfectant, and the like. I'd expected to find a table and chairs, a refrigerator, and maybe some lockers for the nurses to store their personal belongings. I noticed then there was a partition that divided the room into two equal parts and assumed the break room was on the other side of it. Just as I took a step toward the partition, I heard a hushed voice that originated from behind it and froze in my tracks.

"I did not!" The voice whispered in a forceful fashion. I recognized the voice as that of Candace Kobialka. The southern drawl in her tone was unmistakable. "I didn't even know you had the hots for Marco when I started dating him."

"Sure you didn't," Jolene Sarcoxie responded with a heavy dose of sarcasm mixed in with a touch of indignation. Her voice was recognizable too because it reminded me of Marilyn Monroe's seductive tone in *Some Like it Hot*. With brunette hair, blue eyes, and just the right amount of curves, Jolene had a tall, lithe body that matched her voice and undoubtedly made men of all ages take a second look, and, I'd imagine, quite a few women, as well. "And if you truly didn't know I had my eye on him, you should have asked."

"Why would I have to ask?" Candace asked, clearly perplexed. "Maggie is dating Dr. Murphy. Did she have to ask your permission before going out with him?"

"Of course not," Jolene replied. I could tell she'd missed Candace's point when she added, "I had no designs on Mitch. He can't be more than about five-nine, and that's much too short for my liking. If I *had* wanted Mitch, however, I would've gotten him before Maggie even had a chance."

I could almost hear Candace rolling her eyes at Jolene's response. "What gives you dibs on any attractive and available man at the clinic? Although now I wish I hadn't, I had just as much right to pursue Marco as you did!"

"Humph!" Jolene's reply made it clear she had a different opinion. "Oh, come on now, Candace! Take a look at the two of us. If Marco had known I was attracted to him at the time, do you really think he'd have chosen you over me? He wouldn't have given you the time of day."

"Looks are not everything, Jolene! I have a friendly personality, an intelligent mind, a wicked sense of humor, and I'm not exactly as ugly as a pissed-off iguana, either."

"All of those qualities you profess to have are admirable but highly debatable." Jolene's remark was as callous as it was cruel. It cut to the bone like a buzz saw. Personally, I thought Candace, who was just as statuesque as Jolene and had those riveting green eyes and jet-black hair, was more attractive than her antagonist. She wasn't as buxomly, perhaps, but anyone could tell Jolene's huge breasts were an after-market product she'd paid dearly for. *Are men as attracted to fake boobs as they are natural ones?* I wondered. Although mine have always been ample enough in size, they now have a tendency to point down toward my penny loafers when I don't have them hoisted upward with a wired-infused push-up bra.

Candace responded to Jolene's hurtful remark about her appearance with an undignified snort. "Besides, what difference does it make? He ended up with Frankie anyway. If I had my druthers and could rewind the clock, I'd have encouraged you to make a play for him. Then he'd have broken your heart instead of mine."

"Who says he would've broken my heart?" Jolene asked. "If he had been involved with me then, I doubt he'd have ever even looked twice at Frankie. I can almost guarantee you I'd have been his wife, not her."

"Oh, I see." Candace sounded startled, as though she'd just had an epiphany. "And you'd now be the grieving widow of the revered surgeon instead of Frankie. You'd be driving his shiny new Mercedes Benz, living in his mansion on Silver Lake, dripping with diamonds, and rolling in cash. "

I'd had an epiphany too. Jolene's own words had me curious. "If he had been involved with me *then*" led me to believe she was having an affair with Dr. Moretti at the time of his death. Just then, as I was totally focused on the nurses' tense conversation, I passed gas unexpectedly. Unlike Mr. Godfrey's, it was a barely audible toot that took me by surprise, as farts tend to do once you've passed the seventy-years-old mark. We've all seen and heard flatulent old ladies at Wal-Mart passing gas with each step they take through the produce department. It makes one think the cherry tomatoes are spontaneously imploding in their paperboard cartons. I chastised myself for not having better foresight. I should've known not to eat so much broccoli for supper. Rip had forced himself to suffer through a bare minimum of florets and I'd polished off the rest so as not to be wasteful. *How foolishly frugal of me,* I thought. *I knew perfectly well they always blow me up like road-kill on a hot Texas highway.*

I held my breath, hoping Jolene and Candace didn't step around the partition to check out the source of the sound and praying it wasn't followed up by an even louder toot. Abdominal gas often had a mind of its own. There was a long moment of silence as though both nurses had heard the sound and were wondering if it had been a figment of their imaginations, or perhaps Mr. Godfrey, who by now probably had room 213 a match strike away from exploding like the number four reactor at the Chernobyl Nuclear Power Plant in 1986. Apparently, they both decided it was nothing to be concerned about and the contentious tête-à-tête continued.

"I'm not a gold digger like you accused Frankie of being when Marco dumped you for her," Jolene informed Candace. "I was interested in him as a person, not his wealth and position."

"So if you had an interest in him and are so irresistible, Jolene, why didn't Marco choose you to hook up with instead of me and then Frankie?"

"Who says he didn't?" Jolene's response took me by surprise. It seemed to confirm my earlier epiphany, however. "Why do you think he demoted you and made me his operating room nurse?"

"Oh, bullcrap! You just wish he'd had the hots for you!" Now Candace's response was sarcastic, mixed with indignation like Jolene's had been when I'd first stepped into the room. I had to wonder if Jolene and Dr. Moretti truly had engaged in a sexual relationship rather than just a flirtatious one. Not that either option was acceptable for a married man. If so, Dr. Moretti was much more of a player than one would think by his demeanor and professionalism. The exchange between Jolene and Candace had gone full circle and sounded as if it was nearing its end. I decided I'd better slip out of the room before the two nurses stepped around the partition and found me eavesdropping on their conversation.

As quietly as possible, I stepped back out into the hallway. I backed up about twenty feet and waited. No more than fifteen seconds later, the two adversaries exited the supply room with identical scowls on their faces. With as much nonchalance as I could muster, I smiled brightly, and said, "Good evening! It's so nice to see both of you ladies again."

They nodded in unison. Neither Jolene nor Candace looked as though they were as delighted to see me as I had pretended to be to see them.

"I was hoping to run into you," I said, looking directly at Candace.

"Why?" she asked warily.

"I wanted to see if I could get your mother-in-law's paszteciki recipe. My husband would absolutely love them." I knew without reading the recipe the pastries were a chore to make and contained more than my maximum threshold of three ingredients. It went without saying a Polish meat pastry would never cross my husband's lips if I had anything to do with it. I probably should've left it at that, but I didn't. "I wanted to ask you for the recipe at Maggie's party but you left before I had the chance."

Candace's face flushed as though all the blood in her body had raced to her face. My off-the-cuff remark had brought back a painful memory she had no desire to revisit. She turned to glare at Jolene, the reason behind her hasty departure from the Scentsy party. Both nurses immediately turned away from each other and walked off in opposite directions. Over her shoulder, Candace said, "I'll see if I can get it from Kat for you."

"Thank you, dear," I said to her backside as she walked away.

It'd been about fifteen minutes since I'd spoken to Maggie, so I added, "Oh, and also, Maggie told me she's ready to bring you up to date on the patients you'll be taking care of tonight."

So much for finding out if Candace had any notion what her former flame may have eaten before he bit the big one in the clinic's parking lot. At least I did garner some interesting information and had two potential suspects to put on my list. *Had Candace been infuriated enough with Dr. Moretti for choosing Frankie over her and then replacing her with Jolene as his operating room nurse?* I wondered again. *Had Jolene been driven to commit murder because she felt slighted, having been deemed good enough to hook up with but not worthy of marrying, as he had done with Frankie? Or am I just grasping at innocent straws in my quest to find out who murdered a man who might've truly just had an unfortunate run-in with a lupin bean?*

As I pondered these questions, I walked back up the desolate hallway. I'd been filling up with gas the entire time I was listening in on the exchange between the two combative nurses. I was to the point I felt like an over-inflated tire. Therefore, with all of the floor nurses busily checking in on patients, I was unabashedly tooting in synchronization with every footfall, just like the flatulent old ladies in the Wal-Mart produce section. The sound reverberated down the hallway like a bugler playing Taps at a funeral.

I have learned that with age comes a great deal of apathy about what other people think about you. And, subsequently, not giving a flip comes with a lot more freedom to do whatever you damn well wanted. And at that precise moment, I wanted to release the pressure on my belly before it blew up like a seagull that'd just ingested an Alka-Seltzer tablet.

NINE

Rip was watching an episode of *Blue Bloods* when I returned to the Caboose about fifteen minutes later. Being a career lawman, he could relate to the series about a family of New York City police officers.

"What's in the bag, hag?" He greeted me with a laugh.

"Still hilarious," I said dryly, as I set my Scentsy order on the kitchen table. "Even though it's the five-hundredth time I've heard it."

"Sorry," Rip apologized. "Go back outside and re-enter the trailer."

"What?"

"Just do it."

Mystified by his request, I exited the Caboose and then walked back in. This time I looked at him skeptically as I did so.

"What's up, buttercup?" he asked with his arms extended. "Give me a hug. I've missed you."

"You're a dork." I laughed and hugged him. "But I still love you."

"Love you more."

* * *

After I showed Rip the Scentsy warmer I'd purchased, I reiterated the gist of the prickly conversation I'd overheard between the two floor nurses.

"Wow!" he replied. "I'm kind of glad Candace was my night nurse and not Jolene. Jolene sounds like a first-class bit——"

Rip's profanity was interrupted by his phone quacking. His ringtone was that of a duck, and it never failed to amuse him. Yesterday, we were out for a walk as was suggested in his discharge instructions. As we strolled around the pond located on the RV park's property, a duck, that was drifting aimlessly across the water with a few of his buddies, quacked. Rip instinctively answered his phone. "Hello," Rip had said into his phone. When no one responded, he repeated the greeting in the form of a question. "Hello? Can you hear me? Is anyone there?"

Giggling, I'd tapped him on the shoulder and pointed to four Mallards floating at the edge of the pond. "I'm pretty sure it was one of them who wanted to talk with you."

Unlike yesterday, this time it wasn't a Mallard, but rather a scam artist.

"Oh goodness! No kidding?" Rip sounded oddly delighted. He turned to me and exclaimed, "Guess what, honey? We won a million-dollar lottery we didn't even have to buy a ticket for? Isn't that incredible?"

Rip listened to the caller for a second and said, "We only have to wire three thousand dollars to you to collect our lottery winnings? That's very reasonable. In fact, I'm so excited about winning a lottery I never even entered that I'm going to add another couple of thousand bucks to my wire transfer. Consider it my gift to you. Now, go ahead with the wiring instructions. I'll write them down as you give them to me."

"Rip," I began, "what are you doing?"

Rip turned to me and, picking up on the concern in my voice, shook his head and winked before conversing with the caller. "You're very welcome. Uh-huh. Of course. Yes, I understand. That makes perfect sense. Look for the money to come through tomorrow morning. If it doesn't arrive by noon call me back at 1-800-Go2-Hell."

With that, Rip snickered and ended the call.

"You should just hang up on them, Rip. Or, better yet, don't answer any call from a number you don't recognize," I advised. "They consider us older folks as easy prey. Talking to the scam artists only encourages them to keep calling. They truly seem to believe if they call you often enough, eventually, you'll come to your senses and wire the three grand to them."

Rip shook his head.

"It's true, Rip."

"I know it's true. But not answering the call isn't near as much fun."

Now it was me who shook my head. "I'm going to bed."

The next morning, as we were both eating a bowl of steel oats, Rip's phone rang again. The unexpected quacking caused me to drop my spoon, scattering oatmeal across the table.

"Don't answer it," I told Rip.

"It's from a number with a 507 area code."

"Then answer it," I said, changing my tune.

When Rip appeared conflicted, I took the phone out of his hand. I'd recognized 507 as Rochester's area code, followed by the

STAT Clinic's number, and figured Rip probably wouldn't hear or remember anything important the cath lab employee said to him.

The caller was Dr. O'Ryan's receptionist. I put Rip's phone on speaker mode, and cranked up the volume, so he could hear what she had to say and respond to any questions she might have for him.

"This is Colleen Dudley in Dr. O'Ryan's office. Are you doing all right, Mr. Ripple?"

"Yes," he replied.

"Are you experiencing any tightness in your chest, bleeding at the insertion site, or having any other complications?"

"No," Rip said. "I feel just fine."

"Good. I've called to reschedule your follow-up appointment with the cardiologist tomorrow. He'll be out of the office for a couple of days and unable to see you until Thursday."

"Okay," Rip replied.

"Is everything all right with the doctor?" I asked, because Rip clearly didn't give a hot damn about what was behind the doctor's inability to report to his office for two days.

"Yes," she said. "He has some personal obligations he needs to tend to that can't be put off until next weekend."

"That's a relief. I was afraid he'd taken ill."

"Nope, Mrs. Ripple. It's just personal stuff." Colleen obviously had no intention of elaborating. I grabbed a pen to jot down the new appointment time. "Will ten o'clock on Thursday work for you folks?"

"Yes," Rip and I answered simultaneously. I added, "That'd be perfect. Thank you, Ms. Dudley."

"You're welcome, Mrs. Ripple. See you Thursday. Make sure you bring a mask. Facial coverings are still required in Dr. O'Ryan's office."

"Of course. We wore them at his initial follow-up appointment," I responded, while Rip shook his head in disgust. He was clearly done with the Covid-19 pandemic. I put my finger to my lips to keep Rip from making a negative remark the receptionist might overhear. Colleen probably hated wearing a mask all day even more than Rip hated wearing one for the thirty minutes he was being seen by Dr. O'Ryan. And listening to patients gripe about having to wear a mask had to be even more frustrating for the poor girl.

The rest of the day passed agonizingly slowly. While Rip lounged in front of the television with Dolly stretched out on his lap, I poured through a cookbook of heart-healthy dishes, looking for ideas that would satisfy Rip while not prompting the necessity for another arterial stent. As was my tendency, I immediately bypassed any recipe that looked to require more ingredients than there were animals on Noah's ark. I wasn't interested in purchasing fifty dollars' worth of food items to create a five-dollar casserole——like the Shepherd's Pie recipe I found that required, among other things, lamb, rice vinegar, shallots, fresh rosemary, and dry red wine. The wine alone cost more than the entire meal was worth. Besides, the last time I'd cooked with Cabernet Sauvignon, I'd used a cup of it to braise the short ribs. I'd then placed the ribs in the oven before mixing a quart jar's worth of tequila, orange juice, and grenadine to enjoy with Rip during our traditional three o'clock happy hour. By the time I'd finished off my cocktail and the remainder of the bottle of cabernet while preparing supper, I was toast. Rip found me passed out in front of the stove and Regina has teased me about cooking with red wine ever since. It was a lesson well learned.

I went to bed an hour early that evening because I thought it would make Tuesday arrive sooner. I was anxious to hear what Maggie had to say. I sensed whatever it turned out to be would be a catalyst to increase our involvement with the investigation. I prayed once again the path we chose to take was the right one. At this point, I believed that taking any path was better than doing nothing pro-active at all to solve the case.

Three o'clock finally rolled around after a long morning of the doldrums. I whiled away the time by dusting and vacuuming the trailer and scouring the sink, lavatory, toilet, and shower. I wanted the Chartreuse Caboose to look nice when Maggie arrived. Or at least clean, because looking nice was a tall order for an older travel trailer that wasn't equipped with all the newfangled upgrades, like slide-outs, fireplaces, and laundry appliances. Not to mention we had a couch that was liberally coated with orange dust, the kind ten years' worth of Cheetos can leave behind and no amount of scrubbing can remove. I found it exasperating, but I had a feeling Maggie would have too much on her mind to even notice.

My hunch proved to be correct. Maggie looked nervous and out of sorts when I opened the trailer door following her knock a few minutes later. We could've had a three-legged flamingo doing the tango in the living room and I don't think she would've noticed.

"Welcome to our humble abode, Maggie," I said in greeting. "Come on in, sweetheart."

"Thank you." She handed me a pitcher of mango margarita after she stepped inside. She appeared tired, as if she'd gotten little to no sleep the previous night. I asked her about it.

"I'll admit I didn't sleep well last night. But then, I haven't slept particularly well since Dr. Moretti died."

"Oh, dear." I draped an arm around her shoulders while I held the pitcher in the other hand. "I'm so sorry his loss is affecting you so deeply."

I nearly dropped the pitcher of margarita mix to the floor,

which would've caused a very sticky mess and scared the living crap out of the imaginary dancing flamingo, when she responded. "I *should* be affected deeply by his death. I may have been the one who caused it."

"What?" I sat the pitcher down on the end table with so much force some of the liquid inside splashed out and formed puddles in the middle of the table. "What in the world makes you say such a thing?"

"I didn't mean to kill him," she added quickly. "It was purely an accident. But it was probably my fault nonetheless."

"Say no more for the moment. After I wipe off the table, we all need to sit down, relax, and have a bit of alcohol to calm our nerves before we continue this conversation. Since the weather's so nice for this time of year, why don't we sit outside and enjoy it?"

"All right," Maggie replied, her voice quivering.

I hollered out the door for Rip. He was rooting around in one of the undercarriage compartments of the trailer for a socket wrench he needed to tighten up something under the hood of his Chevy truck. "Could you please set up the patio table and three lawn chairs, dear? Maggie and I will be out in just a minute, or so."

I filled two quart canning jars with mango margarita and one with Crown Royal and Coke. Rip had told me he wasn't interested in a frilly drink that day, despite the fact our guest had brought the mango margarita mix to share with the two of us.

I watched Maggie's eyes open wide when I handed her drink to her. She said, "Wow! Those are huge servings!"

"Yes, they are," I agreed, "but our primary doctor only allows us one drink per day."

Maggie looked at me uncertainly. "But, don't you think she meant——"

"Just enjoy it," I interrupted her, already knowing the nature of the question brewing in her mind. "Don't overthink it, dear. It is what it is."

"Okay, I get it. I'd probably do the same thing if I were you or Rip. But after I drink this humongous margarita, I have to drive home."

"Oh, you're right," I said, as I snatched the quart jar out of her hand as though the container was about to transform itself into a fistful of glass shards. "Sorry, I forgot about that."

I drained her drink back into the pitcher and then poured about six ounces of the margarita mix into a kitchen glass. After I handed it to her and returned her corresponding smile, I sat the pitcher down on the counter and put the rest of the two-liter bottle of Coke from Rip's drink back into the fridge. As I did so, I thought about Maggie's remark about possibly killing the surgeon accidentally. It occurred to me the guilt from that belief was what had made Maggie look so uptight today. It also explained her exhaustion, for who could sleep well while thinking they'd been the cause of someone's death? And if they greatly admired that person whose death they thought they were responsible for, the guilt would be completely overwhelming. I was sure that was exactly what was eating Maggie up, like a cancer devouring her from the inside out.

Settled into the lawn chairs a few minutes later, I prefaced the exchange with, "Before you begin, sweetheart, I want you to know that Rip and I have your back. Whatever you say will strictly be confidential. Neither Rip nor I will breathe a word of it to another human being unless you ask us to do so on your behalf. I'm sure whatever happened was an understandable mistake that could've happened to anyone. As far as the authorities are concerned, I'm sure you have nothing to worry about. Rip was in law enforcement his entire working life and will know exactly what you should do at this point."

"Thank you," Maggie said sincerely. "I was hoping that's what you'd say, Rapella. I remember you mentioning that Rip was the sheriff of your county in Texas when he retired, and also that you two had been personally involved in several murder investigations.

Not that I consider this a murder investigation, mind you, but the Rochester police department probably won't see it that way once they realize what caused Marco to pass away so suddenly, without warning."

I took a long swallow of my drink and Maggie followed suit. She needed the alcohol to boost her courage and I needed it to clear my mind. Rip had already drained half of his cocktail. He reached over and patted Maggie's hand which had begun to tremble. "Relax, Maggie! You are among friends."

"Thank you, Rip. I was hoping you could advise me."

"We'll do whatever we can do to help you out," Rip said gently. "Rapella clued me in that you think you might have had a hand in Dr. Moretti's sudden passing. If that's true, I know it was an accident, and they can't lock you up for an accident, my dear."

"What about involuntary manslaughter?" Maggie asked with a catch in her voice.

"Let's not go down that road quite yet," Rip replied. "Why don't you start at the beginning and tell us what happened?"

"All right." Maggie took another large swallow of her margarita, which like a yawn, impelled me to take a long swill of mine. One more lengthy swig like Maggie's and her glass would be as empty as a politician's promise. To give her moral support, I reached over and squeezed her hand. She nodded at me, and said, "Okay, here goes…"

Maggie leaned forward in her lawn chair and prepared to open up like a fire hydrant that'd been plowed into by a cement truck. Rip and I settled back into our chairs in anticipation of a confession neither one of us wanted to hear. We both were quite fond of Maggie Brown and we didn't particularly want to be the vessels she poured her guilt into. If the nurse confessed to killing Dr. Moretti, no matter how innocently, we both knew we'd feel duty-bound to take the information to the Rochester Police Department's homicide department, despite our promise to keep it to ourselves. We both nearly bolted from our chairs when Maggie spoke next.

"I think I killed Marco with cookies."

"What?" My mind immediately went back to the news Wendy had obtained about Moretti's autopsy. A chunk of lupin had been found in his stomach, presumably ingested when eating a cookie.

"How?" Rip asked at the same time.

"Let me explain," Maggie replied. "As you know, Rapella, I have now been out on six dates with Mitch Murphy."

"Yes," I said as Rip remained silent. "I remember you saying at the Scentsy party you were dating the anesthesiologist. What does Dr. Murphy have to do with Moretti's death?"

"His initials more than anything."

"His initials?" Rip asked in surprise. "Since when can a person's initials cause another person's death?"

"When both people have the same initials," Maggie began, "as in Marco Moretti and Mitch Murphy. Both men's initials are M.M., you see."

"Well, I think both Rip and I both understand the two physicians had the same initials. But how could that coincidence have become fatal?"

"When you bake cookies for the man you're dating, put two of them in a paper bag, and then scribble 'M.M.' on the outside of the bag."

"Oh, I see." It was starting to dawn on me what had happened. "Were there peanuts in the cookies?"

"Nope," she replied. "No peanuts. I knew Dr. Moretti was deathly allergic to peanuts so I would've never put anything with peanuts in the refrigerator in the doctors' break room. I didn't want to take a chance a single peanut particle could get transferred to something Dr. Moretti ingested."

"The doctors have their own break room?"

"Yes. I think they see us nurses as being too low on the totem pole to share one with them." Maggie laughed, but I couldn't tell if it was a humorous chuckle or a scornful one. "Except Mitch, of course. He's not like most of the physicians at the clinic."

"Okay." Her remarks about being looked down upon by most of the doctors she worked with flew over my head like a drone taking photos for a real-estate ad. I was still digesting how determined Maggie was to protect the doctor from ingesting something that could adversely affect him. "So I assume Dr. Moretti accidentally ate the cookies you put in a bag for Dr. Murphy? Correct?"

"Yes. Or at least I assume he ate them." There was a quiver in Maggie's voice. She sniffled as a tear ran down her cheek. The reminder of her fatal mistake was getting to her. I began to comfort her. Rip, however, wanted her to cut to the chase, and the sooner the better.

"So, if not peanuts, what was in the cookies that could've killed Dr. Moretti?" Rip asked.

"Lupin."

"Oh," I said with an involuntary gasp. Maggie had done her homework. She'd discovered that a lupin allergy often went hand-in-hand with a peanut allergy. "So Mitch Murphy has celiac disease, doesn't he?"

"Yes." Maggie looked at me as if I'd just morphed into Dr. William Dicke, the medical director at a children's hospital who'd almost by accident discovered the disease in the 1940s. Like Maggie, I had done my research too. Why would God (or Al Gore) have created the internet if he didn't want us to use it? "Rapella, how did you know about the connection of lupin to celiac disease?"

"That's of no real importance," I replied. I didn't want to risk exposing Wendy's involvement in the personal investigation Rip and I were undertaking. "Suffice it to say, I learned lupin is occasionally substituted for wheat so that people who can't digest gluten can safely consume the cookie, cake, or whatever the lupin is baked into."

"Exactly." Maggie began to cry uncontrollably. Her distress was making Rip uneasy. He excused himself, using his recent stent procedure as the reason. He was beyond just milking it. He was now using it as a crutch and a handy excuse for removing himself from an uncomfortable situation.

"I need to go inside and rest. Rapella can fill me in on the details later. I'm sure you'll feel much better about the situation, Maggie, after Rapella chats with you."

"Okay," Maggie replied between sobs. I was afraid she was going to begin hyperventilating. *Should I go inside and get a paper bag, just in case?* I wondered. I decided to roll the dice and hope she could regain control of her emotions without having to take more extreme measures.

Fortunately, Maggie was able to calm down and recover her composure after a few minutes, even though she seemed incapable of putting her thoughts into words. I tried to fill in the gaps for her. "You're saying you put the cookies in the doctors' break room's refrigerator and the late doctor ate them, thinking the M.M. you'd written on the bag stood for Marco Moretti. Is that correct?"

Maggie nodded, still unable to speak.

"If you were so conscientious about not putting anything containing peanuts in the fridge, why would you put something in a bag containing an ingredient you knew Moretti could also be allergic to?" I was trying not to sound judgmental. My next remark failed miserably to meet that objective. "To put initials on the bag he could mistakenly assume was meant for him was even more irresponsible."

Maggie lost it. She put her head in her hands and howled in overwhelming grief. I noticed Rip pull back the kitchen curtain as if to make sure there were no wild animals roaming through the RV park. I put my arm around Maggie's shoulders and apologized.

"I'm sorry if that sounded like I thought you deliberately tried to harm Dr. Moretti. I know you would never do such a thing. I'm just a little confused."

Maggie tried to speak coherently while weeping. "It wasn't (gasp) deliberate, Rapella. I (sob) didn't know (sob) about the lupin (gasp) connection until I researched it the day after his death."

When she stopped to blow her nose, I said, "That makes more sense. It's really not what one would consider common knowledge, at least by those of us who aren't afflicted with celiac disease and/or a peanut allergy. It seems to me that if Dr. Moretti ate those cookies that weren't meant for him in the first place, and an ensuing allergic reaction from those cookies killed him, his death was purely an accident. No one would hold you responsible for his death if it wasn't intentional. I can almost guarantee you'd never be charged with murder in a situation such as that."

"How about 'involuntary manslaughter?'" Maggie repeated her earlier query.

"No," I replied simply. I had looked up the definition before when I'd gotten involved in a similar situation. "The definition of involuntary manslaughter is a death produced by a lawful act performed under the reasonable belief that no harm would come to the victim."

Even as I spat out the definition as if I were Alexa responding to a question posed by the owner of an Amazon Echo, I thought it sounded very much like what had occurred in Dr. Moretti's case. I already knew there was lupin in the victim's stomach, so Maggie's fears of having accidentally killed the surgeon were not unwarranted.

"See, Rapella? See what I mean?" Maggie lost it anew, bursting into a fresh round of uncontrollable crying. The howling intensified to the point Rip opened the door and asked if there were any dogs running free in the RV park. I assured him there wasn't and turned back to Maggie.

"Let me go inside and get you a wet cloth. I'll be right back." I didn't know if she understood me through her weeping, but I went inside and explained to Rip what Maggie had told me.

Rip looked out the open window and saw Maggie weeping and dabbing at her eyes with a tissue. "Good job making her feel better."

"Thanks, Rip," I replied. "Your sarcasm's not appreciated."

When I went back outside with a wet cloth, Rip accompanied me. He soothed Maggie by explaining that he and I would do whatever it took to make sure she wasn't arrested on any charges, including involuntary manslaughter. He made a valid point when he added, "Besides, do you have any proof Dr. Moretti actually ate those exact cookies?"

"Well, no, not really." Maggie calmed down immediately.

"Isn't it conceivable Dr. Moretti had eaten something else containing lupin or peanuts? Did you ask your boyfriend if he ate the cookies you specifically made for him?" Rip asked. I knew he'd forgotten the anesthesiologist's name. To remind him, I spoke next.

"Rip's right. Mitch might have eaten them before Moretti even saw the bag, making the entire 'death by allergic reaction to your cookies' supposition a moot point."

"Yeah, I wish. But, no," Maggie replied. "I asked Mitch and he said he never even saw the bag in the refrigerator. Marco must have eaten them and pitched the bag before Mitch had a chance to even notice the bag with his initials on it. I'm sure Marco thought Frankie, or one of the nurses who all knew of his peanut allergy, had placed the cookies in the fridge for him to enjoy on a break between patients."

"Oh," I replied. "That's too bad."

By the time Maggie left our campsite, I was half drunk from having drained the remaining half of the margarita mix in the pitcher, and Maggie was five pounds lighter from having cried enough tears to have filled the pitcher back up. Even in my some-what inebriated state, I made a vow to myself to find out if it was indeed Dr. Moretti who consumed the lupin-laced cookies Maggie had left for her new love interest. How I was going to accomplish that feat, I had no clue. But I knew I had enough guts and gumption about me to figure out a way. I also had enough wits about me to know the death of the surgeon was driving me to drink and I didn't want to make a habit of it.

TEN

After Maggie had gone home, a little less manic after speaking with Rip, I got to work fixing baked tilapia, steamed asparagus, and a tossed salad with hard-boiled eggs and cherry tomatoes for supper. I planned to discuss my next plan of action with Rip while we dined. I'd figured the bag marked "M.M." would have been disposed of in the break room's trash receptacle and if nothing else, removing the bag might turn out to be to Maggie's benefit. No sense leaving evidence lying around in the event the homicide detectives were to scrutinize the break room as a "crime scene."

I was trying to think of a way to get into the doctors' break room to see if the trash can had been dumped in the week following Dr. Moretti's death. I assumed it had because hospital and medical clinics tend to be very fastidious about things like mopping floors, washing bedclothes and towels, emptying trash cans, and disinfecting every inch of every solid surface in the building. But I had to start somewhere, and there was a chance the janitorial workers were more particular about patients' rooms than they were about ones dedicated to the staff.

Deep in thought, I absentmindedly spilled hot water out of the asparagus pan onto the counter, which then ran down the cabinet and began to puddle up on the floor. I quickly grabbed a kitchen towel off the sink to sop up the spill. The red and white striped towel in my hand lit a bulb over my head.

"Aha!" I exclaimed out loud.

"'Aha' what?" Rip asked from his recliner. He was brushing Dolly's fur with a hair-removing glove and the tubby tabby was purring loudly in approval.

"I just had a doable inspiration," I replied.

"Oh? You had a 'doable' inspiration? That's funny. I just had a shiver run up my spine hearing you say those words," Rip said with a dramatic sigh. "I'm pretty sure I felt a ripple go up Dolly's spine too. We're both afraid to ask, but what was your inspiration?"

"I have to get the salad tossed. I'll explain it while we eat."

"I think I just lost my appetite."

"And Dolly?" I asked playfully. "Has Her Majesty lost her appetite too?"

"On the contrary," Rip began, "she said she needs some comfort food to deal with her stress. She thinks she needs a few chicken-flavored Greenies."

"That chubster does not need a snack. She just had a full bowl of tuna and whitefish delight. That should more than hold her over until bedtime."

"Tell *her* that."

Dolly turned to glare at me and then leveled her sternest stare at Rip, as well. We both chuckled at her reaction before I got back to the task of preparing our evening meal. Out of the corner of my eye, I saw Rip sneak a couple of Greenies out of Dolly's plastic treat container. The green-colored treats were designed to keep cats' teeth clean. All they seemed to do for Dolly was keep her from having a waistline. I watched as she chewed them up as though she hadn't ingested a single morsel in a week and then meowed at Rip in hopes of scoring a few more. Her strategy worked. Rip was a sucker and too soft-hearted for his own good sometimes. Dolly was fully aware of Rip's weaknesses and was not above exploiting them.

Just after we sat down at the kitchen table to eat, I explained my plan to Rip. The cherry tomato he'd just poked into his mouth shot out as if it'd been launched by a slingshot. Rip's reaction was not the positive one I'd hoped for. In fact, he instantly turned as red as the marble-sized projectile that had just zipped by my right ear.

"Your brilliant idea is to pretend to be a candy-striper to get into the doctors' break room so you can root through their trash can? Then you're going to remove the bag that could've possibly held the murder weapon, or at least the article that killed Dr. Moretti?" Rip's statements were spoken as mocking questions, and his tone sounded very irate, and even more disbelieving than angry. "Have you ever heard of the federal offense known as 'tampering with evidence?'"

"Well, of course, I've heard of that, Rip. But would it be considered 'tampering with evidence' if I merely cleaned up the room and threw the cookie bag away with the rest of the trash?"

"It's possible." Rip nodded his head so fiercely he could've hammered nails into a walnut stump with his chin. "And you think no one will question your presence if you're in the doctors' break room collecting their trash? Is that what you're telling me? *This* was your clever inspiration? Your 'doable' inspiration, to be more exact? Are you serious, Rapella? You want to pretend you're a seventy-two-year-old candy-striper and you think no one will think a thing about it. Is that what you're saying?"

"Of course not!" It was the snort of derision at the end of Rip's tirade that pissed me off. I responded in the same fuming nature as he had. "I never had any intention of pretending to be a candy-striper. Candy-stripers disappeared even before payphones did!"

"That was hardly my point!"

"Besides, I didn't say it was a 'clever' inspiration! I said it was 'doable.'"

"That's even worse, and I'm not convinced your ruse is either one, clever *or* doable."

Rip's manner had simmered down. I knew he felt there was no sense screaming at each other across a two-foot-wide table. The neighbors on either side of us could probably hear our hollering from inside their own RVs. We didn't want to be their free entertainment for the evening.

As I spoke, my tone of voice was much milder. "Candy-stripers were typically young ladies: high-schoolers, college students, and even middle-schoolers on occasion. Volunteers' services are of considerable importance to the healthcare system. Not only did candy-stripers help fill this need years ago but often older folks like Henrietta still do. It gives senior citizens like her purpose and something constructive to do with their spare time."

"Henrietta?" Rip asked. "Who's that?"

"She's the volunteer who wheeled you out of the clinic after you were released. Her husband Stanley was the one who died from a rare blood clot after pacemaker surgery."

"Oh yeah, I remember now. Sad deal, huh?" Rip asked.

"Very much so, but Henrietta still chose to volunteer her time and efforts after her husband's death. I'm sure she was lonely and needed something meaningful to do that would allow her to interact with other people. Like you and I, Henrietta is of retirement age, and being alone is not exactly an enjoyable way to spend one's golden years."

"That's certainly true. I thank God for you every day, Rapella. I'm curious though. Has retirement been all you dreamed it would be?" Rip asked with a serious tone. "Do you still enjoy traveling the country in the Kitschy Caboose?"

I refused to rise to the bait when he referred to the trailer with the insulting moniker he'd come up with a couple of years prior. It'd ticked me off then, and it did so today, too. "Yes, I do. Our lifestyle following retirement's been better than I'd ever anticipated." I stuck my tongue out at him for the name he'd given our trailer. "And don't ever refer to the Caboose as kitschy again or you'll be the one keeping it clean and cooking your own meals."

"My apologies, dear," Rip said with an ornery grin. "I stand corrected! I meant to say our trailer was like a 700-horsepower-drawn carriage, transporting the Queen and Her Majesty from one location to another."

"Have I told you what a dork you are lately?" I was glad our interaction had turned silly, as opposed to controversial. "How about you? Do you still enjoy being a full-time RVer?"

"First of all, yes, you told me I was a dork yesterday. And I believe you called me a dork once, and a dweeb twice, the day before that. But who's counting?"

"You are, apparently," I said, laughing loudly. Rip chuckled in return. I was hoping the RVers on both sides of us could hear our merriment and be reassured their neighbors were no longer at risk of thrusting ice picks into each other. "So, seriously, honey. What is your opinion of our full-time RVing lifestyle at this point in your life?"

"I still enjoy this way of life immensely, but the walls of this trailer are beginning to close in on me," he replied. "I think it's time we begin looking for a newer and larger RV. I don't think I'd be comfortable pulling a lengthier travel trailer around. I'd like to switch to a fifth wheel no more than thirty-five, or-six, feet long with about fifteen slide-outs."

"I agree." I knew he was exaggerating about the number of slide-outs, but having at least three of them would definitely be nice. *I'd never buy another RV without a stackable washer/dryer unit either. I'm so tired of lugging dirty clothes to the RV parks' laundry rooms I'm about ready to throw the clothes away and buy new ones every time they're ready to be laundered. And that's saying a lot for a skinflint like me. One of those propane-powered fireplaces would sure be cozy on cold evenings too. And what wouldn't I give for a kitchen with a center island, as well?* A lady named Celia Buckley had shown me inside her fancy rig while we were at the Alexandria Inn over the holidays. I probably left a trail of saliva from the center island in her kitchen, past the roaring gas fireplace, and all the way to the front door, from drooling so much over the pure luxury of the amenities inside her Newmar motorhome.

But we were getting off-track. I pivoted away from my daydreaming and back to the original subject. "The point is that pretending to be a volunteer would be the perfect ploy to get into the break room. I will carry a mop and a rag, and no one will look twice at me, assuming I'm there to freshen up the area as an unpaid helper. Perhaps they'll think I'm involved with the Gray Lady Service if I wear a light gray dress. I remember my daddy talking about those ladies being so valuable to the war efforts during World War II."

"My father talked about them too. I recall him saying the volunteer service was created in 1918 at the Walter Reed Army Hospital in Washington D.C. to provide services for war patients. It wasn't until after World War II that it officially became known as the Gray Lady Service, however."

"How do you remember details like that?" I was often impressed by Rip's ability to recall trivial facts and details, often things he'd learned years or even decades prior, and yet be unable to remember anyone's name for more than ten seconds. *Does Rip have a bunch of wires crossed in his brain?* I wondered. *Or is it selective memory in line with his selective hearing?* My guess was the latter. "Your father probably told you all that over half a century ago!"

"How often do I need to remind you that my mind is like a steel trap?"

"A heck of a lot less often than you do," I said in disgust. "So, what'd you have for breakfast this morning?"

"Biscuits and gravy?"

"In your dreams, buddy. You had oatmeal and cantaloupe."

"Well, I do remember you had a bowl of Cap'n Crunch Berries while I suffered through my oatmeal."

"That was two days ago," I corrected him. "Yesterday and today I ate the same thing you did—oatmeal and cantaloupe. And I only finished off the box of Crunch Berries so they wouldn't go to waste."

"All right, all right, you win," Rip said with an impatient wave of his hand. "My point is, the Gray Lady Service was disbanded in the 1960s and absorbed into a more unified volunteer service within the American Red Cross. I think you should forget the light grey dress and see if you can find a shirt or jacket that has American Red Cross printed on it and pretend to be a volunteer within that organization. The millennials of today wouldn't know what a Gray Lady was if she walked up and swatted them on the ass with a dustpan."

Rip's remark was crude but accurate. His suggestion was top drawer though and just the answer I'd been searching for. I jumped up from my chair at the kitchen table, ran around, and kissed Rip on the top of his bald head. "That's a great idea. Thank you so much!"

"You're welcome," Rip said. "But under no circumstance can you let on you're there in the break room with the sole purpose of finding the bag Maggie's cookies were in. Is that understood?"

"Absolutely!" I replied simply. "I'm going to get on my iPad to search for a Red Cross shirt while you finish up your supper."

"Are you finished with your plate?"

I was too excited to finish my dinner. Before I could reply to his question, he stabbed the remaining piece of tilapia on my plate and transferred it to his.

Within five minutes I found a t-shirt on eBay that looked as if it had actually been part of a uniform worn by an American Red Cross volunteer. I showed it to Rip, and said, "Unfortunately, it won't work."

"Why won't it?"

"With the standard shipping, it won't arrive for five or six days."

"Can you get overnight shipping if you chip in more money?"

"Well, yes, but——"

"Do it! That trash is not going to remain undumped indefinitely, if it's even still in the break room now. If you're determined to get that bag, you can't afford to put it off any longer than necessary." Clearly, Rip was on the same page as I was in not wanting to leave incriminating evidence behind if we could prevent it. He had an affinity for Maggie and felt protective of her. Rip added, "If Dr. Moretti truly did eat Maggie's cookies, the evidence could implicate her in his death. But you've got to exercise extreme caution in removing it from the break room so that you don't look as though you're trying to get rid of incriminating evidence."

"I know. I will," I said. "I promise."

"Okay. I'll hold you to that promise. Now get to ordering that Red Cross shirt."

Under normal circumstances, my penny-pinching personality wouldn't allow me to pay extra for expedited shipping, but this was not a normal situation. This was an "eliminating evidence emergency." So, I swallowed hard, clicked on expedited shipping, and tried not to let the fact the shipping now cost five dollars more than the fricking shirt cost bother me. It was due to arrive tomorrow by noon, which would allow me to wear it to the cath lab the following afternoon. At this point, that's all that mattered.

At five after twelve the next day, I was standing in the office of the Autumn Woods RV Park collecting our mail, which was handled by the Escapees RV Club out of Livingston, Texas, for a reasonable fee. I was delighted to discover that along with our bag of mail, my eBay purchase had arrived as promised. I tried not to think about the twenty-five dollars it had cost us to get it there that quickly. *Desperate times call for desperate measures,* I reminded myself.

I had the Red Cross shirt out of the package before I'd even completed the short jaunt back to the Caboose. I knew when I'd ordered it the shirt would be too big for me. I normally wear a medium or large and the only suitable shirt I'd been able to find on eBay was a 2XL. Looking at the shirt now I was afraid it'd look like it was eating me alive. "Feed me Seymour" from the *Little Shop of Horrors* movie came to mind as I pictured myself wearing the shirt that could double as a muumuu. On the bright side, I decided it would work as my new nightshirt after the cookie caper was completed. The oversized Houston Astros t-shirt I'd worn as jammies for the last six or seven years was quite large too, but extremely comfortable. Sadly, it was getting threadbare, and it'd be nice to have another use for the Red Cross shirt that had cost me forty-five dollars after paying the exorbitant expedited shipping charge.

Little did I know at the time, the pricey shirt would be tossed into the STAT Clinic's dumpster by mid-morning after I used it in my plan to get into the doctors' break room. As it would turn out, not only was wearing it to bed likely to give me nightmares, but it'd also have a huge toxic stain across the front of it that all of the liquid stain removers in the world couldn't "Shout" out!

ELEVEN

"How do I look?" I asked Rip after I'd donned the new shirt. "Do I look like an official American Red Cross volunteer?"

"Actually, you remind me of what the offspring of a candy cane and a pup tent would look like."

"Be serious, Rip."

"I *am* being serious. Isn't there some way you can take the shirt in a few sizes?"

"Yes, of course," I replied. "But that'd take time I don't have. I need to get into that break room as quickly as possible."

"I suppose you're right," Rip conceded. "If anyone asks you why your shirt is so gargantuan, just tell them you recently lost a hundred pounds on the Jamie Craig program."

"It's Jenny, Rip. Jenny Craig. But, yes, that's exactly what I'll say."

Seriously? I thought. *This is the man that can remember that over fifty years ago his father told him the Gray Ladies volunteer service was created in 1918 at the Walter Reed Army Hospital in Washington D.C.? The same man who can't remember the name Jenny Craig even though her weight loss program was advertised on TV numerous times a day for years? How is that even possible?*

"With any luck at all, no one will even notice me go into the break room and check the trash can." I was gathering up a dust rag, mop, and bottle of *Formula 409* as I spoke. These were the props I needed to look like a retiree volunteering her time and elbow grease to clean up after messy physicians in the cardiac clinic.

"Yeah, right." Rip snorted. "Do we still have a thousand in cash in the floor safe we had built in under the bed?"

"Yes. Why?"

"I was just wondering in case I need access to bail money later on today."

"Don't be ridiculous, Rip!" I exclaimed. "How could I possibly end up in legal trouble for merely volunteering my janitorial skills?"

"You'll find a way. You always do."

Rip didn't sound very optimistic I could pull off the hoax I had in mind. I hoped to prove to him I was more clever and conniving than he gave me credit for. I also hoped the bag that had held the cookies Dr. Moretti might've accidentally ingested was still in the trash can. And more than anything, I prayed this scheme, which was riddled with potential pitfalls, didn't land me in the local police station. I might as well have been praying for the sky to open up and rain down one-hundred-dollar bills on Rip and me as we sat in our lawn chairs and watched the sun set that evening. Both things were equally apt to happen.

I walked into the STAT Cardiac Clinic like I was reporting for my afternoon shift with the custodial department. With my mop in one hand and a bag of cleaning supplies in the other, I took the elevator up to Maggie's floor. I wanted to discuss my plan with her before implementing it. For starters, I had no clue where the doctors' break room was located.

My oversized American Red Cross shirt was cinched at the waist with an elastic belt I'd owned for decades. I'd hastily stitched two large pockets on the front out of an old red t-shirt of Rip's I'd saved to use as a rag. Located below the belt line, the humongous shirt now looked more like a smock. Even Rip agreed it helped make me look more believable as a janitorial volunteer. I had decided to wear both a mask and a protective face shield to make myself less recognizable to anyone who may have remembered me from Rip's recent stay at the facility. To further disguise myself, I tied a bandana around my head to hide my silver hair.

Maggie was not at the nurses' station when I arrived on her floor. I loitered around for ten minutes, staring at my phone intensely, hoping no one would ask me what I was doing. No one did. The nurses milling about had enough on their hands without concerning themselves with the strange woman standing in the hallway with a phone in her face and cleaning supplies at her feet.

Finally, Maggie appeared at the nurses' station with her rolling computer. She appeared flushed and breathless. I knew by her demeanor she wouldn't have much time to converse with me. I approached her and greeted her warmly.

"Listen, Maggie, I know you are busy and I won't keep you. I just need to know where the doctors' break room is located."

"Why?" She looked me over, from stem to stern, and shook her head in bewilderment. At last, it dawned on her who I was. "Oh, Rapella, it's you! What are you planning to do?"

"I don't have time to go into it right now," I replied. "Call me later on when you have a break and I'll explain it all then."

"Okay." Maggie sounded uncertain. "The doctors' break room's on the third floor, two doors down from Operating Room Three, or 'OR3' as it says on the door. The break room has no sign on it, as if the doctors don't want anyone to know they actually take breaks on occasion."

Maybe they're afraid if the nature of the room is posted, nosy old ladies will walk into their private space uninvited, I wanted to say. Instead, I said, "Thanks, sweetheart. Now get back to work and I'll talk to you later."

I tried not to dwell on Maggie's arched eyebrows and skeptical expression as I headed for the elevators.

It took a while to find the break room. There was a maze of hallways on the third floor. To get to the operating rooms you had to pass through two doors marked "Hospital Personnel Only." Entry to the corresponding hallway required entering a passcode into a box next to the sliding glass doors.

I had no choice but to loiter nearby. With my phone aimed at, and closed in on, the security code box, I stared at my phone as if reading something on the screen. I moved my head back and forth slowly as if I were reading a book. While doing this, my phone was set on video. It took five staff members before I got a clear shot of the passcode they entered into the digital panel. The first four who entered codes to gain access blocked my view as if they were entering the pin number for their debit card into an ATM.

Studying the video of the fifth staff member, I saw that the security code to open the door was 2633, which ironically would correspond with the word "code" on an old rotary dial phone. I waited until the phlebotomist was out of sight before entering the same code and slipping through the opened door.

As I turned the corner at the end of the hallway, I ran smack dab into a man dressed in a white gown, surgical cap, theater boots, and a mask and face shield similar to what I wearing. He was clearly one of the heart surgeons employed by the clinic. It was only the man's red hair that made him instantly recognizable as Blaze O'Ryan. I apologized for nearly knocking him over.

As he was removing a pair of blue latex gloves, he asked, "Can I help you, ma'am?"

"Um, no, I'm fine," I muttered.

"Who let you back in the operating theater area? This is a sterile environment and only operating room personnel are allowed," the surgeon stated. It was then I noticed that under his name on his gown was stitched MD FACC. It was only after I'd Googled FACC did I discover it stood for Fellow of the American College of Cardiology, a highly prestigious credential in the field of cardiovascular health. It soon became clear Dr. O'Ryan recognized me, or at least my voice, but couldn't recall from where. "Do I know you?"

"I don't believe so, sir." I decided it would likely be advantageous if he didn't know my name. "I'm here to help keep this area sterile. I have volunteered my services to disinfect certain rooms on this floor, rooms other than the operating rooms themselves. I was given the passcode so I could perform my duties."

"Who gave you the passcode?"

This is going to be harder than I anticipated, I thought. *I'll have to come up with a reason to escape this encounter with Dr. O'Ryan.*

"I'll have to look up his name on my phone," I replied casually. "I need to go to the restroom first, however. My bladder is about to explode, and believe me, that wouldn't be a pretty sight. Talk about a bacterial nightmare."

As I spoke I was backing up in the direction of a women's restroom I'd just passed by. As I slipped inside the small bathroom, I said, "Be right back."

I quickly locked the door and leaned back against it, trying to regain normal breathing. During my unnerving exchange with Dr. O'Ryan, my pulse had quickened and my inhalations had become ragged and irregular.

I remained quiet, even when I heard the surgeon rap on the restroom door and ask, "Hey! Are you all right in there?"

Only when he said, "I need to get back to an operation already in progress in OR2," did I decide to respond to the surgeon.

"You go ahead," I replied through the restroom door. "I don't want to hold you up or make you any later for that surgery taking place. I was planning to leave as soon as I'm through in the restroom. My shift is about to end and I need to check my supplies back into the janitorial department."

Dr. O'Ryan did not respond, but eventually, I heard footsteps which became fainter as he walked back toward Operating Room Two. I let out a huge sigh of relief. Exiting the restroom, I scurried past the door with OR2 on it, and then past the third operating room. I found the unmarked break room two doors down as Maggie had instructed. I wondered how she'd become so familiar with this portion of the clinic. She was a floor nurse, not an operating room nurse. It crossed my mind she could've been previously employed in other capacities at the clinic, and I'd have to remember to inquire about it when I next spoke to her.

I knocked softly on the break room door. No one opened the door so I tapped on it again. When I finally felt it was safe to enter the room, I opened the door. I was relieved the room was unlocked and no code was necessary to enter it. Unfortunately, the only trash can in the room had absolutely no rubbish in it, as if it'd just recently been emptied. I sat down on a chair to mull over my next move.

Just then I heard a sound outside in the hallway. I jumped to my feet. When the door opened, I was rubbing my rag over an area on the table I'd just doused with disinfectant spray. With my back to the door, I pretended to be intensely focused on my work.

"Sorry to disturb you," a kind voice I recognized said in greeting. "I'll be out of your way in just a sec."

I turned to see Mitch Murphy open the refrigerator and

remove a can of Dr. Pepper. The irony of Dr. Pepper being his preference amused me. The anesthesiologist was exactly the person I needed to speak to and I could not have planned this chance encounter any better. As Maggie's latest love interest, and the man the lupin-laced cookies were intended for, I knew I needed to use this opportunity to question him.

"Oh, hello, Dr. Murphy." I smiled broadly. "It's so nice to see you again."

"Again?" He studied what he could see of my facial features through the mask and shield I was wearing, and asked, "Were you a patient here?"

"No," I began, "but my husband was and I decided to dedicate some of my time as an American Red Cross volunteer as a way of giving back."

"How thoughtful of you, ma'am." I could instantly see why Maggie was attracted to this kind, polite fellow. Dr. Murphy didn't seem to care how I'd gained entrance into the restricted area, or question my authorization to be disinfecting the doctors' break room in the first place. He was laid back, unlike the uptight Dr. O'Ryan. "I think it was just cleaned by the lady who usually takes care of this area every Wednesday morning."

"Oh, well," I said. "I will just check to see what else I can do to help out."

When Dr. Murphy nodded without speaking, I asked, "Isn't it nice to have a designated break room where you can relax for a few minutes and snack on something from the refrigerator and cabinet?"

Mitch nodded again. He was clearly unsure of where I was headed with my line of questioning.

"You must have been the 'M.M.' who the bag I saw in the fridge a few days ago belonged to," I said in a chitchat manner as if just making small talk.

"Yes," he replied with a laugh. "My new girlfriend left some cookies in the fridge for me."

"How in the world did your girlfriend gain access to the break room?" I asked. "I had to jump through hoops just to get permission to do volunteer custodial work in this area."

Dr. Murphy gazed at me silently for a moment before turning his back to me. He opened up the refrigerator again and withdrew a Kit-Kat bar this time. When he turned back around he resumed gazing at me without speaking. *Kit-Kat got your tongue?* I wanted to ask. Instead, I said, "Oh, duh. She must've got the code from you."

"I don't know how Maggie got the code, but she's worked here a long time so it's not surprising she knew it. She told me she was going to bake me some oatmeal chocolate chip cookies but she didn't warn me she was going to drop some off in this break room for me."

"Warn you?" I asked. "Why would you need a heads up about something like that? Oatmeal chocolate chip cookies sound yummy."

"Yes, they do *sound* yummy."

"They weren't delicious?"

"Umm, I kind of doubt it."

"You don't know?" I asked.

"No," he replied. "I didn't eat them, but someone had taken a bite out of one of them and decided it wasn't good enough to finish. That was my clue to toss them without sampling one. I'd never tell my girlfriend I threw them away and promise me you won't either if you happen to talk to Maggie Brown."

"Oh, yes, I know Maggie. She's a lovely young lady and I'd never purposely hurt her feelings. So mum's the word, but why'd you do such a thing?"

"Maggie can't cook worth a darn. I swear a chimpanzee with a sheet pan and a roll of *Nestlé Toll House* cookie dough could make better cookies than Maggie. And knowing she had to alter the recipe to make them gluten-free made me even more convinced they'd taste awful." Mitch studied my expression for a moment and explained. "For our third date, she offered to make dinner for me. I was excited, expecting her to be an accomplished cook."

"And she wasn't as accomplished as you'd anticipated?"

"Good Lord, no. Not even close. She fixed lasagna for supper and the noodles were so undercooked they snapped in half when I took a bite. The mozzarella cheese had not even begun to melt and there was so much salt in the dish you could've laid slugs on the top of the lasagna and watched them dissolve. As a rule, I never salt anything. I could hardly choke down any of the lasagna." Mitch laughed. I could tell he found her cooking failure amusing. "I had to eat it though or risk hurting her feelings. And, like you, I didn't want to do that. But I learned to always have an excuse handy in case she offered to cook for me again."

I laughed along with the handsome doctor who reminded me so much of Peter O'Toole. Thinking back to an anecdote Lexie had once shared with me, I said, "I have a friend who left her husband after he criticized her first attempt at lasagna. Fortunately, after storming off and going to her mother's house, her mother made her march straight back home to make up with him."

"I understand completely," the doctor said. "You have to choose your battles and lasagna is hardly the issue I'd want to end our relationship over when it's been blossoming so nicely thus far. I felt badly for Maggie, because lasagna is not exactly the ideal dish to attempt when you're trying to make a good first impression. You should start with something easy, like meatloaf."

"Yeah, I agree wholeheartedly. Meatloaf's a good choice, or a pot of stew. Stew's hard to screw up because you can put just about anything in your refrigerator in it and it would still taste pretty much the same."

"Anything other than a pound of salt, which I have a feeling would find its way into any dish Maggie prepared."

"Anything but that," I agreed with a hearty laugh.

I vowed to myself never to share Mitch's sentiments with Maggie about her cooking. But I had to wonder, if he pitched the bag as he'd inferred, would I be able to find both cookies, minus the small bite someone took, in the facility's trash container? I was convinced it was Dr. Moretti who'd seen his initials on the bag and took a bite of one of the cookies he'd found inside. Like Dr. Murphy had suggested, it was probably so god-awful he'd put the cookie back in the bag and returned the bag to the refrigerator. That was undoubtedly how the hunk of lupin had made its way to the surgeon's stomach. *Was the one small bite enough to kill him?* I wondered. It *did* seem to be common knowledge his allergy to peanuts was severe, so the same probably applied to lupin. *This is not good news as far as Maggie is concerned.*

I felt it was crucial to track down the bag, which had been recently removed by a member of the janitorial staff. It sounded as though the room was only cleaned once a week. On Wednesday mornings, Mitch had said. So the trash from the break room could conceivably still be somewhere on the premises. To keep the anesthesiologist talking, I praised his new girlfriend.

"I think Maggie's a keeper, despite her lack of cooking expertise. After all, it's the thought that counts. Right?"

"Oh, absolutely." The warm smile on Mitch's face made it clear he was captivated with Maggie, which warmed my heart. I knew she was crazy about him, as well. "I have no intention of ever letting her go. I may have to encourage her to take some culinary classes down the road, but I'll wait a while before I cross that bridge."

"Good thinking," I replied. "Just out of curiosity, do you know of anyone who might've wanted to kill Dr. Moretti? My husband and I can't imagine anyone would want to harm such a kind person."

"I can't imagine it either. Dr. Moretti was such a thoughtful person and a good friend to me," Mitch replied. He'd had an odd look on his face when I'd changed subjects so suddenly but didn't appear to mind sharing his opinion. "It crossed my mind that it could have something to do with him replacing Candace with Jolene Sarcoxie as his operating room nurse. I've worked with Candace during surgeries a few times when she was Marco's operating room nurse and thought she did a great job. I don't know anyone who likes working with Jolene. Maggie told me Candace was pretty bitter about it," he said. "Maggie said Candace felt as though she'd been demoted, and basically, that's what it amounted to. You know what they say about a woman scorned, don't you? But please don't ever repeat my suspicions to anyone."

"I can understand why Candace would feel that way if she didn't do anything to deserve it. And I promise not to ever tell anybody what you shared with me." As I responded to the anesthesiologist, my mind was doing cartwheels. *It seems clear Dr. Murphy thinks Candace might've killed Dr. Moretti because she was upset about him demoting her to floor nurse and giving Jolene her position?* "Did Candace do something wrong during an operation that might've warranted losing her job as his operating room nurse?"

"Not that I'm aware of. As far as I know, Candace didn't do anything to deserve it. She was very proficient and extremely professional. The swap was totally out of left field, and no justification was ever offered her. I didn't bring it up with Marco only because I felt as though it was none of my business," Dr. Murphy explained.

"Hmm." I shook my head. "Yes, I can see where it might've seemed intrusive of you to question him about his decision to choose a new nurse to assist him during surgery. It was his prerogative, after all. I just feel bad for Candace."

"I do too. She's a nice lady. I'm sure the swap just had something to do with their relationship outside of the clinic."

"Whose relationship?"

"Dr. Moretti and Candace's." Dr. Murphy replied in a tone that suggested I wasn't paying adequate attention to what he was saying. "They'd been going out for a few months before Marco met and married Frankie. Candace continued to work as Marco's operating room nurse for at least six months before he suddenly replaced her with Jolene. Perhaps his new wife wasn't comfortable with him working side-by-side with a former lover and requested the switch. Frankie may not have realized it was like exchanging a garter snake for a King Cobra. It's never easy fraternizing with people you work with. But I guess that's the risk we take when we date co-workers, as I'm doing now with Maggie."

"That's true." I'd listened to the nurses discuss Candace's former fling with Dr. Moretti at the Scentsy party, but Dr. Murphy's comments made it clear their affair had been common knowledge among the clinic's staff. I supposed it was tough to keep it a secret when working relationships turn into sexual ones in a close-knit group such as the employees at the cath lab. I was thinking about how many personal relationships there seemed to be taking place at the clinic when Dr. Murphy brought me out of my reverie with his next remarks.

"Oh well. It's water under the bridge now that Marco's no longer here. Hopefully, Candace can apply to be the new surgeon's operating nurse. I'm assuming they'll hire another surgeon fairly quickly because we're going to be short-handed until they do."

"Yes, probably so," I agreed. "I hope she applies too and that her application is successful."

Just exactly how bitter was Candace about being replaced by Jolene? Could she have played a part in the death of her former flame? It certainly wouldn't be the first time jealousy and revenge were the motives for a murder. As these questions were flitting through my mind, Mitch Murphy was downing the last of his Dr. Pepper and scrunching up the candy bar wrapper to throw in the empty trash can.

I didn't want him to walk out of the break room before I could get another piece of information out of him. "You know, just in case I have to someday fill in for the lady who cleans this room on Wednesdays, I probably should find out where she takes the trash she collects."

"I'm not sure," he admitted. "But she probably hauls it to the bin behind the mobile MRI trailer in the back of the clinic. I've seen a special hazardous waste truck dumping that bin on Thursday mornings "

"Hazardous waste truck"? I didn't like the thought of sorting through trash classified as "hazardous waste".

"Yes." The doctor then explained. "There is a bio-hazard cart there too and it is picked up by a different truck on the same day. Unfortunately, a lot of potentially dangerous stuff, such as bodily waste, used syringes, and occasionally high-powered medications, are disposed of in patients' rooms. Rather than making a practice of sorting through all the trash in each room, the custodians have a tendency to pitch it all into the regular dumpster."

"Oh, goody," I said in a dry tone. "That does make sense, however."

I could tell Dr. Murphy was getting impatient to get back to work, so I wished him a good day and left the break room. I hurried to get to the hallway leading to the sliding glass door that required a code to enter but allowed anyone to exit. That thought brought the Eagles song *Hotel California* to mind, even though the lyrics of the song were just the opposite. I was singing the lines softly as I rounded the corner to the hallway. *"Relax," said the night man. "We are programmed to receive. You can check out any time you like, but you can never leave."* I stopped singing abruptly when I ran into what felt like a brick wall.

"Oomph." The low guttural sound came from Dr. O'Ryan, whom I'd just plowed into for the second time that day.

"Hey, lady!" He exclaimed. The red-headed doctor's temper

was triggered once again by my clumsiness. "Could you watch where you're walking? And why are you still here anyway?"

"I'm sorry." I paused to come up with a reason I hadn't departed when I'd told the surgeon I was going to after finishing up in the restroom. I thought back to the excessive amount of broccoli I'd eaten that had led to a bout of flatulence. "I got hung up in the restroom longer than I'd expected. It seems I'm dealing with some unexpected constipation today. I should know better than to eat a bunch of cheese. Thankfully, I'm heading home in a couple of minutes."

"Thankfully," Dr. O'Ryan repeated dryly.

"You should hear the story about the time I ate way too much broccoli."

The physician's expression was classic. He looked like I'd just asked him if he wanted to hear the tale about my mother going into premature labor and my daddy having to deliver me on the floor of a horse barn using a hoof trimmer and an extension cord. Without responding, O'Ryan shook his head and walked off in the opposite direction.

Thinking back, it might've been better if I *had* headed home in a couple of minutes as I'd told the ill-tempered heart surgeon earlier, instead of going ahead with my plan to find the cookie bag with "M.M." scribbled on its front in the cardiac clinic's disgusting dumpster. But hindsight was 20/20, whereas dumpster diving in hazardous waste could lead to 20 to life.

TWELVE

Although the idea of dumpster-diving didn't sound too appealing to me, I knew it had to be done before the bin was emptied. Dr. Murphy had told me the trash trucks both came on Thursday mornings and it was currently Wednesday afternoon. I walked out the front door and turned right to follow the sidewalk around the clinic. The concrete walkway stopped on the east side of the three-story building constructed out of Austin limestone and a well-worn path in the grass took its place. The Kentucky bluegrass lawn was in need of mowing, I noticed.

I continued to follow the path around to the back of the structure. It didn't take me long to find the dumpster Dr. Murphy had mentioned. The trailer it was stashed behind was huge and had "Mobile MRI unit" spelled out across its entire side. I was discouraged to discover the only way to see what was inside the dumpster was to climb up the side of it and lower myself down onto a mountain of rubbish, which I reluctantly did. The contents amassed in the trash bin were a disgusting mixture: used bed pans, uneaten food from patients' meal trays, a dirty diaper I stepped on. At that point, I nearly added fresh vomit to the dumpster's nauseating contents.

Just as I was about to call it quits because I wasn't sure locating the cookie bag was worth what I had to go through to find it, I spotted a paper bag. Confident the bag would have "M.M." scribbled on the front of it, I grasped it with my right hand. When a brown, furry spider crawled out of the bag within an inch of my index finger, I flung the bag as hard as I could at the inside wall of the metal trash container. Just a nanosecond before the bag made contact with the dumpster's interior wall, a bottle flew out, shattering into a zillion pieces. The dark inky liquid inside the bottle spewed out like a carbonated drink that'd been violently shaken up before the tab was pulled back. Startled, I yelped in reaction to the exploding glass container and ensuing fountain of black fluid.

Clearly, it was not the brown paper bag I'd been searching for but I was concerned about the black inky liquid now covering the front of my red and white shirt. I saw that most of the label previously attached to the bottle was still intact and picked it up to read it. The label read, "Gadolinium Contrast Medium, 50 ml."

I decided I'd better utilize the internet to find out what "Gadolinium Contrast Medium" meant. I was startled to find out the bottle had contained fifty milliliters of a toxic chemical substance found in the dye used to add contrast in magnetic resonance imaging, or MRI scans. Undoubtedly, it'd been pitched into the dumpster by someone working in the mobile MRI unit parked in front of the dumpster. Perhaps the substance had expired, or been compromised in some way. Either way, I felt positive it should've been disposed of in the nearby bio-hazard cart that had a secure, locking lid. *Laziness*, I thought in disgust. *Whoever disposed of it didn't want to be bothered with unlocking the cart where I'm certain toxic chemicals like gadolinium were supposed to be contained.*

Even though I felt sure the chemical was only toxic if consumed, I wasn't positive and it was unclear in the information

I'd read on the internet. I could feel the substance soaking through my shirt and onto my skin. The very idea made me panic. I ripped off my belt and quickly pulled the shirt over my head, hoping I might find something in the dumpster I could use to cover myself long enough to get to the truck where I always kept a sweater in the event I became chilled while traveling.

I was topless, sitting on a pile of repulsive rubbish in the medical facility's dumpster, when I looked up and saw two police officers peering down at me. One was tall and slim and the other officer was short and chunky. It seems a hospital employee had heard me yelp and thought an animal of some sort was trapped and needed to be rescued from inside the dumpster.

I explained, as vaguely as possible, that I had been searching for something that had been mistakenly thrown into the trash when a bottle of a toxic chemical exploded. "In my defense, the bottle of gadolinium should have been disposed of in the bio-hazard cart behind you. I had no way of knowing if physical contact with the substance was potentially harmful so I felt it necessary to remove my Red Cross shirt. I'm a volunteer for the organization, you see."

In response, the tubby officer took the shirt from my outstretched hand as though I was handing him a used condom. If he found my shirt disgusting, I had to wonder what he was going to think when he got a whiff of the baby doo-doo on the bottom of my shoes. The officer quickly cast the shirt aside as if contact with it had seared his skin. I was beyond humiliated and beating myself up for wearing an old raggedy bra when I had a brand new lacy Cross-Your-Heart brassiere in my underwear drawer. I'd been saving it for a special occasion. And what could be more special than having two young cops drag me out of a dumpster with black dye dripping from the C-sized cups of my stained and shabby bra?

I felt sick to my stomach when the two men exchanged a look. Without uttering a word, the look they'd exchanged had spoken volumes. It was obvious they thought the odds of me actually being a Red Cross volunteer were about as good as they were of me being the new director of the cardiac clinic. I was sure they thought I'd picked the shirt out of a Good Will box even though it was large enough for two people my size to share, or perhaps removed it from a three-hundred-pound drunk lying unconscious on the sidewalk. They might even think I was searching for my next meal in the dumpster. Nothing I could say was going to change their minds so I remained silent.

As they reached down into the dumpster and extended their arms to help lift me out, I eyed another paper bag. Astonished to see what looked like "M.M." on a portion of it, I hastily reached out and grabbed it. "Thank goodness! This is the bag I was searching for, officers."

I clutched the bag to my chest as though it contained my wedding ring, my passport, a thousand bucks in cash, and the only remaining photo I had of my deceased parents. Holding the bag tightly against my body only left one arm free. The portly officer said, "Hand me the bag, ma'am, while we help you out of the dumpster."

The last thing I wanted to do was to hand the bag to the officer. I could tell by the weight of the bag it still contained the two oatmeal chocolate chip cookies. Explaining why the cookies were of such dire importance to me would require more information than I was willing to share. When the officer asked again for me to hand him the bag, I took a peek inside the bag before I flung it as violently as I had the bag containing the gadolinium. Unfortunately, just like the contrast dye, the cookies flew out of the bag just before making contact with the wall. I'd gotten enough of a glimpse at the cookies to see a small portion of one cookie was missing and the other was fully intact. I realized then that Dr. Moretti's bite had been extremely small, much tinier than I'd imagined. I wondered if that minute bit of cookie could contain enough lupin to kill the surgeon. It didn't seem likely.

"Were those chocolate chip cookies?" The officers both asked in their most disbelieving tones. The slender cop who'd been relatively silent up until now asked, "You climbed into this dumpster to retrieve a couple of chocolate chip cookies?"

"Well, no," I said defensively.

"Then what are they?" The shorter, chubby cop asked as the slim, taller cop removed his jacket and handed it to me to cover up with, for which I was very thankful.

"Well, actually they are *oatmeal* chocolate chip cookies," I stammered.

The rude cop laughed so hard that spittle flew out of his mouth, landing on his partner's blue jacket, which I'd just put on. I didn't like this officer nearly as much as I'd liked the kinder, more fit one who'd sacrificed his jacket to protect my modesty. The jacket would likely never be free of the dumpster's stench, but at least the other cop's spit would come out in the wash. I liked the bad-mannered cop, who'd likely eaten too many doughnuts while on patrol, even less when he sarcastically added, "So am I to assume it's the addition of oatmeal that makes them so valuable?"

"That's enough, Josh!" The more compassionate, and slightly older, officer whispered just loud enough I could make out the admonishment to his insensitive partner. He'd taken pity on me. He clearly thought I'd been on a quest to find something to eat because I was hungry, homeless, mentally impaired, or all three. I was mortified beyond words. The empathetic officer spoke softly, trying not to sound judgmental.

"Give us your arms so we can get you out. We're going to take you down to the station so we can get you some assistance. We have a lady in our department who can help you contact a family member or get you transferred to a shelter or halfway house. I'm sure she can see to it that you are given a warm meal, as well."

I was too embarrassed to tell the nice man it wasn't food I'd been after when I'd just made it plain it was the cookies I was trying to find when I climbed down into the nasty rubbish. I merely lifted my arms up without speaking. Without admitting to the law enforcement officers my husband and I had butted into what we were convinced was a murder case, and I'd been on a mission to eliminate potential evidence, I could think of no way to convince the two officers I was not in need of intervention. I would call Rip who would claim me at the police station. He'd proceed to blow off a little steam at my impulsive, reckless actions and then laugh about the embarrassing episode later on—— with any luck at all!

If nothing else, even without having the bag in my possession, I could now confirm that the late surgeon had ingested very little lupin and had most likely not been killed by Maggie's cookies. "Most likely not been killed by her cookies" was probably not what Maggie wanted to hear, and I couldn't be sure how much lupin it would take to kill a man with a severe allergy to the substance. I had hoped to be able to give the sweet nurse a definitive guarantee that she was off the hook and could continue her life without guilt and regret. But I couldn't. On the other hand, I *could* positively guarantee I'd never live down the degrading incident I'd just experienced.

"Thank you, Officer Ramsey," Rip said. "I'm going to take your jacket to the cleaners and will return it to the police station for you after I pick it back up. My wife and I both appreciate you loaning it to her. I apologize for the inconvenience."

"It was no inconvenience, Mr. Ripple, but thank you for getting my jacket laundered," the kindhearted cop replied. He had seemed genuinely concerned about my welfare whereas the other officer had appeared irritated he'd even had to deal with a vagrant like me in the first place. "When we realized she was after a bag that had two old cookies in it, we thought maybe she was hungry and needed help. Margaret offered her a ham sandwich, which she refused."

"No, hunger's not the problem," Rip said. "Ever since her recent head injury, she's been very unpredictable. I'm thankful you found her when you did because I was just about to call and see if I could have an APB put out on her. She'd wandered off while I was taking a shower."

"Oh, sure," the friendly cop replied. "We get those silver alerts all the time."

As the wife of a career lawman, I knew APB stood for all-points bulletin and a silver alert was a public notification system to broadcast information about missing senior citizens. I felt ashamed that either one would be deemed necessary on my account. I was also impressed with Rip's ease at telling bald-faced lies, but equally irritated with him. He'd made me sound as though he couldn't bathe without me turning the short unsupervised interlude into a silver alert emergency.

Soon we were buckled into the truck, which the snotty officer named Josh had driven to the police station while I rode in the back of the patrol car driven by Officer Ramsey. Since I'd taken the truck to the cath lab, Rip had been forced to ask the owner of the RV park to call him a taxi to transport him to the police station. *Utilizing a ride-sharing company like Uber or Lyft would've been cheaper*, I thought. *But I'd have died of old age in police custody before Rip would've ever figured out how to even bring up one of their apps on his phone, much less use it to book a ride.*

As expected, once we were on the road headed back to the campground, Rip let off steam. A whole lot of steam, to be clear. I'm shocked my glasses and the Chevy's rearview mirror hadn't fogged over by the time we pulled up to the Chartreuse Caboose. I've learned it's easiest to let Rip rant uninterrupted, apologize to him when he's finally finished, and promise never to do something so ludicrous again. Only then would I try and state my case for attempting such a stupid stunt in the first place.

I was surprised Rip seemed even more incensed than he had in similar situations in the past. This time, he'd at least known what I'd planned to do in advance, even if he had no way of knowing my plan would go so far south during its execution. When he'd cooled down, I explained how I'd been able to confirm Dr. Moretti had ingested such a tiny amount of lupin that it likely had nothing to do with the doctor's death. Obviously relieved by that bit of news, Rip said, "I'm sure she'd be more relieved if you could tell her for certain it wasn't enough to kill him."

"I realize that," I said. "Unfortunately, she'll be emotionally disturbed that her new boyfriend had pitched them out uneaten, and even Dr. Moretti could only tolerate a tiny bite of one of her cookies. We may have to think of a way to be a little vague about it. After all, I did promise Dr. Murphy I wouldn't tell Maggie he thought she was a horrible cook."

"Well, like I've said before, that kind of thing is in your wheel-house, not mine."

"Uh-huh." And, also like before, his comment was not meant as a flattering remark, but rather as a slight. Regardless, I was thankful Rip had gotten his anger out of his system and we could move on from the shameful incident.

Rip reached over and patted my knee. I knew it was his way of saying he wasn't mad at me. His tone was much more amicable when he said, "It is nice Maggie won't have to worry quite so much about being held responsible for Dr. Moretti's death, isn't it?"

I nodded and smiled, but was thinking, *or at least not likely to be held responsible because of an allergic reaction due to the cookies she made. At this point, I'm not so convinced she wasn't involved in Moretti's death in some form or fashion.*

I had Maggie's phone number so I sent her a text.

> Just wanted to let you know I was able to confirm Dr. Moretti only ate a minuscule amount of one of the cookies you made. Hopefully, not ingesting nearly enough lupin to cause his death. That should be a load off your shoulders.

As if she'd been holding the phone in her hand, Maggie immediately texted back.

> That's comforting even though there's still no guarantee, considering how deathly allergic he is to peanuts. Thank you, Rapella. Candace asked for your phone number to send you her mother-in-law's paszteciki recipe. Is it okay to give it to her?

> Yes, of course, Maggie. By the way, I am just curious if you've ever performed any duties at the clinic other than as a floor nurse?

> Nope. I enjoy interacting with patients and their families the way I did with you and Rip. I've had no desire to change jobs at STAT.

> I understand. You are so good at what you do; I'd hate to see you switch to another position. Talk to you later.

> K

I wanted to ask Maggie how she knew the passcode to gain access to the operating room area where the doctors' break room was, but decided the question might make her leery of me. I felt certain I'd need to be able to converse with her in the future and didn't want to put a wrench in our budding friendship if it turned out the doctor's death had nothing to do with her cookies.

Within minutes of ending my text exchange with Maggie, my text tone went off again. It was Candace forwarding me the recipe for the Polish pastry. I scrolled up and back down to see if she'd included a personal note. She had not.

I sent her a response to thank her and say I couldn't wait to try the recipe out on Rip. Even though I'd first expressed interest in the meat-filled pastry only as an excuse to speak to her, I was having second thoughts. I truly did think it was something Rip would enjoy. With a few substitutions, I could even make the recipe fairly heart-healthy. And unlike Maggie, I considered myself a fairly accomplished cook.

> I have a question for the nurse who assisted Dr. Moretti when he performed a stent placement procedure on my husband just prior to his death, but I can't recall her name. I remember she was at Maggie's Scentsy party and with you at the clinic when I spoke to you earlier in the hallway.

> His operating room nurse was Jolene Sarcoxie. It was probably her.

> Oh, yes.

I was playing dumb, hoping to drag a little more information out of Candace. I wanted to determine whether or not she had a strong enough motive to kill her former boyfriend.

> Now I remember. I heard Jolene took over for another nurse who'd had that position previously.

> That nurse was me and Jolene didn't exactly take over my position. It was more of a rollover than a takeover. None of us at the clinic can figure out how she was able to coerce Marco into promoting her and sending me back to the post-surgical floor. I'm sure Marco's wife Frankie wasn't too happy either when she learned about it. It's fairly well known that Jolene's a snake in scrubs, who'll go after any man she sets her sights on.

> Wow!

Her remark reminded me of the analogy involving a garter snake and a King Cobra that her boyfriend, Mitch Murphy, had recently used to compare her to Jolene.

> I'm so sorry you had to deal with all that.

> Thanks, Rapella. It's been tough for me.

Had Frankie learned about the nurse swap her husband had made? I wondered. *Knowing Marco had dated Candace before he began dating her, could Frankie have demanded her husband replace Candace with a different assistant, not knowing what kind of man-eater Candace's replacement would turn out to be? Is it possible the clinic's grapevine doesn't extend as far out as the surgeons' spouses?* I was chewing over these questions before responding.

Candace was unaware I'd overheard her argument with Jolene in the break room earlier in the day. I had to be careful how I responded. My guess was that prior to Dr. Moretti's death, Jolene had not given up on her quest to land the well-respected surgeon, and didn't care if it broke up his marriage before the new had even had a chance to wear off of it. *Dr. Moretti could not have been oblivious to Jolene's attraction to him, could he? Had that attraction led to an affair between the two? Or could there be something Jolene was holding over his head?*

I wondered. *Was she cognizant of a secret so potentially damaging to his marriage or his career, or even both, that he couldn't take the chance of Jolene spilling it? Had he been blackmailed into promoting Jolene?* Something was definitely rotten in Denmark, or Rochester in this case. To keep the exchange from getting too dark or deep, I typed out the following text and clicked on "send."

> I'm sure it has been tough for you, Candace. I'm starting to get the impression Jolene Sarcoxie is never going to win any popularity contests at the STAT Clinic.

I added a laughing emoji to the message.

> You can say that again!

> I'm starting to get the impression Jolene…

I began to repeat my former remark.

> LOL——just kidding. Seriously, I'm sorry she acted like such a horse's ass to you at Maggie's Scentsy party the other night.

> I'm used to it. At least I had the decency to step aside when Marco told me he'd met Frankie, who he claimed was the woman he wanted to marry, even if his admission did hit me like a Lamellar Dissector knife to the heart.

I didn't know how the rather specific knife she'd named was different from any other knife, but I didn't want to look uninformed so I didn't mention it.

That had to be hard on you. I won't keep
you any longer. Thanks again for the recipe.
Please give my regards to Kat.

I'll do that. Have a good night, Rapella.

I wished Candace a nice evening, as well, and ended the text exchange.

Who knew the cath lab would turn out to be akin to Peyton Place? I thought. I could never have imagined the personable, professional, and highly regarded cardiac surgeon could have angered someone to the point they'd want to harm him. But it was beginning to look like the man changed girlfriends more frequently than Kanye West changed the name he wanted to be known by.

And then another thought hit me. *We are only assuming it was the small amount of lupin that killed Dr. Moretti. If an allergic reaction wasn't the cause of Dr. Moretti's death, then what was?* Could the man with the stressful occupation have actually died of myocardial infarction like the medical examiner had suspected? Were we trying to delve into a murder case that had never been a murder case to begin with?

After I talked it over with Rip, we decided we needed to take a step back. We planned to be in Rochester for three more weeks, as it was nearly always cheaper to pay for a full month in an RV site than it was to sign up for two or three weeks.

We would rest and relax, and let Rip recuperate fully for the remainder of the month. We had nowhere we needed to be, no deadlines to meet, and no new destinations on our schedule. With any luck at all, the tox screen results from Dr. Moretti's autopsy would come in sooner rather than later. I'd make sure Maggie knew to let me know if she heard anything. In fact, I would make sure to stop by to chat with her at the clinic on a couple of occasions in the following two weeks to keep the line of communication with her open.

Three days later, Maggie called at eight o'clock in the evening. I put my phone on speaker so Rip could hear both sides of the conversation. Maggie went on to tell us that Dr. Moretti's tox screen results had come back. Apparently, the medical examiner had requested the results be expedited due to the uncertainty behind the surgeon's sudden passing. His foresight had proven correct, and an updated determination of the late surgeon's cause of death had been made. Dr. Moretti's COD was now being classified as a homicide. Even though we'd suspected his death had not been by natural causes, Rip and I could not have been any more gobsmacked if Maggie had told us that Dr. Moretti had come back to life and was inserting a stent into a patient's carotid artery as we spoke.

I couldn't tell if the shakiness in Maggie's voice was from shock, heartbreak, or fear, but she definitely was not handling the new murder classification well. She began to stutter and became more and more distressed the longer she spoke, which wasn't nearly long enough to fill us in on all the details. Finally, Maggie said she'd stop by the following morning to tell us more about it because the news he'd been deliberately killed was just sinking in and had her all choked up. "Tomorrow is m-m-my day off," she began, "and (sniff) I'm not sure I could have performed my nursing duties adequately anyway. Is nine o'clock t-t-too early?"

"Nine o'clock is perfect," I assured her. "I'll have the coffee ready!"

THIRTEEN

I woke up the next day feeling like my blood had been drained and replaced with Elmer's Glue while I slept. Just changing out of my nightshirt was exhausting. I took some over-the-counter cold medicine and struggled to get breakfast down. *Feed a cold, starve a fever*, I reminded myself as I tried to work up enough energy to butter my English muffin. When Lexie called at eight o'clock, I could barely get a greeting out of my mouth because my voice was so hoarse.

"Good morning, Rapella," she said in her usual cheerful lilt. "I can't comment on how you look, but you sound like death warmed over."

"I can't comment on how I look either, Lexie, because I've been afraid to look in the mirror. But my sinuses are draining like an overturned spaghetti pot and my throat feels like I gargled with battery acid."

"I'm sorry to hear you've caught a bug, my friend," Lexie began, "but I was curious how your investigation into the cardiac surgeon's death is going. Anything new to report?"

"Well, not much, other than his death has officially been ruled a homicide. Maggie, one of the nurses at the clinic, is stopping by this morning to give us more details about the tox screen report. We were also able to determine the doctor only took a tiny bite of one of the oatmeal chocolate chip cookies Maggie left in the doctors' break room refrigerator."

"Is that the royal 'we' you just used?" Rip asked from his position on the couch. "Make sure Lexie knows I had nothing to do with that disaster. It was all Calamity Jane and no Wild Rip Hickok."

"I overheard Rip's remark." Lexie was clearly amused and now anxious to hear about my ill-fated shenanigans. "You're going to have to elaborate."

"Well, I don't——"

"Please, Rapella. I'm begging you."

"Oh, all right." I cleared my throat several times and then explained what had happened regarding my dumpster diving experience. I left out nothing, not even that I'd been wearing my oldest, most tattered bra when the two officers discovered me half-naked in the disgusting dumpster.

When Lexie stopped laughing so hard she was having trouble catching her breath, she said, "So I'm guessing it didn't turn out quite the way you'd pictured it would?"

"You think?" I asked in my driest voice, which was easy to do since my throat currently felt as parched as Death Valley in August. Before I could continue, I had a coughing jag that lasted at least thirty seconds. When I went back to the phone, Lexie sounded concerned.

"Rapella, you really do sound awful. I think you should go see a doctor. Maybe he or she can give you something to at least ease your symptoms."

"I don't have time for that today," I replied a few seconds later after I'd nearly hacked up a lung. "Maggie, who might have some beneficial information, is due here in a few minutes. I'll let you know if we learn anything new. So far, we are coming up short in the evidence department. After she leaves, I'll make a run to the pharmacy for some Robitussin."

"Well, I hope your nurse friend can suggest something stronger for your cough. I'm not sure Robitussin is enough. If you don't feel any better by mid-day, you should pop into an Urgent Care Clinic."

"Okay, Lexie. I promise I won't let it get ahead of me. I'll talk to you later on today, or tomorrow at the latest."

"Okay, Rapella." She rang off just as a knock on the door echoed throughout the travel trailer. Maggie knocked a second time before I could get to the door. I motioned her inside and waved off her attempt to hug me. She looked confused and mildly affronted. I pointed her toward the couch. Rip was in the restroom and would occupy the recliner as soon as he joined us, and I would sit on an ottoman as far from the other two as possible. As I poured three cups of coffee, Maggie apologized for arriving early.

"I'm sorry I'm early. I was hoping you'd be up and around," she said. "I was so on edge this morning I felt jittery and short of breath. Nervous energy, I suppose."

"Here's a cup of fully-caffeinated Folgers. I've heard it's just the medicine for jittery nerves." I tried to laugh at my sarcastic quip, but it came out as more of a grunt. She eyed me warily as she grasped the cup from my hands.

"Why do you sound like you ate a bowl of broken glass for breakfast?" Maggie asked, the nurse in her instantly picking up on the vibes of ill health I was giving off.

"I woke up with a bad cold. Don't get any closer to me. I don't want to share this with you." After Maggie nodded, I asked, "Why are you so nervous and upset this morning, sweetheart?"

"Just anxious, I guess. Dr. Moretti's death has affected me so much worse than I ever thought it would."

"Why?" My question sounded like the croak of a dying bullfrog, but the hot coffee was slowly beginning to soothe my throat, making it easier for me to speak. Maggie's remark had caught me off-guard. Without thinking, I asked her a question that caught her off-guard, as well. "Was there more to the cookie deal than you're telling me?"

Maggie sat the coffee cup down on the end table. As though she was debating whether or not to expand on the story, she remained silent. After a long uncomfortable pause, she said, "No. I can guarantee you my uneasiness has nothing to do with the cookies."

"What *does* it have to do with then?" I attempted a casual tone, but even to my own ears, the inquiry sounded distrustful.

"I think I know who killed Marco."

"Really?" I asked. My lower jaw had dropped so fast my upper dentures went with it. I apologized, turned my back to Maggie, and put the plate back in place before asking, "Who?"

"Well, everyone knew Jolene had the hots for Marco. Eva thought when Marco gave Jolene Candace's job, Candace was angry enough to want to get revenge against Marco. And Charmaine told me she thought he and Jolene were hooking up. If Candace found out about that, she would definitely be beyond livid. Charmaine also thought——"

"Charmaine and Eva *thought* these *things?*" I did too, but didn't want to say so at that point. "Did Charmaine have proof the two were involved in a sexual relationship or just suspect it? Or did she *know without a doubt* the two were having an affair? The difference in thinking and knowing is highly significant."

"Well, she said Eva told Monica, who told——"

"Stop!" I held my hand up as if I was stopping traffic so a herd of third-graders could cross a busy intersection. "That's a lot of 'thoughts' and no evidence. With every word you say, the accusation becomes more circumstantial. Which means the claim is a product of a busy gossip mill and, thus, very problematic. You have absolutely nothing concrete to stand on when you say Candace is likely responsible for the surgeon's death. Don't forget, Maggie, she is considered innocent until proven guilty, as aggravating as that is at times."

Even as I made the last comment, I realized I'd also been guilty of thinking a certain suspect was guilty beyond a shadow of a doubt before they'd had their day in court. I'd had no proof, just a gut feeling someone was a cold-blooded killer before I had any evidence they were guilty of the crime. Over time, I've learned my gut has a tendency to lie to me. And then sometimes it even tries to cover it up, which is not easy for a gut to do.

"Maybe so, but we all knew Jolene had the hots for Marco," Maggie repeated, less enthusiastically this time.

"Honey, I had the hots for my fourth-grade teacher in primary school," I said. "That certainly didn't mean I 'hooked up' with him, as you put it. Wanting and having are two different things."

"You wanted to have sex with your adult teacher when you were, like, nine years old?" Maggie had taken my remarks way too literally. She looked at me as though I'd told her I was turning tricks during recess.

"Of course not!" I exclaimed. "Like you said, I was nine and Mr. Marshall was thirty. But I was convinced I'd marry him someday. Incidentally, I found out years later he was gay *and* his life partner was our hunky mailman."

Maggie chuckled and I followed suit. I was happy to see my made-up story had lightened the mood and taken the edge off of our tense discussion. To be honest, my fourth-grade teacher had been a surly sixty-year-old spinster named Ms. Boswick, who I called Ms. Bossy Witch, which had landed me in the principal's office several times. I once dreamed she'd fallen into the well on our property. Even though in my dream I'd seen it happen, I decided not to tell anyone because she'd written "talks too much in class" on my report card. *What a revengeful child I must've been*, I thought. *Glad I grew out of it.*

Our laughter about my childhood crush on the fictional Mr. Marshall appeared to summon Rip from the restroom. He looked from me to Maggie and asked, "What are you ladies cackling about?"

"Nothing that would interest you," I responded. I noticed my throat was much better now that I'd finished off my first cup of coffee. I jumped up and poured myself a refill. Maggie's cup was still two-thirds full.

Maggie laughed again and said, "Oh, I think Rip would be fascinated by what you——"

"Hush! That was just between us girls." I shook my index finger at the nurse. We both began chortling again and Rip just shook his head waiting for us to settle down and catch him up on the conversation. When we quieted down, he asked, "So, Maggie, what did Dr. Moretti's tox screen show that changed his death from natural causes to death by homicide?"

The amusement on Maggie's face faded faster than the lawn chair cushions we'd just purchased during our recent visit with Lexie Starr and Stone Van Patten. "The lab work showed Marco had a chemical called Agent VX in his system," she said seriously and solemnly, with a hint of relief thrown in the mix.

Agent VX meant nothing to me, but Rip almost dropped the coffee cup he was holding. "VX nerve agent? How did Dr. Moretti get a toxic chemical like that in his system?"

"I don't know," Maggie replied. "But apparently it can be very lethal."

"Yeah, duh," Rip said, rather rudely. Even though his response was somewhat demeaning, his knowledge and memory amazed me once again as he explained, "That's what killed Kim Jong-nam in 2017 inside the Kuala Lumpur airport in Malaysia. The nerve agent was splashed on his face by two female attackers. He didn't even ingest any of the deadly chemical."

"Isn't that the dude from North Korea President Trump called Rocket Man?" Maggie asked.

I was going to impress her with my knowledge and confirm the man was one and the same. Thankfully, Rip responded before I had the chance.

"No," he said simply. "Korea's ruler is named Kim Jong-un. Kim Jong-nam was his half-brother. It was widely believed his assassination was ordered by Kim Jong-un, however."

"Why would Kim Jong-un kill his own half-brother?" Maggie asked.

"For one thing, Kim Jong-un is a ruthless dictator. But it was also because his half-brother was reportedly working with the CIA and Jong-un considered his half-brother talking to American spies as treacherous." After Maggie nodded in understanding, Rip continued. "The remarkable thing about all this is where would someone in Rochester, Minnesota, be able to obtain VX nerve agent and know enough about how to handle it safely without exposing themself to the very toxic chemical?"

Neither Maggie nor I knew enough about the chemical to even hazard a guess. We both shrugged and waited for Rip to speak again. I have to admit I was a bit crestfallen when he did.

"If nothing else, now that the Rochester Police Department knows Dr. Moretti's death was a homicide and are aware of what was used as the murder weapon, they will undoubtedly be able to follow up on it and solve the murder case. I'm sure they'll have the killer behind bars before the week is over."

I knew Rip's words were meant not only to give Maggie comfort but also to let me know our part in investigating the surgeon's death had come to an end. I'm not sure why this disappointed me, but it did. I guess I'm the kind of person who likes to finish what I've started. Stepping aside to let the local homicide detectives handle a murder case without my interference just wasn't in my DNA.

Rip decided to drive to an auto parts store to buy new windshield wiper blades for the Chevy truck while Maggie and I continued to gab for another hour. Once the door had closed behind my husband, I asked Maggie, "Do you have any idea of anyone besides Candace who might have wanted Dr. Moretti dead?"

"Not really," the nurse replied. "I know of a number of people who might've had an issue with him, but no one I know despised him enough to kill him."

"What about his wife? Could she have found out something was going on between Dr. Moretti and Jolene?"

"She could have, I suppose." Maggie sounded uncertain, even about her own response. "But I think Frankie would've filed for divorce and taken him to the cleaners before she'd have murdered him."

"Why do you say that?"

"Because he made good money, and it's kind of like the blood from a turnip thing. You can't draw alimony from a dead guy. At a party at the Morettis' home last month, Frankie got a wee bit tipsy and told a few of us nurses that before she and Marco had tied the knot, she'd been persuaded to sign a pre-nuptial agreement. The terms in the prenup left most of Marco's assets to his three adult children from his first marriage if the couple's marriage ended in divorce within the first ten years. I got the impression then that part of Marco's appeal, as far as Frankie is concerned, was his money. My guess is she's pretty content with her current lavish lifestyle."

"Okay," I consented, while still wondering if Frankie had previously had any overwhelming incentive to kill her husband. She apparently lived in a mansion on Silver Lake that had a shiny new

Mercedes Benz parked in its garage. None of which would likely remain hers for long if Dr. Moretti died and the bulk of his estate went to his kids. *Or would it?* I wondered. *After all, he had died. She hadn't divorced him.* While I had the chance, I wanted to ask Maggie about several people I considered suspects, starting with the one she most suspected of killing Dr. Moretti. "Do you feel Candace was bitter enough about Marco dropping her for Frankie to truly want him dead? He also demoted her as his operating room nurse in favor of a flirtatious fellow co-worker. That had to sting."

"Yes, she was extremely upset by both incidents." Maggie seemed confident about this one. "From the very beginning of their relationship, Candace was afraid Marco would soon cast her aside for a more desirable woman. I'm guessing she became so clingy Marco felt as though she was suffocating him."

"It sounds like she lacks self-confidence."

"Yes, Candace is very insecure. She grew up with a younger sister who won several beauty pageants, including Miss Minnesota, and felt like she was a disappointment to her parents. Her sister was a gifted singer and a straight-A student, leaving Candace to think she wasn't pretty enough, smart enough, or talented enough."

"That's too bad." I felt sorry for the kind nurse with the poor self-image. "You'd think her mother would have noticed her older daughter felt unworthy and would've done whatever it took to build up Candace's self-esteem."

"Yeah, I agree. I really like Candace. Even though I think she may be a killer, it pisses me off that Jolene has taken to tearing her down, making Candace think she's even less desirable than she'd already imagined."

"Jolene is a bully," I said. "Do you think *she* could've had something to do with Dr. Moretti's death? Perhaps he told Jolene he'd never leave Frankie for her."

"I guess that's possible," Maggie replied. "Eva, Monica, Charmaine, and I all think Jolene threatened to tell his wife, Frankie, that she and he were having an affair if he didn't give her Candace's job as his operating room nurse. The position is more interesting, deemed more respectable by the medical field, and comes with a bigger paycheck. Returning to the floor nurse position was basically a demotion for Candace, and her pay took a hit too. We all think Jolene had enough nerve to even demand Marco leave Frankie for her or lose his job and reputation as an esteemed cardiac surgeon."

"We're back to a lot of 'thinking' and not a lot of 'proof,'" I said. "But the hypothesis is worth considering." I made a mental note to write all of this information down in my notebook as soon as Maggie left. I didn't want to forget any of it, but I could hardly make notations in a notebook in Maggie's presence without causing her to become self-conscious and curious as to my objective. She might even glance at the page with my suspect list printed on it and see her name was listed as suspect number three.

"What about Dr. O'Ryan?" I asked, thinking about suspect number four. "Could he be responsible for his colleague's death? I doubt it's any secret he felt the director's position should've gone to him, not Dr. Moretti, due to his previous work experience."

"I highly doubt it. Blaze had just accepted a position at the Mayo Clinic that pays more than the STAT Clinic. Next Friday is to be his last day at the cath lab. He told Eva, who is *his* operating room nurse, that he prefers the more laid-back atmosphere at the clinic. He just couldn't turn down the higher salary and the future career opportunities working at Mayo would afford him."

"Will Dr. O'Ryan be in charge of the entire cardiology department at Mayo?" I asked. There was something about Maggie's last response that was niggling at my mind, but I couldn't quite put my finger on it.

"No," Maggie began, "but he will be one of the head surgeons, and he'll have the opportunity to train new recruits, which he seems to enjoy."

I was running out of suspects, so I said, "Let's say for a moment it turns out not to be Candace, as you suspect. If you had to render a guess, who else might you suspect of being responsible for Dr. Moretti's death?"

"Pratyush Patel," Maggie answered without pause.

"Pratyush Patel?" I was taken aback by her response. His name was not even included on my suspect list. "The cardiovascular technologist? Why in heaven's name would you suspect him of killing Dr. Moretti? He was actually crying when he told Rip and me about the surgeon's death. He described him as his mentor and one of his closest friends. What could possibly make a guy like that want to kill a guy he told us felt like a brother to him?"

"That might have been Pratyush's cover story, but secretly I think he was jealous of Marco. You see, Pratyush had a huge crush on Frankie after he and she met at the same party where Marco met Frankie. He actually took Frankie out on two dates before Marco asked her out. Pratyush fell hard for Frankie, but she never gave him another look after she went out with Marco. He told me once he felt like Marco stabbed him in the back and stole his girl. Pratyush went on to date me for a while. But clearly, I didn't measure up to Frankie so he dropped me after about six months."

"And now Pratyush is dating the Mayo Clinic volunteer you mentioned at your Scentsy party and you're dating Dr. Murphy," I pointed out. I wanted to ask Maggie if there was any doctor who hadn't hooked up with every single nurse at the STAT Clinic because I was beginning to lose track of who was dating whom. I didn't want to look like a disapproving old fogey though, so instead, I said, "It sounds to me like it all worked out for the best in the end."

"Yes, I suppose so."

FOURTEEN

The following day marked Rip's final follow-up appointment with Dr. O'Ryan, who had taken on a few of Dr. Moretti's patients after his death. With Dr. O'Ryan's days working at the lab numbered, he could only take on patients like Rip who were about to be released from the clinic's care. The rest of the late doctor's patients had been split up among the remaining two surgeons at the clinic.

After twenty minutes of scanning old *Good Housekeeping* magazines in the waiting room, Rip's patience had reached its conclusion. Apparently, there wasn't a single article about flower arranging or air-frying tips that interested him. When he turned to a page that read, "12 Clever Uses for Kitchen Foil," he slammed the magazine down on the table. "If I'm not called back in the next five minutes, I'm leaving and they can reschedule my appointment to a time when the doctor can actually see me when he says he will. My time is every bit as valuable as his."

"Hush, Rip!! I'm sure they'll call you back soon." If Rip was not sitting in the waiting room, he'd be home sitting in his recliner in front of the television with a fat cat sprawled out across his chest. I didn't really think the time he spent watching *Gunsmoke* reruns was as valuable as the heart surgeon's time saving lives. As Mitch Murphy had recently stated, we all need to choose our battles. Bickering about whose time was most valuable wasn't a battle I wanted to engage in right then. So I told Rip I was going to go get a cup of coffee out of the vending machine near the elevators.

Purely by coincidence, I ran into Eva Clemens, who was stepping off the elevator when I walked up.

"Hello, Eva!" I greeted her. "Do you remember me from Maggie's Scentsy party?"

"Of course," she said. "You're Rapella Cripple, or was it Nipple?"

"It's Ripple, but you were close. If it'd been either Cripple or Nipple, I'd have legally changed my name fifty years ago. So how are you doing?"

"I'm fine. Why are you here, other than to buy a cup of the most gag-worthy coffee in the entire city? There's a Starbucks directly across the street if you'd prefer more palatable brew."

"I would, but I don't have time, and you know what they say…"

"Bad coffee is better than no coffee?" Eva guessed.

"Well, that too," I replied. "But I was thinking that beggars can't be choosers. Rip had a ten o'clock follow-up appointment with Dr. O'Ryan. He's still waiting but should be called back at any moment."

"Don't count on it," Eva said drily. "Dr. O'Ryan's been known to keep patients stewing in the waiting room for over an hour. I've been working here since the clinic first opened its doors and I've never seen a patient get called back to a room on time. The patient scheduling leaves a lot to be desired."

"We're learning that right now," I replied. "And, unfortunately, it's not uncommon in medical settings. Maggie said you are Dr.

O'Ryan's operating room nurse. What will happen to your job when he leaves for his new job at the Mayo Clinic?"

"I was told I would serve as a backup until a new surgeon can be hired to replace Blaze, but I'm considering the idea of retirement. As in the case with Marco's replacement, I'd have to apply for the position as the new surgeon's operating room nurse and beat out the other nurses who put in for the job. I'm just not sure I want to go through all that at my age."

"I don't blame you, Eva. Dr. O'Ryan's departure might be a sign it's time for you to hang up your scrubs for good."

"You might be right, Rapella," Eva replied. "I was surprised when Blaze applied for the opening at Mayo. I thought he loved working here."

"Isn't his new job more prestigious with a higher salary?" I asked. At her nod, I added, "Speaking of old clichés, 'Money talks and bullcrap walks.'"

"That's true. And Blaze has a third child on the way. He and his wife, Olivia, are expecting a boy this time to go along with their twin daughters. He's been over the moon about having a son."

"And I'm sure he wants to provide well for his growing family. I'm also sure he's an exceptional father and husband, but his bedside manner could stand to be a little friendlier."

"True again. But don't let Blaze's brusque manner fool you. He's an exceptional surgeon even if his deportment with patients is less than stellar. We were all shocked when Marco was promoted to the director's position instead of Blaze. My guess is the board of directors preferred working with Marco because he was so much more compliant, more compassionate, and more cooperative. Even so, Marco's expertise as a cardiac surgeon didn't hold a candle to Blaze's." Eva glanced at her watch and said, "I better get back to work. It was great to see you again, Rapella."

"You too, dear. Have a good day."

I soon learned Eva had not exaggerated about the poor quality of the vending machine coffee. It was just a couple of minutes after I returned to the waiting room with my "gag-worthy" coffee that Rip was called back to a room. Monica Corry, one of the nurses I'd met at the Scentsy party, weighed Rip, took his temperature and blood pressure, and told us the doctor would be with us momentarily. It was another half-hour before Dr. O'Ryan opened the door to the room that might've passed as a large closet. Claustrophobia had taken over for impatience by the time the clock struck eleven and Dr. O'Ryan waltzed in with a clipboard in his hands.

"How are you doing, Mr. Ripple?"

"Other than the fact my butt is numb from sitting in this chair for so long, I'm doing fine."

"Good to hear." Clearly, the surgeon would not know sarcasm if it jumped up and spat in his eye. Dr. O'Ryan then placed a stethoscope over Rip's heart to listen to its rhythm, which I had no doubt was beating more rapidly than it had been when we'd first arrived at the clinic. "Your pulse is a bit fast, but otherwise it sounds good. Feeling any pain in your chest?"

"Nope."

"Have you experienced any redness or bleeding at the incision site on your wrist?"

Rip shook his head.

"Any shortage of breath or excessive lethargy?"

"No," Rip answered.

"Have you been taking your blood pressure as advised?" Dr. O'Ryan asked.

"Yes." As Rip responded, I handed the doctor a piece of paper that we'd notated his blood pressure readings on four times a day since his stent placement procedure.

The surgeon scanned the readings and handed the list back to me. "All right, then, Mr. Ripple. Everything looks fine. You should be good to go. If, and when, you have any symptoms of another clogged artery, or chest pain related to any cardiac issue, just call the clinic and make another appointment."

We both nodded in consent. Neither Rip nor I mentioned that we'd be many miles away from Rochester, Minnesota, in our home on wheels if and when another clogged artery or cardiac issue raised its ugly head.

"That's it?" Rip asked the doctor. "I waited a full hour for what I could've told your nurse over the phone in about thirty seconds?"

"We like to see our patients in the office." Dr. O'Ryan replied in what sounded like a defensive tone. "We can tell a lot about how someone is feeling by observing them in person."

To cut Rip off at the quick, I said, "We understand. Say, I heard congratulations are in order, Dr. O'Ryan."

"For what?" He looked baffled by my remark. "What exactly did you hear?"

"Two things, actually. I heard you and your wife are expecting your third child and also that you've been awarded a new position at the Mayo Clinic."

"Oh, that." He sounded disappointed. "Yeah, thanks!"

"Have you always lived here in Rochester, Dr. O'Ryan?" I asked, even though I already knew he'd moved to Minnesota from Indiana.

"No. I moved here right after my wife, Olivia, and I got married fifteen years ago. I was finishing up my residency at the Indiana University School of Medicine and soon landed my first job at the Mayo Clinic here in Rochester."

"Does Olivia work?" Again, I knew she didn't but was fishing for information.

"She had a pretty good job in upper management about thirty miles away from where I lived, but after we got engaged, she quit so I could pursue my career as a heart surgeon. We met at a party and hit it off instantly. Four months later we were husband and wife and she's now a happy homemaker."

"Oh, I see." Ironically, like Blaze and his wife, Olivia and I had met at a party too. She hadn't sounded much like a happy home-maker when I'd chatted with her. "Being a homemaker is a very respectable job."

"Taking care of two, and soon to be three, children is a full-time job."

"I agree, Dr. O'Ryan." I sensed I'd ruffled his feathers when he defended his wife's occupation. "I actually met your wife at Maggie Brown's Scentsy party. Olivia's a beautiful young lady and could work as a model if she ever wanted to work outside the home again."

"Why would she want to do that?" Dr. O'Ryan asked with a quizzical expression.

"Oh, I don't know." I needed to be careful how I responded. "She may find being a housewife is not stimulating enough at some point. That happened to me years ago so I took on a few part-time jobs here and there to curtail the boredom. Olivia's very nice and the two of us had a fascinating conversation."

"About what?" Dr. O'Ryan asked. As he and I conversed, Rip took our exchange in silently, his head swinging back and forth as though he were watching a pickleball game. Dr. O'Ryan's atten-tion, however, was focused directly on me. He stared into my eyes as he waited for me to reply. It made me feel a bit wary.

"Oh, just girl stuff," I replied casually. I decided to change the subject. "Are you looking forward to returning to the Mayo Clinic?"

"In some ways," he responded after seemingly giving it some thought. "I'm very familiar with the facility so it will be like going home when I start my new position in two weeks. It's a little more structured than the STAT Clinic, which has a more laid back atmosphere, but my hours won't be as erratic, which is nice. I'm happy about the career move, considering I'll also be making more money. An extra mouth to feed will increase our monthly financial obligations."

"Yes," I began, "kids have a way of doing that to a family."

The surgeon had suddenly gotten chatty. I thought it was a good time to segue into another, more pressing, topic. I did feel a moment of guilt, however, knowing that by delaying the doctor, other patients would be left sitting in the waiting room for an even longer amount of time, a few perhaps threatening to leave like Rip had.

"I'm sure you are still unsettled about the unexpected passing of your fellow surgeon, Dr. Moretti." It was meant as a rhetorical question so I was surprised when Dr. O'Ryan responded.

"I've been in the business of fixing broken hearts, so to speak, for so long now that nothing surprises me anymore. Dr. Moretti's time was clearly up. It could've just as easily been you or me." After a moment of thought, he added, "Although I am probably more attuned to my cardiac health than you are."

"And you don't think Dr. Moretti was attuned to his?" My response sounded catty, even to my own ears. Stunned he hadn't already heard the latest news, I felt compelled to fill him in. "Not that it matters because his death has now been classified as a homicide. He was poisoned. Rip is a lifelong law enforcement officer, and we both find it mind-boggling that the highly accomplished surgeon was murdered. Who could've possibly wanted him eliminated?"

"I couldn't tell you." Dr. O'Ryan ran his fingers through his cherry-red hair. "I hadn't heard his death was intentional."

"Yep!" I said. "He was killed with VX nerve agent. We heard the authorities now have a suspect in mind and are going to issue an arrest warrant this afternoon."

"Did you say VX nerve agent?" The doctor looked like he'd just seen his grandmother leaving a dive bar with a drunken sailor.

Oddly, he didn't inquire about who the arrest warrant was to be issued for. After I nodded, he said, "I have to continue on with my next patient now. You can check out with Colleen at the front desk."

Without another word, Dr. O'Ryan picked up his clipboard and left the room. I looked at Rip and shrugged my shoulders. Shaking his head, he said, "I don't think he appreciated your questions and comments. It's probably a good thing I won't have to see him again."

"How can he be so callous about a colleague's death, especially when it was a cold-blooded murder?"

"I don't know, Rapella," Rip replied. "How can he be an hour behind schedule when he only spends five minutes with each patient? If you hadn't held him up, he wouldn't have spent two minutes with me."

We had no way of knowing how much time he'd spent with the patients who'd had appointments before ours that day. To put an end to Rip's single-mindedness, I said, "What do you say we stop for lunch while we're out?"

Just then, Dr. O'Ryan opened the door and stuck his head back into the room. "Can you two wait here for a moment?"

"Sure," I replied. "Why?"

"I need to check something in Rip's medical records. It won't take long."

"Okay."

Six or seven minutes later, Dr. O'Ryan reentered the room. He was breathing heavily like he'd had to sprint up several floors worth of stairs. "Everything checked out all right. You are free to leave now."

Without waiting for a response, the doctor ducked back out as quickly as he'd ducked in. Rip immediately returned to the topic we'd been discussing before Dr. O'Ryan had requested we delay our departure while he scanned Rip's medical records.

"Grabbing lunch while we're out would be awesome." Rip's expression had been downcast while waiting for Dr. O'Ryan to return to the room, but his face lit up now as if a switch had been flipped.

"The Salad Brothers Café and Deli we ate at the other day is only a couple of blocks from here."

"Oh, great." The light that had illuminated Rip's face switched off as quickly as it had switched on. With as much derision as he could muster, he added, "I was sure *hoping* to have a salad for lunch."

Rip looked so let down I felt compelled to say, "I don't think a sandwich will hurt you any, as long as it isn't accompanied by French fries. I saw on the café's lunch menu they offer a Rueben with coleslaw for only ten bucks."

"We ain't left yet?" Rip's good humor had returned. His face lit back up and remained bright all the way to the truck. As we approached the Chevy in the parking lot, Rip looked up, his features darkening as though the *Goodyear* blimp had drifted over the top of us, and asked, "What the hell?"

FIFTEEN

The rear tire on the passenger side was flat. Not just low, but flat. As flat as a road-killed opossum that's been run over a hundred times, and then backed over twice for good measure.

"There must be a nail in it. Was that tire low when we left the campground this morning?" Rip asked.

"Not that I noticed."

"You didn't look at it before you got in the truck?" He'd asked a ludicrous question in my opinion. The idea of me checking the tires before stepping into the truck was like Rip checking the calendar to ascertain it was after Labor Day before donning a white shirt.

"No," I began, "why would I?"

"Because it's on your side!" he exclaimed angrily. I was glad Monica wasn't checking Rip's blood pressure now or she'd have immediately laid him back on the table and attached electrocardiogram leads to his chest.

"I didn't actually examine the tires on my side of the truck because that's something you usually do, but I think I would've noticed if one of them was too low."

"Damn!" Rip muttered after he'd studied the tire closer. I could actually smell his blood pressure ratcheting up another notch. It smelled like burnt rubber mixed with a hint of turpentine. Rip punched the tire with his fist, presumably to punish it for its betrayal, and said, "Somebody slashed it with a knife. That's twice in the last few months we've had a tire intentionally ruined."

"I'm calling AAA," I said firmly. "You're in no condition to change the tire yourself."

"Fine." Rip surprised me by not arguing the point. When a tire had been deliberately flattened several months ago in Rockdale, Missouri, Rip had insisted on taking care of it himself, but at that time he wasn't recuperating from recent stent surgery. "Who would do such a thing?"

"Who knows?" I replied. "Maybe it was just a young hooligan, or a random thug. I highly doubt it was personal. I don't know anyone in this area who'd even recognize our vehicle, for one thing. For another, we haven't done anything to incur anyone's wrath. Just relax and don't let it upset you, Rip. That's why we pay for auto insurance coverage every six months and why we maintain our AAA membership."

With a grunt, Rip got into the truck, banging his hand on the steering wheel in frustration. Leaning against the fender, I called AAA's road service number and arranged for an emergency vehicle to be dispatched to our location. Within ten minutes, a fellow named Harry arrived and swapped out our spare for the ruined tire. I signed a form he handed me, and said, "You too" when he wished us a good day. I then crawled back into the truck where Rip's temper had only barely begun to cool off.

"Now we get to go to a tire store and spend another hundred and fifty bucks on a new spare," he grumbled.

I merely nodded. Once again, not a battle I chose to involve myself in. But I couldn't help wondering. *Could this tire-slashing episode have happened because we've been investigating the truth behind Dr.*

Moretti's death? Has the killer caught wind of the fact I've been snooping around, asking people questions about things that are none of my business? I don't believe it was a young hooligan or thug any more than Rip does. There was at least one person who would recognize our truck. Maggie. She'd seen it parked next to the Caboose when she visited us at the campground. And of course there was Henrietta, the volunteer who'd watched me peel away from the curb when I was driving Rip home from the clinic the day after his procedure. But the likelihood of Henrietta slashing our tire was about equal to the odds of Rip wearing a Princess Ariel costume on Halloween. She knows nothing about us and probably doesn't have the strength to slash a tire if she wanted to. I suddenly realized it was also possible several nurses from the clinic had seen me get out of the Chevy when I arrived at Maggie's Scentsy party. *Could one of them be responsible?*

With so many names now on my suspect list, I didn't know who I could trust. Rip had pretty much forbidden me to do any further investigating once Dr. Moretti's death had been reclassified as a homicide. That made no sense to me whatsoever. Why would I investigate a death by natural causes? As soon as Dr. Moretti's death *needed* to be investigated, Rip had cut me off like a withered rose blossom. I was silent all the way back to the campground, deep in thought.

If the incident truly was personal, how can I not be concerned? How can I sit back and do nothing? If the person responsible was disturbed enough to slash our tire as a warning, what might they do if they feel the warning was not taken seriously?

Our plans to have lunch at *The Salad Brothers Café and Deli* were scrubbed. Rip drove home and I fixed us each a turkey sandwich. After lunch, I took out my notebook and circled Maggie's and Blaze O'Ryan's names on my list of suspects. I then stored the notebook back in the nightstand next to my side of the bed. There was something about the heart surgeon that rubbed me the wrong way. *I would like nothing more than to be able to determine he was behind Dr. Moretti's death,* I thought candidly. *And I pray it wasn't my new friend Maggie who'd murdered the surgeon. Accidentally or otherwise.*

It was not like me to set my sights on a particular suspect, but for the first time ever I was determined to prove the red-headed Irishman was behind the good doctor's murder.

———

At two o'clock, Rip headed to a National Tire & Battery auto repair shop to purchase a new spare. He'd decided to get a new battery and an oil change while he had the truck at the *NTB* store located on 3rd Avenue SE, just blocks from the Autumn Woods RV Park. I knew the truck was probably due for an oil change, but I felt the new battery was wasteful when it undoubtedly still had plenty of life left in it. But Rip was in no mood to bicker with me about frivolous purchases. So I let it go.

I stayed behind to watch *Jeopardy* on television, a game show I enjoyed on a near daily basis. It often made me feel dim as a twenty-five watt bulb when high schoolers in their teen tournament knew the answers to clues that I had no idea about. I felt vindicated that day when I knew it was iodine that was sometimes found in table salt to make up for human deficiencies of the element. Sometimes it only took small victories such as this to keep me going.

I washed our lunch plates and hung the dish towel on the oven handle. As the iconic Final Jeopardy tune began to play, my phone beeped. It was a text from Maggie.

> Are you and Rip planning to attend Marco's funeral? Now that the tox screen results are back, the homicide department has released his body for burial.

> Do you know when and where it's going to be?

I asked this question knowing it wouldn't be easy persuading Rip to attend the services.

> It's scheduled for tomorrow at two and is to be held at Manfranz & Pine Funeral Home. Just thought I'd pass on the information in case you wanted to attend. It will be an emotional service, I'm sure.

> Thanks for the info, sweetie. I'll talk it over with Rip and most likely see you tomorrow at the funeral.

There was no way in hell Rip would agree to my suggestion we attend the surgeon's funeral. I knew it was going to take some powerful persuading. *Or an outright lie,* I thought. Waiting for Rip to return from NTB, I was as nervous as a stand-up comedian would be his first time behind the microphone at a local comedy club.

"I don't think attending Dr. Moretti's funeral is either appropriate or necessary," Rip said when I brought up the subject. After he'd gotten home, I decided to give him time to take his blood pressure and for me to muster up the nerve. I finally broached the subject while we relaxed over our afternoon cocktails. I was aware of Rip's dislike for attending funerals. He'd once confessed to me he'd "almost rather be the poor stiff in the pine box than have to dress up and mingle with the dearly departed's grieving family and friends."

I didn't enjoy funerals either, as a rule, so I couldn't honestly say I blamed him. But I thought it was important to go so I could evaluate all of the funeral goers' demeanor and body language. Due to the fact everyone on my suspect list was highly likely to be in attendance, I felt the odds of running into the surgeon's killer at the funeral were high. It was one of those circumstances where the killer might feel it'd look suspicious if he or she wasn't in attendance.

"I know, Rip. I feel the same way," I said tactfully. It looked like I was going to have to punt, also known as *lie my ass off*. I didn't like lying to my husband, mind you. But I also wasn't above manufacturing a cock-and-bull story when it came down to having no other option. "Maggie mentioned being emotional at the funeral and was hoping we could be there to offer her moral support. She said something like, 'Rip reminds me of a teddy bear. Just knowing he's there will make me feel protected like he's my own personal security blanket.'"

I'll admit that my justification to Rip for attending the funeral was a stretch. But, as it turned out, adding the teddy bear fabrication was pure genius on my part. Rip caved in like an overloaded life raft when he heard Maggie had specifically asked us to be there for her and thought of him as being her own personal security blanket. He'd formed an attachment to the young nurse, and I'd used his affection for Maggie to my advantage. I knew I should be ashamed of myself and I was sure I would be if, and when, the glow of success had faded away.

"Oh, all right. I guess we could go," Rip consented with the look of an individual making a painful sacrifice for the cause. "The man *did* open up a main artery for me just prior to his death. I suppose the least I could do is attend his funeral."

"Yeah, you're right, honey." I nodded solemnly, trying not to look overjoyed. "I reckon we really should attend the services, just for Maggie's sake if nothing else."

When we walked into the Manfranz & Pine Funeral Home at one-forty-five the next afternoon, we were immediately met by Dr. Moretti's widow, Frankie, who thanked us for coming even though she'd never seen us before. I explained that her late husband's last surgery was performed on my husband so we felt obliged to pay our respects at his memorial service. We offered our condolences and then I drug Rip over to the far corner of the room where I'd spotted Maggie.

"Your teddy bear has arrived," Rip said as we approached. Maggie looked at him as if wondering if he'd downed three quart jars' worth of Crown and Coke for lunch. I just smiled and asked her how she was doing before it became apparent I'd made up the "security blanket" story to encourage Rip to attend the funeral.

"I'm doing okay," she replied. "It seems weird to see all my co-workers wearing dresses and suits instead of scrubs. You two look awfully nice today."

"Thanks," I said. "You clean up pretty good yourself, sweetie."

I left Rip to chat with Maggie while I mingled with the other folks who'd come to say goodbye to their fallen comrade.

"Hello again, Jolene," I greeted Dr. Moretti's former operating room nurse. "It looks like the entire staff of STAT Cardiac Clinic is here. Who's running the show at the cath lab?"

"For the first time ever, to my knowledge, the board of directors approved closing the lab from one-thirty to four to allow anyone who wanted to attend Marco's funeral to do so without having to use personal leave."

"That was nice of them to do."

"It sure was," she replied. "I didn't have any vacation time left. Once I get a week's worth of vacation time built up, I book a trip to somewhere warm. I just used all the time off I had left to go to Sanibel Island a couple of weeks ago."

"That explains your nice tan."

"Yes. We spent a lot of time on the beach."

"We?" I made sure my interest came off as casual.

"Um, well," Jolene's face flushed. "I went with a friend."

"That must have been a lot of fun."

Jolene's tanned face suddenly looked as if it had sustained third-degree burns during her time on the small island off the coast of Florida. When her eyes grew misty, as well, she excused herself to go use the ladies' room. I wasn't sure what to make of her reaction.

The next person I ran into was Blaze O'Ryan. "Long time, no see," I said in greeting. He looked at me as though he didn't know me from the funeral parlor employee standing behind the guest book table handing out memorial folders. The folders listed pall bearers and other information about the deceased, along with a photo of him on the front. The photo was deceiving. The man pictured looked as if he could be Dr. Moretti's son. *It must have been taken when the surgeon was still in med school,* I thought. In the photo, he had a stethoscope around his neck and was wearing a white jacket with his name stitched across the left chest area. I noticed that none of the clinic's staff members were among the six names listed as pall bearers, which I found odd. I realized a lot of people don't socialize with their co-workers that much, spending all the time they can tolerate with those individuals at work. *They may not socialize with their co-workers much at the STAT Clinic,* I thought, *but they sure hooked up with them a lot.*

When Dr. O'Ryan continued to stare at me in confusion, I identified myself. I could've told him I was the ungainly Red Cross volunteer who'd nearly ran him over like a charging bull moose – twice – but chose to say, "My husband, Rip, and I were just in to see you yesterday for his final follow-up appointment."

"Yes, of course. It's nice to see you again, Mrs. Ripple. Why are you here?" He asked this question as though he was asking me why I'd come up on stage to accept an Oscar I hadn't even been nominated for. It was apparent he felt as though Rip and I were crashing a funeral we had no business attending.

"Dr. Moretti saved my husband's life just minutes before losing his own. We felt obliged to pay our respects at his memorial service," I replied, repeating the words I'd just said to the late surgeon's widow.

Dr. O'Ryan remained silent. He appeared to be ready to move on, so I quickly asked, "Are you here alone? I haven't seen Olivia."

"She wasn't feeling well this morning," he replied. "It's been a rough trimester for her so far. She's been experiencing intermittent bouts of nausea and the baby's been kicking a lot this last week. She didn't know Marco very well, anyway. I think she only met him once before he passed."

"I'd have stayed home too, if I were Olivia," I said. "She's probably exhausted."

"Not as much as me, I'll bet." After Dr. O'Ryan's response, I raised my eyebrows to encourage him to elaborate.

"I've had a heavy workload for the last several weeks. Taking on some of Dr. Moretti's patients after his death has had me working long hours. The week before that he had to make an unplanned trip to Florida to visit an extremely ill aunt."

"That's too bad. I hope she's recovered from her illness. I'll bet you'll be glad when Friday comes." Friday was his last day, and I'd heard he'd have over a week to unwind before he began his new position at Mayo Clinic.

"Yes, in some ways." Dr. O'Ryan glanced at his watch. "I better keep mingling. I have to be back to the clinic before four. I still have several patients to see this afternoon. I'm not sure we didn't leave one waiting in a patient's room when we left the lab."

I laughed, but his tone and expression made me question if he'd been joking or not. Considering how long Rip and I had waited the previous day, it made the seriousness of his remark even more unclear.

As Dr. O'Ryan walked away, I saw Eva Clemens and Monica Corry walking up to the open casket. They both stopped and stared down into Dr. Moretti's puffy face. As Rip and I had walked past the casket, I'd thought he'd looked as if the mortician had used twice as much embalming fluid as necessary. His face looked bloated and his lips looked like someone had smeared black lipstick on them. Of course, knowing nothing about the effects of VX nerve agent on a body, I chalked it up as some of the consequences of being poisoned to death. Along with other side effects, of course, such as one's heart and lungs failing to perform adequately, both of which could be extremely disturbing and equally lethal.

I watched as Eva wiped a tear off her cheek and Monica blew her nose on a tissue she'd removed from her pocket. After they'd moved on, Candace Kobialka walked up to pay her respects. As a former girlfriend of the deceased, I was sure she was dealing with even more emotions than her friends, Eva and Monica, had been forced to deal with. I watched as she took what appeared to be a note card out of her purse. She looked left and right and then tucked it down beside Moretti's body. I assumed it was a personal note she'd penned for him. It reminded me of when Rip and I had gone on a tour through the Holy Land in Israel for our twenty-fifth anniversary. I had written out a note to protect us in our travels and stuck it in a crack at the infamous Wailing Wall, an ancient lime-stone wall in the Old City of Jerusalem. The difference being I didn't glance around first to make sure no one was watching me. She hadn't turned completely around, however, and failed to spot me standing directly behind her, eyeing her tuck the note down inside the casket. As you can guess, I was dying to see what was written in Candace's message. Please excuse the cliché. "Dying to see" is probably a phrase I shouldn't use at a funeral.

Soon afterward, I saw Frankie Moretti dab at her brow with a handkerchief as she walked over to stand next to the casket. She gazed down at her husband's face with an odd expression on her own. It was a mixture of sadness and remorse, along with what appeared to me to be just a hint of relief. She looked pale and unstable, as though she might faint. I hurried over and offered her my arm. I didn't want her to fall to the floor. Nor did I want

Frankie to be the one to discover the note that'd been tucked inside her husband's casket. Thankfully, Frankie took my arm and let me lead her over to a chair. She thanked me, and said, "I got a little light-headed there for a moment."

It occurred to me then that whoever had murdered her husband might have a bone to pick with her as well. I felt Frankie should be examined immediately as her symptoms seemed to mirror the ones I'd witnessed with Dr. Moretti in the waiting room following Rip's procedure. Surrounded by medical professionals, I wasn't sure who to turn to for help. I chose Dr. O'Ryan. I raced across the room and grabbed his arm. "Come with me. I think something is seriously wrong with Mrs. Moretti."

I recognized the look on Dr. O'Ryan's face as panic, which is not exactly encouraging to the person in need of emergency medical attention, or to their family and friends who are gathered around them. He was at Frankie's side within seconds. Dr. O'Ryan soon was as sweaty as the woman in front of him who was denying she needed assistance.

Although she was almost speaking in a whisper, I heard her tell him she would be fine once she'd had a moment to collect herself. She stated she'd had Covid-19 in early January but had tested negative just days later.

"I'm glad you recovered so quickly," I replied, thinking back to my recent conversation with Dr. O'Ryan. "I hope it wasn't a couple of weeks ago while Dr. Moretti was in Florida visiting his sick aunt."

"My husband didn't have a sick aunt in Florida. In fact, he didn't even have a healthy aunt in Florida. But he did have to attend a health seminar in Omaha a couple of weeks ago while I was sick with Covid. The seminar was required by the clinic's board of directors, but it was probably instrumental in keeping Marco from catching the virus from me." As Dr. O'Ryan stared at Frankie in disbelief, Frankie shook her head and dabbed at her brow once again. Before continuing, she refreshed her lipstick. "You must be thinking about someone else, ma'am. As far as I'm aware, Marco only had two aunts and both live in Minneapolis."

"Oh, yes," I replied. "I must've been confused. I've met so many nurses and physicians at STAT Clinic that I've gotten them all mixed up."

But I wasn't confused. Dr. O'Ryan, who was still standing next to Frankie, was obviously befuddled, however. He's the one who'd told me about his colleague's recent trip to Florida and he now looked like Frankie had poked him in the eye with her tube of lipstick. Frankie clearly had no idea her deceased husband had spent a week in Florida shortly before his death. She was under the illusion he'd been suffering through some boring seminar in the Nebraskan town situated along the Missouri River near the Iowa border. Omaha is not exactly known as "party city." My guess was that Dr. Moretti had been living it up on a beach on Sanibel Island with Jolene. While his newlywed wife was home suffering with body aches, coughing, fever, and other symptoms, he was probably walking hand in hand on the sand with his girlfriend. As Frankie moped around, missing her husband and feeling miserable, I could imagine him rubbing lotion on Jolene's back, or the pair sitting side by side in lounge chairs, enjoying a large piña colada with two straws.

For the first time, I was pissed off at the man lying stiff as a board in the casket I could've reached out and touched. I felt sorry for Frankie and hoped Dr. O'Ryan didn't bring up her misconception about Dr. Moretti's whereabouts in early January. For what good would the truth do now, other than upset her and make her want to kill her already dead cheating spouse? I shot Dr. O'Ryan a look of caution. Almost imperceptibly, he nodded, and said, "If you need anything, Mrs. Moretti, I'll be standing close by."

While he stood with his back to me, and the broad-shouldered doctor blocked Frankie's view of the casket, I walked over and stood over Moretti. I wanted to look as though I needed a private moment with him, and in a way, I did. As I whispered, "You deceitful jerk, you didn't deserve a woman like Frankie," I reached down and felt around for the small card Candace had slipped into the crevice between Dr. Moretti's body and the wooden side of the mahogany box. Leaning over to block everyone's view, I unfolded the card and read what Candace had typed in bold, all capital letters.

YOU GOT WHAT YOU DESERVED FOR WHAT YOU PUT ME THROUGH.

I gasped in surprise. It was clear to me the note had not been typed on a whim. Candace must've been full of bitterness when she decided to leave a message in the man's casket. *Wow!* I thought. *Not knowing who might find that card next to a man who was the victim in a homicide case, leaving a hand-written message like that in his casket was a very brazen thing for the jilted nurse to do. Fortunately, Candace was wise enough to not sign it.*

I snapped a quick photo of it lying on the surgeon's chest with my phone. I glanced around first to ensure no one was looking my way. To my relief, everyone's attention was focused elsewhere. It was then I noticed Frankie was surrounded by her husband's three adult children from his first marriage, who Maggie had pointed out to Rip and me earlier. They all appeared to be consoling each other on their loss. The two sons and one daughter took turns hugging and kissing their step-mom. It was nice to witness the warm relationship Frankie shared with her step-children, whom she'd told the STAT nurses at a party at the Morettis' home would inherit the bulk of Marco's estate if their marriage ended within ten years of their wedding. I assumed death was different than divorce when it came to a pre-nuptial agreement, but I really wasn't sure. When Rip and I had gotten married, both of us were eighteen and I was six months pregnant with Regina. Rip owned a hunting rifle his father had given him on his sixteenth birthday and a 1963 Chevy Nova. He would've been more apt to ask me to pretend I was a virgin than to sign a pre-nuptial agreement.

It was obvious Candace was a lot more bitter about Moretti dumping her for Frankie and giving her job to Jolene than she'd let on. But now that I had this information, what could I do with it? Who could I tell about it? I felt as if I'd found the smoking gun and my only option was to put the gun back where I found it and keep the knowledge of it to myself. I suddenly realized that not only were Candace's fingerprints probably on the note card, now mine likely were too. I slipped a bottle of disinfectant out of my satchel and using a handkerchief in my pocket, I scrubbed the card as well as I could without drawing attention to myself in hopes of obliterating any usable fingerprints from the card. And, to be clear, it was mine I was worried about, not Candace's. I then tucked the note card back down into the crevice, out-of-sight of any funeral attendees.

I've faced tougher challenges than this, I told myself. *When we get back to the trailer, I'm going to circle Candace's name on my suspect list and concentrate on her as I continue my low-keyed, covert investigation into what, and who, was behind Dr. Moretti's death.* It's not that I didn't have confidence in the Rochester Police Department's homicide division; it's just that I felt obligated to do my best to finish the job I'd set out to do. If I got to the point I knew without a doubt who the killer was, I'd take all of the information and/or proof I'd collected to the police station and turn it over. At that stage, I'd be more than happy to let them take the ball and run with it. I didn't need credit for my efforts; I just wanted the satisfaction of knowing it was a job well done.

Driving back to the RV park, I noticed Rip was more quiet than usual. I asked him if something was bothering him.

"Not really," he replied. "It's just that when I mentioned to Maggie I was flattered that she considered me her security blanket, she didn't seem to have a clue what I was talking about. It was an awkward exchange."

"Oh, don't be embarrassed by Maggie's forgetfulness. She's probably still in shock. It's a condition called Mortalimotionalism Syndrome."

"Mortalimotionalism Syndrome?" Rip repeated. "I've never heard of that condition before."

"Oh, yes." I decided to utilize a skill that had always helped me thrash Rip in a game of *Scrabble*. The skill involves coming up with a detailed-enough definition for a made-up word that the word becomes believable. I'd once fooled him with the word "Quixsum" where the "q" miraculously landed on a triple-letter square. I'd gotten Quixsum from the name brand of an adding machine I'd used when working part-time in a fabric shop. Since name brands are not allowed in *Scrabble*, I described a *quixsum* as "a hole in a watchband for the prongs that are used to adjust the size." When I Googled watch band parts later on I discovered the official name for a hole in a watch band is "hole." Imagine that!

Although I usually used that trick to beat the pants off Rip in a board game, for now, I'd use it to quell his hurt feelings. "Mortal-imotionalism Syndrome occurs when an individual feels somewhat responsible for, or involved in, the death of someone they felt a certain kinship with. It can cause forgetfulness, confusion, or disbelief, among other symptoms. Sometimes it takes weeks for both the physical and mental effects of the syndrome to dissipate."

"Seriously?" Rip asked. "They have an actual syndrome named for that?"

"Oh, sure. It's no different than other syndromes: post-traumatic stress, Down syndrome, Turner syndrome, just to name a few."

"Actually, Rapella, post-traumatic stress is considered a disorder, not a syndrome, as in PTS<u>D</u>."

"Whatever…" I pointed to a Subway sandwich shop sign up ahead. "What do you say we stop for a sandwich? I'd planned to grill some salmon for supper and serve it with a kale salad, but it'd be nice to not have to mess with cooking tonight."

I knew salmon and kale were both near the top of the list of food items that Rip disliked. Without even a word in response, he steered the truck into the Subway parking lot and turned off the motor. He'd instantly forgotten all about syndromes and disorders ——real or fictional ones such as Mortalimotionalism Syndrome.

SIXTEEN

> You'll never believe what happened!!!

My iPhone dinged just seconds after I powered it up the next morning. I found the text from Maggie that she'd sent at eleven-fifteen the previous evening, over an hour after Rip and I had gone to bed.

> What happened, Maggie?

I could barely breathe waiting for Maggie to return my text. It's hard to judge by a text, even one ending in three exclamation points, if the sender is mad, sad, upset, amused, or deathly ill. I was praying she was shocked and my prayers were answered.

> After you and Rip left Marco's funeral, Frankie went back up to the casket to weep over her husband's body. She was smoothing out his shirt with her hand when she spotted a note someone had placed next to his body.

Maggie went on to tell me the wordage in that note which, of course, I already knew.

My bad, I thought. *I must not have gotten the note card pushed down as far as it'd been when I'd reached down beside Dr. Moretti's body to withdraw it.* Perhaps I'd subconsciously left it in such a way it would be discovered by one of the funeral attendees. I can't say for sure, not knowing where my head had been at that precise moment. I'd been fond of Candace, but if she had murdered a man in cold blood, she needed to be punished for her crime. Dr. Moretti, like every other human being, deserved justice if and when someone took their life from them.

> Oh, my! What happened next?

I asked this question hoping she'd respond exactly as she did.

> There were several detectives at the funeral and everyone in attendance was questioned. They took photos of the guest book too, so if you or Rip signed it, I'm sure you'll be questioned by homicide detectives, as well.

> Yes, of course. We'll be happy to report what little we know.

Or most of it, anyway, I thought. I hadn't even told Rip about what I'd witnessed at the funeral, lest he drive me straight to the police station to report it. There was no way I was going to tell the detectives I'd seen who placed the note in the casket, removed it, read it, and then placed it back beside the murder victim's body in such a way someone else at the gathering would re-discover it. They would have to rely on their own investigative skills to determine the source of the note. I had no desire to make it that easy for them.

Not that we'll have much of any use to tell them, Maggie. Were they able to determine who wrote the message?

No. It doesn't seem as though the detectives were able to garner much useful information from all the questioning they did. So, unfortunately, no one knows who placed that note card in Marco's casket.

Wrong, I thought. *Two people know who stuffed the note card down into the beautiful mahogany box next to Dr. Moretti's right sleeve: Candace Kobialka and me. But neither one of us are apt to tell the homicide detectives the source of the typed message.* At this stage of the game, I didn't want to tell anyone what I'd witnessed, not even Maggie who I now thought of as a friend.

It's kind of creepy to know the killer was among all of us at the memorial service, isn't it?

It's very creepy. I need to get back to work, but first I wanted to give you a heads up to expect a call or visit from the detectives.

We appreciate it, dear. Will you be working on the floor tomorrow night?

No, I'm working the day shift tomorrow, as usual. Candace has the night shift. Why do you ask?

It's nothing important. I just had a question about the Polish pastry recipe Candace gave me. Thanks sweetie. Keep us posted if you hear anything new about the case.

Will do, Rapella.

We never did get a call or visit from the homicide detectives. Most likely no one knew where to find us, with Rip and I not having a permanent address in Rochester. I doubted they would put too much effort into finding us in the future, either, because what possible motive could the victim's last patient or his wife have to murder the surgeon who had potentially saved that patient's life? Perhaps if the surgery had gone sideways and the patient was deceased, disabled, or disfigured, but not when the patient's life-span was undoubtedly lengthened due to the skill and expertise of the now-dead surgeon.

That evening I told Rip I was going to go to a nearby mall to see if I could find a satchel to replace the worn-looking one I'd been carrying around for the last several years. Weathered or not, I still loved the purse and would return home and tell Rip despite scouring the entire mall, I was unable to find one I liked. That little white lie would give me ample time to go to the cath lab and try to track down Candace. I would use the pretense of wanting to thank her again for her mother-in-law's paszteciki recipe for the visit.

"Good evening, Candace," I greeted her when I walked up to where she was sitting behind the desk at the nurses' station. "Have you got a moment? There's something I'd like to speak to you about."

With a wary expression, she asked, "What could you want to speak with me about?"

"I was just wondering if a person could make the paszteciki suitable for a vegetarian by substituting some kind of vegetable for the minced meat."

Candace visibly relaxed. "Oh, definitely. My sister, Lily, and her husband, Pete, are vegetarians, vegans, or pescatarians, depending on what day you talk to them. I swear they change stance on their eating preferences daily."

"What in the world is a pescatarian?"

"That is someone who doesn't eat meat or poultry but *does* eat fish." Candace laughed, and added, "Every once in a while, such as Thanksgiving, Lily and Pete reclassify themselves as flexitarians, which are those who normally maintain meatless diets but occasionally eat meat, chicken or fish. I can totally understand a person being a vegan or vegetarian, but Lily and Pete's inconsistency can be exhausting. You never know what to fix for supper if they're invited."

"No doubt." I couldn't help but like Candace as much as I wanted to detest her for having potentially killed her former flame. I knew I had no choice but to set aside the affection I felt for this kind woman who might've committed a sadistic crime. "Listen, Candace, I'm actually here to show you something that could potentially change the entire course of your life."

As though she had an inclination it had to do with Dr. Moretti's death, she stiffened, looked around, and stood up. She motioned for me to follow her to an unoccupied patient room. A very slim woman by nature, I could tell Candace wasn't packing. The closest thing to a deadly weapon she had on her was a ball-point pen. Besides, I could scream outlandishly loud when the need arose. In a tight pinch, I could mimic the sound of a cat ensnared in a vehicle's serpentine belt. My ear-piercing shriek had once given a roof rat a fatal heart attack when it made the mistake of surprising me in my former kitchen in Rockport, Texas. So I felt relatively confident I was in no danger being alone with Candace. I walked directly into the empty room ahead of her.

Candace closed the door behind us and whispered, "What is it? What do you have to show me?"

"Candace, dear," I said softly, so as not to rile her up. "I saw you stick that note card inside Dr. Moretti's casket yesterday at the funeral."

"What note card?"

Okay, so you're going to play dumb, I thought. *No problem*. I took my phone out of my purse and showed her the photo I'd taken of the typed message.

"I've never seen that note card before," Candace replied. Her voice faltered and her hands were trembling like she'd accidentally stepped on a live wire. "What kind of proof do you have that it was me who typed that message?"

"I have no proof whatsoever it was you who typed that message," I said honestly. "But I did witness you take the note card out of your clutch and stuff it into the wooden casket next to Dr. Moretti's right sleeve. It would be your word against mine; a former jilted girlfriend, with motive up the yin-yang, versus some older woman with no dog in the race, no motivation to kill the man, and no reason to lie about it. Which of us do you think a jury would believe? I was hoping it wouldn't come to that, however. I wanted to give you the opportunity to turn yourself into the authorities. It would be much better for you in the long run. The ensuing interrogation you'd have to go through would be brutal, I'm sure. Homicide detectives have a way of squeezing the truth out of a person."

"B-b-but," Candace began to stutter.

"The ball's in your court, Candace, and it's up to you to decide what your next move is." I put my phone back into my purse, turned away from the nurse, and reached for the door knob. Candace's next move was not one I'd anticipated.

The next thing I knew I was waking up on the floor with a throbbing headache. I could hear Candace whispering, "Rapella? Are you all right? Wake up, Rapella. I'm sorry. I'm so sorry. I didn't mean to hurt you. Please wake up!"

When I was able to open my eyes I was staring right into the eyes of the woman who had attacked me from behind, but I was too disoriented to emit my loud eardrum-splitting scream. The fact Candace looked and sounded regretful, and even worried, rather than murderous confused me. Just then she picked up a pillow from off the hospital bed and brought it down toward me. I was getting ready to squeal like the aforementioned trapped cat when she gently lifted my head and placed the pillow under it. I was relieved Candace hadn't planned to use the pillow to smother me. I grasped the wet washcloth she handed to me to hold against my sore head and struggled to sit upright on the floor.

"I'm so sorry, Rapella." Repeating her earlier sentiments, she said, "I didn't mean to hurt you. I've never struck another person in my life until just now."

"Why did you hit me then?" Although metal bedpans had gone the way of most modern car and airplane parts and were now customarily made of plastic, I noticed one next to her. I then realized she'd clobbered me over the head with the now obsolete metal bedpan. I felt a sense of relief that the portable potty was unused. "I was only trying to help you, Candace."

"I know you were. I was just scared and didn't know what to do. I didn't want you to leave the room without me having an opportunity to talk to you about the note card. I wouldn't blame you if you called the cops and had me arrested for assault with a deadly weapon."

"Relax, Candace," I said. It was obvious I hadn't been mortally wounded. The headache would pass in time and I'd be none the worse for wear. "I'll be fine. I'm nearly certain I'm not concussed. Nor do I plan to call the police. Besides, I'm not sure if a bedpan could be considered a deadly weapon."

Having been married to a career lawman for over fifty years, I knew it actually could be. Technically, any object that could potentially cause death could be construed as a deadly weapon, and if you were to batter someone over the head repeatedly with a bedpan, it's conceivable you could eventually beat them to death. I'd told Candace I didn't plan to call the cops, but I've done a lot of things in my life I hadn't planned to do. For instance, I hadn't planned to get pregnant with Regina at eighteen years old. And I hadn't planned to get married to Rip in a shotgun wedding six months later. But, as they say, shit happens! So for now, reporting the assault to the police was just a tool in my belt I prayed I wouldn't have to use.

"I'm so sorry," Candace repeated. "I can get you an ice pack to hold against the hematoma on your head. It should help the swelling go down."

"That'd be great. If anyone asks, I tripped and hit my head on the footboard of the bed."

The relief on Candace's face was palpable. I hadn't been able to wrap my head around the idea she could kill anyone in cold blood. Even after she'd pummeled my skull with an outdated metal bedpan and rendered me unconscious, I still found it hard to believe. *I will give her a chance to convince me she had nothing to do with Dr. Moretti's death before I take the photo I took and my witness statement to the Rochester Police Department*, I decided.

A few minutes later, as I sat on the end of the hospital bed holding an ice pack against my noggin, I listened to Candace explain that she'd fallen head over heels in love with Dr. Moretti during the few months they'd dated. After meeting Frankie at a formal event Candace and Dr. Moretti attended together, the surgeon was instantly smitten. With his left arm around Candace's waist, he'd asked the Italian beauty, Frankie, for her phone number and used his right hand to scribble it down on a lacy napkin. When he dropped Candace like a red hot manifold two days later, he had not only broken her heart but also humiliated her in front of all of her co-workers. They all knew she'd been having visions of wedding bands dancing in her head. They were also aware she'd been searching destination wedding locations around the globe and eyeing a sleek white dress on an online wedding gown site.

Jolene had encouraged the other nurses to tease Candace, but most of them quit ragging her once they saw how hurt she was by their mocking. Jolene, however, continued to rib Candace unmercifully. Candace did her best to hide her pain from everyone, but it still ate at her when she was alone at night and she admitted she cried herself to sleep for weeks afterward.

"Maybe you should've thumped Jolene on the head with a bedpan——a used one, at that." I was trying to lighten her spirits with a bit of levity, and it appeared to work.

Candace chuckled, and replied, "That option is still on the table."

I laughed too, and asked, "Why did you feel compelled to leave a note inside Dr. Moretti's casket? You knew he'd never read it and it might end up being used as evidence against you."

"Evidence of what, Rapella?" She asked, her voice having raised several notches. "I didn't kill Marco. I swear. I might've been tempted to, but I'd never harm a soul."

"Don't forget you're talking to a woman with a knot the size of a golf ball on her head that *you* put there."

Candace fell all over herself apologizing again. I was praying she'd reacted out of fear when she'd thumped me on the head and also that she hadn't killed Dr. Moretti. But I was going to pretend I didn't suspect her because she'd already walloped me once and I wasn't totally convinced she wouldn't attack me again. So I smiled and listened to her explain why she'd left the edgy note in his casket. "My therapist had told me at our last session I needed to find a way to get my feelings off my chest so I could begin to concentrate on my future. I needed to 'let it go,' she said. 'Maybe write it down on paper and then dispose of it,' she suggested. I thought about her idea and decided typing the note might be a good way to get past the heartache and move on. I truly thought it was worth trying since I had nothing to lose. Apparently, it wasn't such a splendid plan, after all. And, sadly, now I have a lot to lose once you talk to the homicide detectives."

"I have no intention of telling a soul I saw you put the note card in Dr. Moretti's casket. But, sweetie, I highly doubt your therapist meant for you to 'dispose of it' in the casket during his funeral," I replied. "I'm sure she meant to burn it, or wad it up and throw it in a trash can where no one else would ever read it. You might've taken your therapist's suggestion a bit too far."

"Gee, you think so?" Candace asked sarcastically. She laughed and I joined in. When another nurse I'd never met before, but recognized from Dr. Moretti's funeral, opened the door to see what all the laughter was about, I said, "We were just giggling about my clumsiness."

"Mr. Ferguson in room 210 is requesting pain medication," the solemn nurse informed Candace.

"Thanks Chantell. I'll go check on him momentarily." With a grateful smile in my direction, Candace said, "I'm so relieved you weren't hurt worse, Rapella."

"Me too," I said, hoping Candace meant every word of her last remark, as I had meant mine.

"Well, I better go take care of Mr. Ferguson," Candace said. "My boss tends to prefer we focus on treating paying customers and leaving klutzy visitors to fend for themselves."

I grinned at her quip. "And I better get headed home before the clinic decides to bill me for your services. Thank you, Candace, for tending to my sore head after I smacked it on the footboard while trying to pick my lipstick up off the floor."

Hoping Chantell didn't notice I wasn't wearing any lipstick, I made sure she was watching as I handed the ice pack back to Candace. I didn't want to cause any trouble for Candace even if I had reason to believe she might have had something to do with Dr. Moretti's death.

As I swallowed two Tylenol at the water fountain on the ground floor of the clinic, I thought to myself. *So, is Candace a good actor, or had she truly not killed Dr. Moretti? And if she didn't kill Dr. Moretti, who did?*

I realized at that moment my work had just begun.

SEVENTEEN

I woke up early the next morning with only a moderately scratchy throat and a slight headache. The cold symptoms I'd experienced the previous day had subsided and the knot on the back of my head had gone down significantly too. The hematoma, as Candace had called it, was only sore when I pressed on it. I'd kept the attack to myself, feeling nothing good could come from telling Rip about it.

After the brewing light on the coffee maker had shut off, I poured myself a cup and went outside to sit in a lawn chair under the awning. It was a drizzly day, but unseasonably mild. I thought it was a good time to take stock of what I knew and didn't know about Dr. Moretti's death. I had my notebook and a pen to take notes and jot down ideas.

Looking back at the timeline, Dr. Moretti had begun the stent placement procedure on Rip at about one-thirty in the afternoon. The operation had taken about two hours. At almost exactly three-thirty Dr. Moretti had spoken to me in the waiting room to let me know all had gone as expected and Rip would be out of recovery soon. The surgeon was exhibiting signs of having been poisoned at the time. That meant the VX nerve agent had to have been ingested, or utilized in some other fashion, just shortly before three-thirty.

It stood to reason the chemical had been put in a bottle of water or some other beverage. Afterward, the spiked drink had either been handed to Moretti or he'd taken it out of the refrigerator in the doctors' break room. I wished now I'd known to look for an opened water bottle in the clinic's dumpster. Of course, there were undoubtedly dozens of empty water bottles in the trash receptacle. Locating the exact one used to employ the nerve agent might've proved as difficult as finding a specific bird in one of Tyson's massive chicken houses. Like water bottles, chickens all tend to look alike. Not to mention, it perceivably could've been deadly for me to handle. In retrospect, I was glad I hadn't thought to search for it.

I knew from experience getting access to the break room required the killer to first gain access to the operating room floor. So the killer knew the passcode was 2633. To me, this seemed fairly significant. It seemed to point the finger in the direction of a staff member at the STAT Clinic, as opposed to an individual who wasn't employed by the cath lab, such as a former patient or family member.

There has to be a limited amount of staff members who had access to the passcode, as well, or what would be the point of restricting access to the area in the first place? I asked myself. *Would the cardiac nursing staff have the code? Perhaps if Maggie had once worked as an operating room nurse, such as Candace had, and the code was not changed on a regular basis, it'd make sense Maggie knew the code. But I'd already asked her about it and Maggie had told me she enjoyed interacting with patients as a floor nurse and had never worked in any other capacity at the clinic. Even so, she'd admitted she'd entered the doctors' break room to put the bag of cookies in the refrigerator for Dr. Murphy.*

Naturally, I made a notation in my notebook. "Find out if the pass-code is changed on a regular basis or remains the same indefinitely. Find out if the nurses at the lab routinely had access to the code, as well as the rest of the lab's employees."

On the other hand, if more than one person knows a secret, it doesn't remain a secret for very long. My guess is that every nurse in the clinic knew the passcode even if they didn't openly admit it or weren't intended to have access to it. But whoever entered the break room that day with the intention of killing Dr. Moretti must've been an individual whose presence there no one would question. Otherwise, it would've been pure lunacy for the killer to attempt such a stunt because surely there were security cameras located at strategic locations all around the clinic. A person can't even back into another vehicle accidentally in the middle of nowhere without there being an incriminating video clip of the mishap popping up in the courtroom as evidence. This is not some-thing I've experienced personally, of course. I would've left my name and insurance information on a post-it note under one of the car's windshield wipers if I was unable to track down the dented car's owner at the time of the fender bender. And then, with a clear conscience, I'd pray a strong gust of wind would blow the post-it note somewhere three miles away.

A second notation was made in my notebook. "Find out if there's any kind of security camera in the break room, or even in the hallway outside the break room." *Any video footage of who was present on the operating room floor would be useful,* I thought.

Knowing the day and time of Dr. Moretti's death should make it easy to see who was on duty at the clinic around three-thirty that afternoon if I could somehow gain access to the work schedule. I wondered if I shouldn't try to determine who was on duty at any time on the day Dr. Moretti died. The killer could've left the bottle of water in the refrigerator well before three-thirty, not knowing when the victim might actually drink from it.

For that matter, how could the killer know who might grab the spiked bottle from the fridge? There were a number of doctors who shared that break room, including at least four surgeons and an anesthesiologist. I'd suspect other staff members, such as Pratyush Patel, the cardiovascular technologist, had free use of the room too. Had it been a targeted attack, or a random one, with no specific victim in mind? I'd never considered that possibility before and wondered if the homicide team had. Either way, anyone who wasn't on the clock at the clinic the day the murder took place could be eliminated from my suspect list as an unlikely candidate for committing the murder. It was not altogether impossible, of course, but highly improbable. I wrote down, "Find out which staff members were working the day Dr. Moretti was killed."

From the tox screen results, I knew Dr. Moretti had been poisoned with VX nerve agent, but how much did I really know about the toxin? How quickly did it bring on death? How accessible was the chemical? How much was required to kill a human being? Was there any reason the cardiac clinic would keep the nerve agent on hand in the facility? If not inside the clinic, where could a person obtain enough of the chemical needed to murder someone? There was a lot I didn't know, including how beneficial it might be to know everything there was to know about VX nerve agent. *Knowledge is power*, I reminded myself. *It couldn't hurt any to do a little research.* I picked up my notebook again and jotted down, "Google VX nerve agent."

I had finished off the coffee at this point and went inside the trailer to refill my cup. Rip was moving around in the kitchen wearing nothing but his azure-colored boxer shorts. I slipped by him and placed my notebook back in my nightstand. There was no sense getting his blue knickers in a twist and I wasn't prepared to be questioned about why I was still poking around in the murder case.

"What's shaking, bacon?" Rip asked me as he came up behind me and kissed the back of my neck. "Speaking of which, what's for breakfast?"

"Not bacon, you can be sure of that," I said with a chuckle. "What'd you have for breakfast yesterday?"

"Oatmeal and a banana."

"That's correct. And what'd you have the morning before that?"

"Umm, the same thing?" Rip asked in the form of a question.

"Right again. So, what would you guess you're having for breakfast this morning?"

"Oh, geez," he grumbled. "Could you just put a little arsenic in my coffee and get it over with?"

"I was kidding you," I said with a laugh. *Could the nerve agent been put in a cup of coffee rather than water or food?* I wondered. "I'm going to fix you a couple of flapjacks. I bought some sugar-free syrup to try. A lady I talked to at the grocery store told me it was almost as tasty as the real thing."

"Swell. Is this like that hamburger patty made with soybeans and tofu that you told me was 'almost as tasty' as real beef, when it actually tasted exactly like soybeans and tofu? Or worse yet, the tofu turkey you served for Thanksgiving last year? If the word 'tofu' is in the description of any food, I don't want any of it."

"I promise there is no tofu in the syrup."

With a long-suffering sigh, Rip agreed to try it. He was pleasantly surprised when he could hardly tell the difference between the sugar-free variety and the fully-loaded syrup with enough sucrose in it to make a horse do the Foxtrot.

After Rip had cleaned off his plate, I said, "Speaking of putting arsenic in your coffee, how much do you know about VX nerve agent?"

"Why do you ask, Rapella? I thought we were done with investigating Moretti's death."

"We are, but I was just thinking about what a horrible way it must've been for Dr. Moretti to die. You seem to know at least a little about everything, Rip, which always amazes me, so I thought I'd ask out of curiosity." Slipping a compliment in never hurt when I was appealing to Rip for something, whether it was eating out at a sushi restaurant, going to see a chick flick at the theater, or sharing what he knew about a toxic chemical.

"Well, I'm only vaguely familiar with the nerve agent. I know it is one of the most toxic of the known chemical warfare agents and is tasteless and odorless, making it hard to detect. It can be deadly in several ways: ingestion, inhalation, or skin exposure, including the eyes. Death usually occurs within ten minutes, so Dr. Moretti may have suffered at the end, but not for long."

"That's comforting to know," I replied. I didn't want to look overly interested so as not to raise suspicion. "Do you know of anything we need at Wal-Mart?"

"Dolly's short on Greenies and there's not much litter left."

"All right. I'll put those two items on my list and go shopping after I wash up the breakfast dishes. So what's on your agenda today?"

"Not much," he said. "Would you like me to take you to Wal-Mart?"

Oh, hell no! I almost said out loud.

"Thank you, honey," I said instead. "But I know the last thing you want to spend your day doing is shopping for cat treats, litter, and groceries. Why don't you clean out that box of tools in the undercarriage storage compartment like you said you wanted to do a while back?"

"Actually, dear, I said I 'needed' to clean out the toolbox, not 'wanted' to. But I guess I could at least spend a little time sorting out and separating all the screws, nails, bolts, and washers. They're a jumbled mess. I've got an old plastic tackle box with dividers that'd be ideal for storing them."

"That sounds perfect." I grabbed my purse and the keys to the truck, kissed Rip, and scampered out of the Chartreuse Caboose before he changed his mind. I was hoping to get an opportunity to speak to Dr. O'Ryan today. Afterward, I *would* have to stop by Wal-Mart. That way I wouldn't feel like I'd been outright lying to Rip again, but rather wasn't being altogether truthful. I hadn't exactly promised him I'd step back and not have any more participation in investigating the murder case, but my lack of involvement had been implied. I'd likely have to explain what took me so long at the store when I got home. In situations like this I always thought WWLD, or "What Would Lexie Do?" Immediately I knew exactly what she'd do in this situation.

I waited for about five minutes and pulled off the road into a McDonald's parking lot. I then sent a text to Rip's phone.

> Maggie just called and asked if I'd stop by and see her at the clinic. She didn't say why, but I thought I should stop and see what she wants.

> Of course, dear. She's getting awfully attached to you all of a sudden. She dropped me like a security blanket that was riddled with moths.

> Don't be silly. I think she's just upset and needs some maternal-type friend's shoulder to lean on. I shouldn't be too long, either at the clinic or at Wal-Mart.

All right. Don't forget the Greenies, by the way. Dolly said to tell you she will pee on your slippers tonight while you're sleeping if you show up without them.

Tell her to chill out. I have never let Her Majesty down before and there's no reason for her to think I'll start doing so today. Tell her I said she could stand to miss out on a few treats. She now weighs twice as much as an average Yorkie.

Dolly said, and I quote, UP YOURS WITH A CAT LITTER SCOOP!

I responded with a laughing emoji, put my phone back in my purse, and pulled back onto the street. As I pulled into the parking lot of STAT Cardiac Clinic six or seven blocks further down the road, I was trying to think of a way to get a private moment with Dr. O'Ryan. I could make up some minor issue Rip was having pertaining to his stent placement procedure, but the surgeon might want Rip to come in so he could run an EKG, take x-rays, or something of that nature. And, as you can well imagine, that would not fly well with my husband.

My problem was solved the second I stepped into the main lobby of the cath lab. The entire staff of the clinic seemed to be milling around in the large, airy room. A large banner was draped across the wall that read, "Congratulations Dr. O'Ryan! We will miss you." Clearly, it was a going-away party for the departing surgeon. I saw the guest of honor standing next to a table with a large cake on it. His wife, Olivia, was sitting in a chair next to the table with her right hand caressing her extended belly as expecting mothers are wont to do.

I walked over to greet Olivia. She looked pale and sullen. She remembered my name which pleasantly surprised me. "Hello,

Rapella. It's nice of you to come to Kelly's farewell party. His last day here at STAT is tomorrow."

"I wouldn't miss it." I recalled that Olivia always fondly referred to her husband as Kelly, rather than his given name of Kellan, or his nickname, Blaze. "You don't look like you feel well, dear. Is there anything I can get for you?"

"Thanks, but I'm okay. Just a bit tired today."

"Do you mind if I sit down next to you?" I asked. I rubbed my left knee and said, "My knee's giving me fits today. It must be going to rain."

"Be my guest." Olivia spoke with no inflection in her voice, whatsoever, as if she didn't care whether I sat down next to her, hopped around the room on my bum knee, or ran outside and stepped in front of a bus to put an end to my misery. I sat next to her anyway. It was the only chair available and I needed to catch my breath after sprinting from the truck to the clinic's front door.

"Say, Olivia, I have a question you might be able to answer."

"What's that?" Again, there were no modulations in her voice.

"Do you know if the passcode to the area where all of the operating rooms are located is ever changed?" I asked, trying to sound as blasé as possible.

"Why do you need to know?" This time Olivia showed more reaction.

"Oh, I don't know, I might want to drop something off for Eva Clemens while she's busy assisting your husband, or his replacement, I should say, with an operation." I tried to determine by her expression if she bought my explanation.

"I don't really know," she replied with a shrug. "I've never actually been on the second floor. In fact, I'm rarely in this building at all. I would think they'd change it regularly, but who knows? I think you could drop the item off in the nurses' break room and they'd make sure Eva got it, if nothing else."

"Good idea. I should've thought of that. I know Maggie would get it to her if I asked her to."

"Yes. Maggie seems nice. I'm surprised she's not here today. It must've been her day off." Olivia went back to looking glum and fatigued. She resumed rubbing her belly. I assumed the baby was kicking her bladder like a striker would kick a soccer ball to score a goal.

After an uncomfortable pause in our conversation, I decided to change the subject. "At my husband's last follow-up appointment with your husband, Dr. O'Ryan talked about your whirlwind romance. It must've been love at first sight."

The new topic appeared to brighten Olivia's state of mind. "Just meeting each other was a miraculous stroke of luck. Talk about a small world. My roommate, Kim, talked me into going to an engagement party at the Verve Nightclub in Terre Haute, about half an hour from our apartment in Newport. The bride-to-be worked with Kim at the bank. They were both tellers there. Since Kim was driving, I got a little tipsy and ended up tripping and spilling my entire drink down the front of this handsome guy sitting at the bar. It was Kelly and he was so nice about it. Turns out his roommate worked with the groom-to-be at a muffler shop and had talked him into going to the party. Within ten minutes, Kelly had my phone number and the rest is history."

"How incredible is it that it was exactly the same scenario that took you both to the nightclub?" I asked. "What a marvelous coincidence it turned out to be."

"I don't believe in coincidences," Olivia replied. "I think it was fate."

"Then I'm sure you are absolutely right," I concurred. "Enjoy your husband's much-deserved party."

I was just getting ready to walk over and speak to Candace, who I spotted having a conversation with some woman I didn't recognize by the elevators, when a man dressed in an expensive-looking black suit quieted everyone down as if to make a toast to Dr. O'Ryan. He asked the surgeon to come up and join him by the cake table. He then raised his voice and began to speak.

"Thank you all for attending Blaze's going-away party, but I hope it was all for naught," the distinguished gentleman said.

Everyone in the room began whispering amongst themselves and the man had to quiet everyone down again. I saw Dr. O'Ryan glance over at Olivia and wink, as though he had a notion where the man was going with his last statement.

"We here at STAT Clinic are a family," the gentleman began again. "As you are all aware, no doubt, I am Terrence Smith, the President of STAT Clinic's board of directors. I speak for all of us when I say we're not ready for this extremely skilled surgeon to leave the nest."

When a number of people began to murmur amongst themselves, Mr. Smith waved his hand to shush the crowd and turned to look Dr. O'Ryan in the eye. "We will make it worth your while, Blaze, if you will accept the position of Director of Cardiology here at STAT, the position once held by Marco Moretti. We will forever mourn the loss of such an accomplished surgeon as Dr. Moretti, but I, and the rest of the board of directors, feel like you'd be the perfect person to fill his big shoes as director of this clinic. What do you say, Blaze? Can we count you in?"

Dr. O'Ryan could not have accepted the offer any faster than he did. By his reaction, I got the feeling he was not only unsurprised by the offer but had totally expected it. Olivia, on the other hand, looked as though her water had broken. It hadn't, thank goodness, and after the shock had subsided she jumped to her feet and applauded wildly. She sat back down when her husband added, "But I still plan to do a little teaching at the Mayo Clinic on my days off here at STAT."

So much for spending time with your three young children, I thought. I knew Olivia was thinking the same thing by the disgusted expression she now wore. As a show of moral support, I patted Olivia on the shoulder and stood up to cross the room to speak with Charmaine, Eva, Monica, Candace, and Jolene, for a few minutes before heading back to the truck. I still had to stop at Wal-Mart before returning to the RV park because I wouldn't put it past Dolly to pee in my slippers if I arrived home without a bag of her favorite treats. I also wouldn't put it past Rip, the ultimate prankster, to pour water on my slippers and then blame it on our beloved pet.

I greeted the nurses when I approached them. Like Dr. O'Ryan, none of them were stunned by Terrence Smith's announcement. Although they *were* surprised Blaze had applied for a position that would've had him return to working at the Mayo Clinic. Eva, who worked side-by-side with the surgeon in the operating room, said all Blaze ever did was complain about the decade he spent working there and often mentioned he preferred the laid-back atmosphere of the cath lab. Although, Dr. O'Ryan *had* expressed a desire to teach aspiring young physicians during their residency, Eva told us.

"That's admirable," I said. The nurses all agreed.

"It truly is like one big family here," Eva said. "Besides, Blaze was the only logical choice to replace Marco as the director."

"Exactly," Monica said, while the other nurses nodded their heads. Monica then turned to me to explain. "The other two surgeons at the clinic, Dr. Jifi and Dr. Marr, both joined the staff only four years ago."

"Choosing Dr. O'Ryan as the new director makes absolute sense then," I replied.

Charmaine then took my next remark right off the tip of my tongue when she said, "I wonder why Maggie isn't here. She was on the schedule for the morning shift but called in sick. I hope she's all right."

"I'm sure she's all right physically," Candace replied. "But

Maggie may not be doing so well mentally. I heard she made an emergency appointment with her shrink for today. It's probably a good thing, too. She's been a little off her rocker since Marco died."

And you haven't, Candace? I thought. *I didn't see Maggie putting a bitter note in the victim's casket!*

I thought I was alone in my opinion until Monica said, "You ain't exactly seemed normal either, Candace. You've been acting like your dog chewed up all your favorite heels."

I'd have expected Candace to react defensively to Monica's remarks, but her face remained stone-cold sober when she replied. "I guess I'm just disgusted with the progress the detectives had made in the case. I have moved on since Marco and I split, but I still feel like he deserves justice. You'd think the authorities assigned to this case would've figured out who left that nasty note in his casket by now."

My mouth opened and closed so fast I had to have looked like a Venus flytrap snatching an insect out of the air. It disturbed me how Candace could say such a thing about a note she herself had typed and left in Dr. Moretti's coffin without batting an eye. Her acting ability was even more impressive than I'd originally thought. Could I trust a single thing Candace had told me? I no longer believed so.

Everyone, including me, agreed with her assessment about the team of homicide detectives. At this stage of the game, I couldn't let on I knew it was Candace herself who left the note. She had clearly not "moved on" since Dr. Moretti dumped her for Frankie.

I noticed then that Jolene had tears streaming down her cheeks. I asked her if she was all right.

"I'll be okay. I still can't believe he's gone, and likely at the hands of someone I know." Jolene wiped her cheeks off with her right sleeve.

"What makes you think you knew the murderer?" I asked, curious if she had some kind of insight that pointed to the fact the murderer was among the clinic's staff.

"Well, um, it's just, um," Jolene stammered as she wiped tears from her face. She appeared flustered by my inquiry. "It's just that I can't imagine who could've wanted to harm him. I suppose it's just as likely I've never met the killer."

All the ladies nodded in agreement, but not a one of them looked moved by Jolene's tears. Nary a nurse offered her any solace. I had to wonder if Jolene had any clue how disliked she was among the clinic's staff. I chose not to break with the crowd and said nothing.

I chatted with the nurses for a few more minutes about insignificant subjects, such as why the president of the board of director's wife, who always seemed to stand two feet behind him, didn't have the unsightly mole on her chin removed.

"Five minutes in a dermatologist's office would be all it'd take to be rid of it," Charmaine remarked. "When I spoke to her earlier, I could hardly concentrate on what she was saying because I couldn't take my eyes off that mole, which was quivering like leaves in an aspen grove as she talked."

I excused myself after Charmaine's mole remarks and headed outside to the truck. Even though I found the behavior of both Candace and Jolene unnerving, it was Eva's comment, which all of the nurses had agreed with, that kept going through my mind as I drove to Wal-Mart. *Blaze was the only logical choice to replace Marco as director.*

As I lifted a box of kitty litter into my basket that felt as if it weighed as much as I did, I thought, *If all of the nurses thought Dr. O'Ryan was the only logical choice, surely he felt that way as well. I recall the first time I met him he said he should have been rewarded that title in the first place, instead of Dr. Moretti, and he deserved to have it now that Dr. Moretti was deceased. That being said, the only way he could have been chosen to replace the former director was to first eliminate the current director, Dr. Moretti.*

I now felt as though it was no longer necessary for me to begin trying to check everything off the list of tasks I'd made earlier that morning. I felt confident I knew who had killed Dr. Moretti, and why!

EIGHTEEN

For breakfast the next morning, I made Rip a plate of poached eggs and toast. It was a rare treat for Rip, something he'd always loved, and something I have always thought looked too repulsive to fork into my mouth. I focused on my bowl of cereal and tried not to look at my husband to keep my nausea at bay while he ate the runny eggs.

I'd been awakened by the sound of an owl hooting from the limb of a pine tree that hung over the trailer. I'd gotten up, turned on the coffee maker, and went outside to sit under the awning while enjoying a cup of bold Columbian brew since the mild weather had continued. I wanted to enjoy the warmth while I could. The forecast was for the temperature to be more seasonably cool the next few days with a slight chance of snow that evening. Not being big fans of snow is one of the main reasons Rip and I had spent most of our lives in south Texas. I hadn't wanted to wake up Rip, so I'd put a robe on over my night shirt before slipping out the door.

I heard the owl again, which now seemed to have flown to another tree at the far end of the RV park. I'd always loved the sound of nature, everything from the soothing sound of a rippling stream to the awe-inspiring call of a trumpeter swan, which we'd heard numerous times while visiting Billy and Bryce, who lived on one of the thousands of lakes that Minnesota is known for. When I inhaled deeply, I could smell the pine trees that dotted the campground. The scent brought to mind Maggie's Scentsy party.

Thinking back to my conversation with Olivia O'Ryan at that party, I recalled her mentioning she got her nails done every Thursday morning around nine. I scrutinized my own nails and realized they were in desperate need of a manicure and gel polish. Today was Thursday. I decided I would be getting my nails done at the mall this morning too. It would be a good opportunity to chat with the pregnant woman about her husband.

I entered the south end of Apache Mall on US Highway 54 and began walking down the center aisle that divided the stores on either side. I came to a nail salon called Coco Nail Designs right next to Macy's. It was nine-fifteen. I glanced around and didn't see Olivia either at a nail station or in the waiting area. I turned to exit the shop when a manicurist called out, "Ma'am, what would you like to have done this morning? We're offering a great deal called the *Coco-Loco Special* on a mani-pedi combo. Today only, it's just fifty dollars for the full meal deal."

"Oh, yeah?" *Wow!* I thought. *That really was a great deal!*

"We can get to you in about fifteen minutes if you don't mind waiting."

I'd have liked to take advantage of the *Coco-Loco Special,* but getting my nails done was not my prime objective that morning. Olivia apparently wasn't getting her nails done that day and I didn't feel like wasting a lot of time at the mall if I couldn't speak to her while getting mine done. *Unless*, I thought, *she had an appointment at a different salon.*

"Oh, nuts!" I said. "I wish I could wait that long but I have a dental appointment I need to get to in an hour. By chance, is there another nail salon in this mall?"

"Yes, but their wait is usually longer than ours." The manicurist sounded as if I'd offended her. "The Avia Nail Care Salon is at the far north end of the mall next to the food court if you want to give it a shot."

"Thank you, dear."

I stepped out of the shop and took approximately six steps when I looked up and saw a frazzled-looking Olivia racing toward me. Her hair was mussed up as though she'd had to walk through a wind tunnel on her way to the mall and her second and fourth buttons were unfastened. She'd clearly dressed in a hurry when she realized she was running behind schedule. She slowed down briefly as she passed me. "Oh, hello, Rapella. I'm late for my appointment or I'd stop and chat."

I nodded, then turned around and followed her back into Coco Nail Designs. The Vietnamese manicurist I'd just accidentally insulted gave me an odd look, and asked, "You again?"

"Yes, I'm sorry, ma'am. I decided to heck with my dental appointment." I remembered Olivia saying she got a manicure every Thursday, not a mani-pedi. When you ask for both at a nail salon, they usually work on your toenails first so they can completely dry while you're getting your fingernails done. I needed to be next to Olivia to chat with her. Upon entering the salon, Olivia had headed straight back to the station manned by a tall brunette. A blonde manicurist at the station next to the brunette's was just putting a final coat of topcoat polish on her customer's nails. After seeing this, I resumed speaking to the Vietnamese lady.

"As good a deal as your *Coco Loco Special* is, I only have time for a manicure today. I decided if I still don't make it to my dental appointment on time, my abscessed molar can wait for another day. After all, it only hurts when I chew."

"No problem," she replied. The petite woman looked as though it *was* a problem, but I ignored her look of skepticism. "Have a seat and we'll get to you as soon as we can."

"Thank you. Could I please have my nails done by the blonde in the far corner? She always does a remarkable job." The blonde was the only manicurist in the salon who wasn't Asian. I hoped my request didn't make me look as though I was bigoted, because that was far from the truth. I knew my request might offend the manicurist again, but I had to take that risk. I'd never met the blonde nail technician in my life, but if I wasn't seated right next to Olivia it would be difficult to converse with her.

"Oh, you want Sarah?" she asked.

"Yes. She knows my nails better than anyone." The manicurist, who wore a nametag that read "Coco Ho", indicating she was the owner of the salon, gazed at me silently as if trying to determine if I was joking or not. Nails were not exactly like hair, where it truly was beneficial if the hair stylist was familiar with your hair and how you like it cut, colored, and/or styled. I was certain Coco was thinking I was *Cuckoo for Cocoa Puffs* as she nodded and turned back to the lady whose nails she was clipping.

Luckily it only took five minutes for the blonde to finish up with the customer she'd been working on. Coco Ho walked up and whispered to her. Both ladies turned to stare at me. I noticed Sarah shake her head, and then both of them shrug. Finally, Sarah waved me back to her station.

"What a nice coincidence we'd both have our nails done here today," I said to Olivia as I passed the brunette's station. Ironically, Olivia was the woman who'd told me she didn't believe in coincidences.

"Uh-huh." Olivia didn't appear to be as delighted to see me as I was to see her. It was obvious this was another so-called coincidence she didn't believe in. Before I could dwell on that thought, Sarah motioned for me to have a seat in her swiveling chair.

"Good morning, ma'am," I said. "I'm sorry I got you mixed up with another blonde nail technician who usually does my nails. I just realized it was at the Avia Nail Designs salon, where I usually go."

"Would you prefer to go to your regular manicurist, ma'am?" Sarah sounded patronizing, as if she'd suddenly realized she was dealing with an older woman with an age-related cognitive deficiency.

"Oh, no, dear," I replied. "I'm sure you'll do an adequate job."

"All right," she said in an amused tone. "I'll do my best to do an 'adequate' job. What color did you pick out?"

Nail polish color had never even crossed my mind. I pointed to Olivia and said, "I'd like the same color my friend is getting."

As Sarah began to trim and buff my fingernails, I turned my attention to Olivia. "I'm afraid I didn't get the chance to congratulate you on your husband's promotion. I'm sure you are both delighted."

"Thank you. Kelly is thrilled with the way it all worked out."

"How do you feel about it?" I'd picked up on the fact she'd only mentioned her husband was thrilled about his promotion to the director position.

"I'm happy that Kelly is pleased with the turn of events. I'm not that thrilled about him teaching at Mayo on his days off, however."

"I understand completely." I recalled her concern about how little time he spent with their twin daughters, and there'd soon be a third child to care for. Spending his spare time teaching at Mayo would leave the majority of the child-rearing to Olivia. "You'll need a hand with your three young ones."

"Yes," Olivia said. "The higher salary that comes with the

director's position is always welcome though. I may have to hire a nanny."

"Good thinking. And who turns their nose down at extra money?"

Olivia smiled but didn't respond. I wouldn't let her hesitancy to converse with me deter me, however. Instead, I plowed ahead.

"I'm happy Dr. O'Ryan is pleased with his new position. I'm sure the fact he only got the promotion because of the murder of his colleague has got to bother him, though." I was going out on a limb, hoping to spur a telling remark from the new director's wife.

"Of course. I'm sure it does." Olivia sounded dubious, as if she hadn't really witnessed any signs of grief from her husband and was as disturbed as I'd been by his cold-heartedness. His lack of emotion was disconcerting to me. As his wife, it surely had to be distressing to her, as well.

I was already out on a limb, so decided to go out on it even further. "I can't imagine where Dr. Moretti's killer was able to obtain something like VX nerve agent. Can you?"

"No, I can't." Olivia made a comment to her nail technician that I couldn't hear before turning back to me. "I wondered the same thing. It's just crazy to think someone would kill a surgeon as gifted as Marco with a chemical weapon like a nerve agent. And it's pretty scary too!"

"I agree it's crazy. But why do you think it's scary?"

"Because if someone wanted Marco dead, how can we be sure he won't come after other surgeons at the clinic? They haven't caught the killer yet, and the homicide department seems totally inept to me. They've made no progress so far, and seemingly very little effort to determine who was responsible for Marco's death. For instance, they seemed to have completely given up on determining who left that incriminating note in his casket. Clearly, it was his killer."

Clearly, it was his killer. Her simple statement echoed over and over in my mind. It truly did seem clear that Candace, the author of the message, was the killer. Was it wishful thinking that had me looking for someone besides her as the perpetrator of Dr. Moretti's murder? Olivia's next comment brought me out of my reverie.

"Like I said, someone may be targeting the entire clinic. Are Doctors Jifi and Marr in danger? What if Kelly is next on their hit list, especially now that *he's* the director of the cath lab? I can't fathom the thought of raising three young children entirely on my own."

"I guess you're right, Olivia. I hadn't thought of that." I responded truthfully. I really hadn't thought of that possibility. Even though I'd dismissed that theory initially, there actually *could* be someone out there that was angry with the clinic itself. Perhaps a loved one had died during or after a cardiac procedure and the killer held the cath lab, and its entire staff, responsible. In retaliation, the responsible party might have been compelled to exact revenge by murdering the surgeon who'd performed the surgery. But what if the killer's motive for revenge involved more than just one particular surgeon? *If that's the case, could other staff members be on the killer's radar, as well?* I asked myself. *Was Olivia on to something the Rochester Police Department should be looking into?*

"I'm almost regretting Kelly took the offer to take over Marco's position at the clinic," Olivia said. "I made him promise he wouldn't eat or drink anything at the lab that he didn't bring from home or purchase himself."

"Good thinking, Olivia. They all need to keep an eye out and be aware of their surroundings. Like you suggested, there could be a killer on the loose who has an ax to grind with the STAT Clinic, rather than just Dr. Moretti alone. Have you spoken to the homicide detectives about this theory?"

"No, I never mentioned it. I got the impression they didn't trust the medical examiner's autopsy report on Marco because the nerve agent that showed up in the tox screen is next to impossible to find.

I recall that an act by Congress years ago required the disposal of all of the country's chemical warfare substances."

"That *is* odd," I replied. Olivia had undoubtedly Googled the chemical after hearing Dr. Moretti's tox screen results. I planned to do the same thing when I got home. "But how often are tox screen findings incorrect?"

"I have no idea. It's not something that I'd ever thought about until Marco died." Olivia wiped a tear that had escaped. "I'm just praying Kelly and the rest of the staff at the clinic aren't in danger."

The thought that Olivia could be on to something discouraged me. The pool of suspects could've just grown expeditiously and I didn't relish the idea of trying to determine who all had been treated at the clinic in the recent past. There had to be a number of patients in the clinic's history whose procedures had not gone as well as expected. Cardiac surgeries were inherently risky. *How could I obtain a list of patients who had walked into the clinic under their own power and exited it in a body bag?* I wondered. HIPAA laws would likely prevent me from ever finding out what patients, or their families, might have a reason to want the cardiac surgeon dead.

As Sarah worked away on my nails, I was totally focused on my conversation with Olivia which had morphed into small talk. We discussed her two toddlers, and the fact the baby in her womb was making her have to pee every twenty minutes. I laughed when she said, "I have to go so bad right now I feel like my bladder might explode."

"Like a propane tank in a trailer fire?" I asked.

"Yikes!" Olivia gasped. "Yes, I guess so."

I didn't tell Olivia Rip and I lived in a trailer 24/7 and the nightmare of the Caboose catching on fire while we were asleep was never far from my mind.

As we were discussing her latest sonogram, I took notice of Olivia's nails which were nearly finished. I'm pretty sure my heart skipped a beat as my head spun around like an eagle who'd just heard a fish jump out of the water. As I'd requested, my nails were the exact same shade as Olivia's. They were hot pink and sparkled as though diamond dust had been mixed in with the gel polish. The tip of each nail was highlighted in fluorescent purple. Rip would be surprised by my thinking outside the box and getting something besides the pale pink polish I normally wore on my fingernails. *Maybe this color scheme will make me look more youthful and daring*, I thought, trying to think on the positive side. *Or, more likely, I'd be seen as eccentric, delusional, and slightly colorblind.*

The only thing more shocking than the color Sarah had painted my nails was the bill. It was then I realized just how great of a deal the fifty-dollar *Coco Loco Special* was. When not part of a combo deal, the manicure by itself was forty-five dollars. I was tempted to rip my shoes off and demand a pedicure for an additional five bucks. But I had other things I needed to get done. For instance, I had to go straight home and scrub my nails with acetone nail polish remover.

"Why would you not pick out the color yourself?" Rip asked when he noticed my fingernails shortly after I returned to the Caboose. "Your nails look horrendous."

"I know." I decided honesty was justified in this situation. "Olivia just happened to be sitting at the nail station next to me, and——"

"Who?" Rip asked, interrupting me.

"Olivia O'Ryan, the red-headed heart surgeon's wife."

Rip raised his eyebrows but didn't ask how I knew Olivia and was able to recognize her at the nail salon. "Okay. Go on."

"I hadn't been able to make up my mind what color to get so I told the nail technician to give me the same color Olivia was getting at the station beside us. I had no idea she would get such an outlandish base color and then outline it in an even more bizarre shade."

"Could you not have stopped the manicurist as soon as she began to paint one of your nails?"

"Well, yes," I began, "but I'd have had to be paying attention to do that."

Rip just shook his head. "I'm going to run into town to run the truck through a carwash."

"All right," I replied. "I'll be here removing the nail polish from my nails."

Rip shook his head again and walked out the door.

After the polish had been completely removed from my nails, I sat down at the kitchen table and Googled VX nerve agent. The information I found was enough to convince me it was time to bring Rip back into the investigation. By the time I was done, I was certain I now knew who had murdered Dr. Moretti. It seemed so clear cut, I felt it was time to take the evidence I'd managed to garner to the Rochester Police Department.

Nerve agents in general, I learned from researching the term on the internet, were liquid at room temperature and could mix with water and other solvents. VX nerve agent, specifically, is both odorless and tasteless, and as Rip had also said, was one of the most toxic of the known chemical warfare agents. As little as one drop on the skin can be fatal. Exposure to the chemical can cause death within minutes. The more I read, the scarier I thought the chemical to be.

And as Olivia had mentioned earlier, on January 13, 1993, a treaty known as the United Nations International Chemical Weapons Convention Treaty was signed and the United States agreed to destroy its stockpile of aging chemical weapons, including VX nerve agent. The treaty was ratified and went into effect in 1997.

In one online article, I discovered the Department of Defense stored chemical warfare agents, either in bulk containers or as assembled munitions, at eight locations in the continental United States. One of those eight sites was the Newport Chemical Depot, or NECD, which opened in 1941 in Newport, Indiana, as the Wabash River Ordinance Works. The depot stored only one warfare chemical agent——VX nerve agent——and was designed specifically for the purpose of storing the highly toxic chemical. Destruction of the nerve agent began in May of 2005 and was completed in August of 2008. The NECD facility officially closed in 2010.

Dr. O'Ryan did his medical training at Indiana University School of Medicine in Terre Haute, Indiana. Newport was no more than half an hour from Terre Haute. *Was this a coincidence?* I asked myself. Like his wife, I didn't always believe in coincidences, particularly ones this striking. I wasn't sure how the physician could've acquired something as poisonous as the nerve agent. It *had* to be stored away so strategically that even acquiring a drop of the chemical would've taken an act of God. But somehow, act of God, or not, my gut told me Dr. O'Ryan had done exactly that. And he'd stored it away until the day he used it to kill Dr. Moretti so he could finally land the position he felt had been his destiny all along.

It occurred to me that Dr. O'Ryan would've had to have a great deal of knowledge about the chemical to be able to handle the sample without poisoning himself with it. A mere drop of the nerve agent on your skin could paralyze or kill you. *How had he obtained that much knowledge of VX nerve agent?* I wondered.

After recording all of the information I had obtained via the internet, I decided I was going to bring it up while Rip and I enjoyed our daily cocktails at three o'clock that afternoon. I was sure my husband would agree we should take the information to the local police department.

At three o'clock I mixed a Crown and Coke for Rip and a tequila sunrise for me. I grabbed my notebook, as well, and headed outside. Moments after Rip and I had settled into our lawn chairs to imbibe in our drinks, my phone rang. I ignored it at first because I figured it was a scam artist wanting to sell me an extended warranty on a car I'd totaled ten years prior. After the fifth ring, I glanced at it and saw that it was Maggie calling. I quickly answered it before she could hang up.

"Maggie?" I asked. "Are you okay?"

"Yes, I'm fine," she said. "But you won't believe what has happened."

I could sense shock and disbelief in her tone, which alarmed me. "Oh, no! I'm almost afraid to ask what happened. You sound like you're hyperventilating."

"I probably am," she replied. "Blaze O'Ryan was found dead in the doctors' break room about an hour ago. He didn't show up in the operating room for a stent placement procedure he was scheduled to perform at one-thirty. And, ironically, it was to be his very last patient on his very last day at the clinic."

"Oh. My. God."

My response got Rip's attention. He asked, "What is it, Rapella? What's wrong?"

I turned to him and said, "Dr. O'Ryan was just found dead at the clinic, on his final day of work there, and just before his very last procedure."

I then turned my attention back to the phone. "Maggie, what happened to him?"

"No one knows yet. Eva Clemens got concerned when Blaze

was 30 minutes late to surgery and went to look for him. She found him in the doctors' break room. Eva called 911 and began chest compressions on Blaze. But, of course, by then it was too late."

"Oh my goodness, Maggie," I said, finding it hard to put my thoughts into words. "I think Olivia must've been right."

"Right about what?" Maggie asked at the same time as Rip. I had switched the phone to speaker mode so Rip could listen to both sides of the conversation.

"While we were both getting our nails done this morning, she expressed being concerned about her husband and the rest of the staff at the cath lab."

"Why was she concerned?" Maggie asked. "Talk about an ominous premonition."

"I know, right? She told me she was worried about the rest of the clinic's staff being potential targets of the individual who killed Dr. Moretti. She thought the killer could possibly be someone who felt they'd been victimized in some way by the STAT Clinic and have his or her sights set on killing every staff member involved."

"That thought had never even occurred to me," Maggie said. "I could be in danger too, couldn't I?"

"Well," I began, looking at Rip, who merely shrugged. "I suppose it's possible. I'd certainly be careful, if not take a leave of absence until after the killer is behind bars."

"Did Olivia discuss this theory with the detectives?" Maggie asked.

"She told me she never mentioned it to them." I had considered the idea but had come to the conclusion it was an unlikely scenario. Apparently, for the umpteenth time in my life, I'd been wrong. "Can you think of any specific patients who might've felt compelled to exact revenge on both Dr. Moretti and Dr. O'Ryan?"

"I can think of a few whose outcome wasn't as positive as they might've liked, but only one who actually died on the table during surgery. He was a fifty-one-year-old construction worker and his family had been incensed. It was a fluke thing, and surely not the fault of Dr. Moretti and his operating team. But I suppose the man's family, or at least one member of his kin, might've felt differently."

"What happened during surgery that would cause the patient to die?"

"An undiagnosed thoracic aortic aneurysm burst when they cut him open. It was obscured by a rib on the scans they'd performed prior to surgery."

"I can understand where a loved one of the patient might be upset at the clinic for missing the aneurysm even though I wouldn't hold the surgeon responsible for the patient's death. Perhaps you should report that patient's name to the homicide department," I advised.

"Yes," she began, "I guess I should. I will call them now. Oh, and there was another patient a few months ago that died in the recovery room an hour after having a pacemaker implanted. But that man's death was due to a rare thromboembolism and was of no fault of Dr. Moretti's or Dr. O'Ryan's either."

"That's a blood clot if I'm not mistaken," I said.

"Yeah."

I swallowed hard but remained silent. A couple of thoughts were coursing through my mind after I'd ended the call with Maggie. The first one was that my belief Dr. O'Ryan was the individual who had killed Dr. Moretti in order to be promoted to his position as Director of Cardiology at the clinic had just been blown out of the water. The second thought was that I now knew without a single doubt who had really killed Dr. Marco Moretti. It was someone I would've never thought could even kill a fly that'd been buzzing around their head for ten minutes.

But I shouldn't have been surprised. *How often*, I thought, *did it turn out to be the person I least expected?*

NINETEEN

After speaking with Rip about my suspicions, he agreed we should take the information to the Rochester police station. But before we did, I wanted to have a conversation with the killer to make sure I wouldn't end up looking like a moron like I'd done more than once in the past. I never wanted to accuse someone of murder again, only to find out there was more to the story than met the eye. This suspect had enough issues to contend with right now, and a false accusation could send her completely over the edge. I had to be dead sure before I contacted the police. Again, I apologize for the unintentional pun.

I told Rip I was going to run to the store to pick up a couple of items I needed to make dessert for that evening and then we'd go to the police station as soon as I returned.

"Why don't I drive you to the store and then we can go directly to the police station from there?" he asked.

"Well, we could do that, but..." I paused as I tried to think of a reason that wouldn't work. I finally finished the sentence. "One of the items will melt if I don't get it home to put in the freezer right away."

"That's no problem," Rip replied. "We'll go to the station and stop at the store on the way home."

"That won't work either," I said.

"Why not?"

"Because the second item needs to be cooking in the oven while we're gone, which it can be doing while we're at the police station." Knowing he was going to question me about these two items, I had to think fast.

"What two things do you need to pick up?" Rip had a puzzled expression.

"I was going to surprise you." I quickly thought about what I already had in my freezer in the house, as I wouldn't have time to actually stop at the grocery store, and Rip was unlikely to check it out while I was gone. "I wanted to make a dessert that wouldn't be too unhealthy for you. I need to get some sugar-free vanilla ice cream to put on a low-sugar peach pie. I don't want the ice cream to melt, but I *do* want the pie to get done in time. I can only find the low-sugar peach pies in the freezer section."

"The dessert is sounding less and less appealing to me with each word that comes out of your mouth," Rip said.

"It'll be no different than the sugar-free syrup which you thought was tasty enough. You wouldn't even have been able to tell the dessert is nearly sugar-free if I hadn't told you."

"Well, all right," he said. "We'll go to the police department after you get back from the store."

After texting Maggie at the clinic to get the address, I asked my phone to take me to 1216 Champions Drive. I figured the chances were high the killer wouldn't be home, but felt it was worth the try. I was surprised when Olivia O'Ryan answered the door after the first knock.

"Oh," she said, clearly startled to find me on her doorstep. "I thought you were the police."

"The police?" I asked. "Why were you expecting them? Are they coming to arrest you?"

"Of course not," she declared. Her eyes were red and puffy as though she'd been sobbing. And I had no doubt she *had* been crying as part of her performance as the grieving widow. "My husband was viciously killed this afternoon at the clinic. I just know it's the same person who killed Marco Moretti, as Kelly drank from a water bottle that had the same toxic nerve agent in it."

"I know it's the same person who killed both surgeons, as well," I said.

As though I hadn't even spoken, Olivia continued. "The Chief of Police came by an hour ago to notify me of my husband's death and said the homicide detectives would be by later on to discuss it further."

"I wouldn't be surprised. I'm sure they'll want to apprehend and question his killer."

"His what?" she asked, aghast at my remark.

"You heard me," I said. "I said they'll want to take your husband's killer into custody and interrogate her. It's interesting how you knew your husband's death was due to drinking water spiked with the nerve agent. I was told his COD had yet to be determined."

"It was just an assumption on my part."

"Of course it was." The sarcasm in my voice was obvious. By her livid expression, I could tell it had rubbed Olivia the wrong way. "Now I understand why you told your husband to only drink out of bottles he brought from home at the clinic, He might still be alive if he'd done just the opposite."

"How dare you!" Olivia was livid. "How could you say such a thing? You know as well as I do the murders of these two prominent heart surgeons were committed by an angry former patient, or someone close to them. My husband's murder is proof of that theory. I can't believe you could accuse a grieving wife of murdering her own husband, a widow who's pregnant with the victim's child, no less."

"I have a feeling it's *because* the 'grieving' wife is pregnant that she felt the need to kill her husband," I replied. When she only stared at me in disbelief, I continued. "For a moment, I thought there might be something to your theory. I even briefly suspected a volunteer at the clinic named Henrietta Stringer, whose husband Stanley died from a blood clot that formed shortly after his pacemaker surgery. But then I realized it was ludicrous to think that such a kind woman would go on a killing spree after her husband of nearly fifty years died of a rare post-surgery complication. In fact, it was absurd to think of anyone doing something that radical unless there was another motivating factor at play. At that point, I put two and two together and came up with you, Olivia."

"And how did you come up with such a crazy idea like that?" She was holding on to her swollen belly with both hands as if it was a basketball and she was standing on the free throw line ready to attempt a basket. I prayed the overwhelming stress Olivia was undoubtedly experiencing didn't cause her to go into premature labor. I was in no mood to try my hand at delivering the monster's baby, as sweet and innocent as the newborn boy would surely be. To keep Olivia's mind off potential Braxton Hicks contractions, I kept talking.

"It occurred to me there was a reason you were trying to promote the idea with me that a disgruntled former patient, or the loved one of the patient, was carrying out a vendetta against the clinic. You figured out I was digging into what, and who, was behind Dr. Moretti's death. Hoping I'd run your theory past the homicide detectives, you first killed Dr. Moretti, who sadly was just collateral damage in this scheme of yours. That way when your husband was killed, it'd look like your theory had been right all along."

"And just where could a person like me even come up with VX nerve agent to use as a weapon in this so-called killing spree you're accusing me of committing?" Olivia now wore a smug expression. I was anxious to wipe it off her face.

"I recall you telling me you worked at a storage facility," I explained. "You let me believe it was the kind of facility where people rented units to store junk they couldn't fit in their basement or garage. Your husband told me you were in upper management. I've never heard of someone having a job with that kind of status at the sort of storage facility I'd imagined at the Scentsy party where I spoke with you about your former job. Nor could I believe employment at a typical storage facility could be as stressful as you'd indicated. But, at a storage facility such as the Newport Chemical Depot in Newport, Indiana, there could definitely be upper management positions with a ton of anxiety built right into the job description. I also thought it odd you knew so much about the act by Congress to dispose of all of the chemical warfare agents."

Olivia remained silent, glaring at me while she rubbed her extended belly. Still standing on her front porch, I continued to talk. I was surprised she hadn't slammed the door in my face. I was ready to thrust my foot in the door jamb should that idea occur to her.

"Dr. O'Ryan also told me you lived about thirty minutes away from Terre Haute, exactly the distance between the university he was attending and Newport. I realize now why you wanted him to be offered the director position at the cath lab. I'd be willing to bet it was after he was offered a position at the Mayo Clinic that you developed the scheme to kill the two surgeons. You seemed pleased he'd been offered the director's position at the STAT Clinic, but disturbed by his desire to still teach at the Mayo Clinic. I don't know why you didn't want him to return to Mayo and I don't particularly care. But I do believe you should turn yourself in at the police station rather than wait for the police officers to come haul you away in handcuffs in front of all of your neighbors. I can just imagine the scuttlebutt that will arise when folks in this ritzy neighborhood witness you being cuffed and scuffed right here in front of your high-falutin' mansion."

"Listen, Rapella," she finally said. "Come inside for a moment. I want to show you something. Have a seat on the couch while I go get something I think will change your mind." I complied, hoping desperately she really would have proof it couldn't have been her. I wanted Olivia to be able to change my mind about her killing her husband. I really, really did. I walked into her house with the naivety of a newborn zebra in the Serengeti National Park, having no idea I was about to become prey to a predator.

I waited on the couch while Olivia went to retrieve whatever it was she wanted to show me. I knew it was one of the worst decisions I'd ever made when she came back into the living room a couple of minutes later and turned the dial on three different locks on the front door. She held a small vial in her hand. It became clear at that point it wasn't my suspicion that she was the killer she wanted to change; it was my ability to go to the police station with my story.

"See this vial?" she asked with a distinct sneer. "I took it from the Newport facility back then because I was so fascinated by its power to destroy. Just holding this vial makes me feel invincible. It contains a very small amount of the toxic chemical I killed both Marco and Kelly with. And, trust me, there's enough left here to take you out with, as well. I happened across this vial in 2008 while we were in the process of destroying the entire supply of the warfare chemical at NECD, where I was in charge of the disposal of the VX nerve agent stored there."

"You seriously think I'm going to drink anything you hand me?"

"You don't have to drink it, Rapella," she replied with an evil grin. "Having your skin exposed to the chemical will work just fine."

"You don't want to do that, Olivia," I said, trying not to sound as panicky as I felt. "What will your twins think if they come into the room and see my dead body?"

"The twins are too young to be traumatized by something like that. They'd climb over your body to get to one of their toys without a moment's hesitation. Besides, they're staying at my sister's house for a few days while I handle the funeral arrangements for their daddy. Jill picked them up five minutes prior to your arrival." Olivia's tone was so cold she'd probably dropped the temperature in the room by at least ten degrees.

"I hope for the girls' and your unborn son's sake, Jill adopts all three of them after you are imprisoned for the rest of your life." I was angry now, knowing her three children would lose both of their parents in different but equally tragic ways. "You'd never get away with killing me too when the detectives already know you've killed both Dr. Moretti and your husband. My husband was going to call them while I was over here talking to you. They're probably on the way already."

"I don't believe you, Rapella," she said. "You're just a nosy old fool who should've minded her own business."

I was nosy, no doubt, and I was old, by some folks' accounts, but I was hardly a fool. To stall for time, I made up a story to tell my would-be assassin. "My mama didn't raise no fool, Olivia. Well, she did raise one, but it was my brother Bubba who joined the carnival at eighteen and tried to rob a liquor store with a very large knife a year later. He learned a valuable lesson that day when he was shot in the head with the store owner's tiny little 22-caliber handgun. Bubba's head wound eventually healed and he did some serious time in the slammer. Sadly, he now has a tendency to walk sideways like a crab and can't look at anyone with both eyes at the same time."

"Are you through jabbering?" Olivia was too astute to not realize I was stalling for time. "I could care less if your brother is loony tunes like his sister."

"Listen, Olivia," I replied. "Before you splash the toxin on me, or whatever you plan to do with it, please explain why you'd kill the father of your children right before your third child is born. Those precious kids needed both of you to grow up happy and healthy and turn out to be decent, law-abiding adults. Now they'll have neither. Not that their mother gives a hoot about being lawful."

I was still stalling for time. Why? I don't know. I guess I was praying a miracle would happen and save me from the same fate that had befallen the two cardiac surgeons. Fortunately, Olivia was anxious to tell her story. After all, what could it hurt to confess her sins to a soon-to-be dead audience?

"You are right about one thing," she said. "I didn't want him to go back to the Mayo Clinic."

"Why?" I asked, recalling her reaction when her husband declared he still planned to do some teaching at the Mayo Clinic, even though he was accepting the offer to be the new director at STAT. "Why would you not want him to go back to Mayo?"

"Because Kelly was apt to run into Michael there."

"Who's Michael?" I was curious but alarmed. Once a killer begins to spew all the details about their crime to you, your own life has been put on the clock. At that stage, it was only a matter of time before you were snuffed out like a campfire during a rainstorm.

"Michael DeWitt is a cafeteria worker at Mayo who I've been having an affair with for over a year. It would've been awkward for Michael seeing Kelly there and I'm afraid he would've made it apparent he and I were seeing each other. He's been begging me to divorce Kelly for some time now."

"Why didn't you?" I asked.

"Because I got pregnant. That's why!" She sounded annoyed. She glared at her belly as if it was the baby's fault. "I don't know who the father is, but I knew if it turns out to be Michael, it would be very obvious when the baby is born."

"Is that because the baby might not have red hair like his father?" I was confused.

"No," Olivia began, "even if Kelly is the father, the baby might not have red hair. It's because the baby could potentially have dark skin like Michael, who is black. I didn't want to have to explain the baby's skin color to Kelly in the delivery room."

"Yeah," I agreed. Olivia's story had taken a turn I hadn't expected. "I can totally understand how that'd be an uncomfortable conversation. But why kill your husband? And Dr. Moretti? Why not just file for divorce?"

"Money, of course." She looked at me as if trying to figure out how I could be as dense as a concrete post. "Once I figured out what I was going to do, I purchased a two-million-dollar life insurance policy on Kelly. I wanted to have enough money for Michael and me to run off to some Caribbean island and live out the rest of our lives in paradise, raising my twins and the baby. He's Jamaican, so that would be the logical place to buy some beachfront property and retire. If I divorced Kelly, there'd be no reason he wouldn't be granted joint custody of our children, and that wouldn't work out too well with Michael's and my plans."

"It sounds like you and Michael have it all figured out." The sarcasm in my voice was unmistakable.

"Do you think I'm stupid, Rapella?" Olivia asked. Before I could reply affirmatively, she added, "Michael knows nothing about who killed Kelly, or Dr. Moretti. I'm sure not giving him something to hold over my head if our future together doesn't pan out like I planned."

"Good thinking, Olivia," I replied dryly. "But you forgot one thing."

"What's that?" she asked.

"For your future to pan out the way you've planned, you first have to get away with murdering two heart surgeons and one nosy old lady who is anything but a fool, as you implied earlier. You don't think the detectives who'll be stopping by soon to speak to you will question you about the dead body in your living room? My husband knew I was coming here so they'll search this place from stem to stern until they find me."

"Kelly had a hidden safe room constructed in the basement when we had this house built a few years ago. It is so well-concealed; no one will ever find it. I can drag your body downstairs and stash it in there until after the detectives stop by to chat with me. Once I get rid of you, I'll be in like flint."

"It's Flynn, actually, and you're just kidding yourself if you think you'll get away with all three murders. All you'll have really accomplished is to make certain you'll receive the death penalty for killing three people."

"Capital punishment was abolished in Minnesota after a botched execution in 1906." Olivia looked pleased with being able to squash my attempt to make her afraid of getting the needle for killing me. To have looked that factoid up, I realized, Olivia must've had some reservations about executing her murderous scheme.

"How your punishment is carried out is irrelevant," I replied. "If I figured out who killed the two surgeons, don't you think the detectives would've eventually figured it out too? It's a moot point now, however, since my husband is leading them straight to your house."

"Then they better get here fast. Before I splash the nerve agent on you, I want to know more about how you figured out it was me." Olivia was clearly intrigued and curious to know what had given her away. It was as if she wanted to make certain she didn't make the same mistake if and when she killed her next victim.

"Like I said earlier, I remembered you telling me you worked in a storage facility. It wasn't until I realized that Newport, Indiana, was one of eight storage facilities for the VX nerve agent that I started to suspect you. Your husband told me you were in upper management. Being in charge of a facility that stores such a lethal chemical would have to be stressful. One thing I don't understand is why you had to kill Dr. Moretti if your main objective was to kill your husband and cash in on the insurance policy you bought on him."

"I didn't *have* to kill him," she replied. "But like you said, I needed it to look as though a killer with a grudge against the clinic was responsible for both murders. I had considered killing the anesthesiologist, Mitch Murphy, too, before I killed Kelly."

"Why didn't you?"

"I ran out of time. It occurred to me that since my twins were born prematurely, Mikey might come early too, and I couldn't afford to put Kelly's death off much longer. I really did care for my husband, Rapella. But I loved Michael and I couldn't live out my dreams with him as long as Kelly was alive. Don't you see?"

"Well, sure I do. And what jury wouldn't also understand that Dr. O'Ryan *had* to die so as not to screw up your dreams of an idyllic life on the beach with your boy toy?" I knew Olivia had now given me way too much information to let me live to pass it on to the authorities. "So you're telling me Dr. Murphy would've been dead too if you'd been able to carry out your original plan? You were prepared to wipe out three physicians at the clinic just to hide the fact you were having an affair?"

Olivia shrugged nonchalantly. "Yeah, I guess so."

"By referring to your unborn son as Mikey, it appears evident you're convinced Michael is the father of your baby."

"No, but I hope he is. The odds are in his favor, at least." I wished I'd had access to a sandblaster to use to wipe off the smile now plastered on her face.

"How did you have the time and opportunity to see this Michael guy?" I asked, although I really wanted to ask her if she didn't think a cafeteria worker was quite a step down from being married to a heart surgeon. I didn't want to anger her though. Nor did I want to sound as though I were prejudiced against blue-collar workers whose jobs were every bit as important as professional personnel. I guess if the unlikely pair planned to live out their lives on a beach in Jamaica, she wasn't particularly concerned about class and status anyway. And even when the woman was threatening to kill me, for some illogical reason, I didn't want to be rude or sound prejudiced.

I realized now Olivia was a sociopath. She would have no more regard for my life than she'd had for the two heart surgeons. I was in extreme danger. I could only stall her for so long before she made her move to eliminate me. Still stalling, I said, "You haven't explained how you were able to get away to spend time with Michael."

"My sister watches the girls for me on Tuesdays and Thursdays, the same days Michael has off at the cafeteria."

"You told me Jill had Thursdays off and watched the twins just long enough for you to get your nails done every week."

"I lied. Sue me. I only have my nails done once a month."

I don't know why it surprised me that she had lied to me. After all, I'd been lying to her too. Besides, sociopaths aren't usually of the trustworthy sort. Curious if her sister was complicit in Olivia's murderous scheme, I asked, "Did Jill know she was watching your kids so you could sneak around behind your husband's back? Is she aware you killed both surgeons?"

"Of course not," Olivia replied. "Jill is too goody-goody to understand. I told her I was taking a class at the Rochester Community and Technical College with the goal of becoming a dental hygienist. She agreed to watch the girls while I attended class twice a week."

"So she apparently bought your deception," I replied.

"Yes. She was aware RCTC offers a program in dentistry."

"You'd have thought Jill would know her own sister better."

"She had no reason to believe I would make something like that up."

"So you did your homework," I said. "How admirable of you."

"Thank you," Olivia said, as though my remark had been meant as a compliment. "This morning, after Kelly left for work with the lunch I'd made for him, along with the bottle of poisoned water, I stopped by Michael's apartment on the way to the mall. Our goodbye kiss turned into something more, if you know what I mean."

"I get it. And I don't need you to elaborate on it," I said. Olivia's admission explained her disheveled appearance when she'd arrived late to her nail appointment. "It's so nice to hear you haven't let two murders and your pregnancy affect your love life."

"I considered an abortion, but Michael has always wanted a child of his own. He's convinced the baby is his. At thirty-nine, I'm pushing the envelope when it comes to my reproductive years. I was afraid I'd never be able to conceive again." Olivia was being awfully chatty, and it'd given me time to think.

"I'm glad to hear you chose life over an abortion. Your debauchery was certainly not little Mikey's fault. Do you have a photo of Michael, by any chance?"

"Yes. I have one photo of him on my phone. Why?"

"I was just curious. My husband and I were at the Mayo Clinic the other day when he got a referral to STAT and I saw a handsome dark-skinned man in the cafeteria. I was wondering if that might have been Michael."

Olivia didn't take the bait. So I added more to the hook. "The man was sure chummy with a good-looking nurse who, like us, was eating her lunch in the cafeteria."

"Like how chummy?" Olivia asked. She was considering taking a bite of the bait. I needed to add just a tiny bit more of an incentive. Sociopath, or not, I knew she still had the capacity to experience jealousy.

"Well, they talked and laughed all through lunch and then he kissed her goodbye."

"They kissed? My phone is in the kitchen. I want you to tell me if Michael is the man you saw with the nurse." Olivia was so incensed she was nearly foaming at the mouth. She reminded me of a rabid raccoon my father once had to euthanize after he discovered it in our outdoor privy when I was about six. I felt a sense of relief wash over me when Olivia said, "You best not move. I'll be right back out before you could make it to the front door."

She was correct about that. It was a long living room and I'd never be able to sprint to the front door and unlock all three locks in time to escape her house. I knew she would grab the phone and be back so quickly I'd have only a split second to react. The moment she exited the room, I grabbed the solid wood chair I'd been sitting on, stepped behind the kitchen door, and raised the chair above my head. I had adrenalin coursing through my veins. It allowed me to hold the heavy chair over my head just long enough to incapacitate her without harming the baby she was carrying.

My scheme worked perfectly. Olivia reentered the living room in a matter of seconds. She never saw the chair coming down on her head and dropped to the floor like a bag of cracked corn. She had placed the vial of VX nerve agent in her front jeans pocket as she'd exited the room, so I'd had to roll the dice on it not busting open and killing all three of us within minutes. It seemed preferable to the sure death I'd have faced if I'd done nothing. Fortunately, luck was on my side and the vial remained intact. While she lay dazed on the floor, I carefully removed the potential murder weapon from her pocket.

Before I even had the chance to call 9-1-1, three cops used a battering ram to gain entrance through the O'Ryans' front door. Rip was behind them when they stormed the room. I pointed to Olivia, who was still lying on her back on the floor. She was awake but, thanks to a goose egg on her forehead and a swollen belly, she was unable to get to her feet.

A few minutes later the police officers had her cuffed and sitting upright. I briefly explained what she'd told me.

"You surely don't believe any of that nonsense, do you?" Olivia asked the detectives. Her phone lay beside her with a shattered screen. "I would never do anything like that, or tell Rapella I had. She's a crazy old woman, a total nut job."

I pulled my own phone out of my pocket. I had slid it in so that the microphone port was exposed and had taped the entire conversation. "I think this recording of your confession might prove differently. It'll show which one of us is a total nut job."

"You no-good bit——" The officers yanked Olivia to her feet before she could finish her remark. It was a gentle yank, to be sure, because none of the three officers wanted to harm the child inside their detainee. I breathed a sigh of relief and turned to speak to Rip while one of the officers was reciting the Miranda rights to Olivia. Something told me her right to remain silent would be ignored by Olivia.

"How did you know where to find me, Rip?"

"I opened up the freezer to get some ice and saw a frozen peach pie and a quart of sugar-free vanilla ice cream. I knew then you were engaged in something you hadn't wanted to tell me about." Rip was calm but clearly angry.

"I planned to tell you eventually, but I didn't want you to worry and I didn't think it would come to a life-and-death situation like it did."

"Exactly," Rip exclaimed. "You didn't think. You never seem to think about what might happen if you take it upon yourself to do the local police officers' job. It seems to me you've also established a habit of getting yourself into life-or-death situations every time you butt into a murder case. Are you trying to give me a fatal heart attack, or what?"

"No, honey, of course not," I said, feeling guilty for causing him such angst. "I'm so sorry. I truly didn't mean to worry you."

"Just promise me you'll tell me next time you set out to confront a potential killer so I can accompany you. Okay?" Rip said. "That's all I ask."

"I promise," I replied, vowing to keep that promise this time. I knew if Olivia wasn't a chatterbox with a jealous side, I could've been dead right now, having suffered the same fate as the two doctors. I knew it'd only take a drop of the nerve agent on my skin to kill me. Whether or not, in her current state of expecting a baby, she could've managed to drag my body to her basement to hide it in the safe room, we'll never know. I repeated my previous question to Rip. "So how'd you know where to find me?"

"I tried to call you but the phone went directly to voice mail."

"I had put my phone on airplane mode when I turned the video function of the camera on. It was filming the inside of my pocket but I had it situated in such a way it would pick up the audio good enough to implicate Olivia in the two murders. I just now turned it off and will forward the video to the homicide department." I then repeated myself one more time. "How'd you know where to find me?"

"You had jotted Maggie's phone number down on a post-it note. I called her to see if you were with her or had been at the cath lab once I realized you weren't really going to the grocery store. She told me you'd texted her earlier to get the O'Ryans' address. I got the address to their house from her and called the police, just in the event you were in some kind of jeopardy. By the time we arrived, you had eliminated the danger, but it could've turned out much differently."

"You're right," I said. "Again, I'm sorry. I promise to keep you in the loop if something like this ever happens again."

"I'm praying it doesn't," Rip responded. "We've been involved in far too many murder cases in the last few years. At this point in our lives, we don't need that kind of excitement. Capish?"

"Yes, capish. I agree." When Rip spoke in Italian, I knew he was serious.

"I love you, Rapella," Rip said, holding my hand as the police officers led Olivia to a squad car parked in her driveway. "Don't ever forget that."

"I won't. I love you more!"

TWENTY

O livia was charged with two counts of first-degree murder and booked into the county jail. As it turned out, during her interrogation, she told the detectives she had nothing to do with slashing the tire on our truck while we were at the cath lab for Rip's last follow-up appointment with her husband.

It was presumed that when I mentioned to Dr. O'Ryan at Rip's appointment that the tox screen results showed VX nerve agent had been used to kill Dr. Moretti, he'd suspected his wife had killed the surgeon on his behalf. He knew if anyone familiar with Dr. Moretti could've had access to the deadly chemical it was Olivia. To give him time to confront her before homicide detectives showed up at their front door, he stalled us by saying he needed to check something in his medical records, while actually rushing out to the parking lot to slash a tire on our vehicle. The fact the Chevy was the only vehicle with Texas tags in the parking lot, which contained a dozen cars at best, was clearly his clue that the truck belonged to us.

Further investigation showed the surgeon had canceled the rest of his schedule that day, pleading a severe headache, and had likely gone straight home to question his wife. Apparently, Olivia had denied any involvement in the surgeon's murder when confronted by her husband and Dr. O'Ryan had believed her. I'm sure that confrontation between the couple sealed the deal on his death the following morning.

We went to her husband, Kellan "Blaze" O'Ryan's, funeral services where everyone in attendance was in a state of shock and disbelief. The entire staff at STAT Clinic thanked me for my determination in seeing that justice was served on behalf of their two slain colleagues. Mitch Murphy was especially thankful for my interference. When he practically worshipped at my feet, Rip rolled his eyes, but he couldn't help looking a bit proud of his persevering wife. Or, at least, that's the way I chose to interpret his expression.

Olivia's son was born in jail where she was being held without bail while awaiting her murder trial. He was one month premature. "Mikey" had snow-white skin and red hair, just like his daddy, Blaze. After a short stay in the newborn intensive care unit, or NICU, he went to live with Olivia's sister Jill. Jill was as shocked as anyone at the actions of her sister. At Blaze's funeral, I overheard Jill tell Maggie she planned to adopt all three of Olivia's children and give them the best life she could afford.

Unfortunately, the two-million-dollar life insurance policy taken out on Dr. O'Ryan by Olivia had been rendered null and void when it was determined it was the policy's beneficiary who'd killed him. The portion of his estate that was inherited by his three children was helpful, but not enough to raise three youngsters for the rest of their childhood. This information was worrisome. I'd listened as Jill continued to converse with Maggie.

"The first thing I'll do once they're legally mine is change Mikey's name to Kellan O'Ryan Jr. It's the only thing I can do to honor the boy's father at this point," Jill said. I wanted to assure her that raising his three children was also a way to honor the late surgeon, but one doesn't make responses, even complimentary ones, when one is eavesdropping on the conversation in the first place. I overheard Jill then say, "My job at a bookstore barely supports me, much less three young kids."

Maggie later told me, "When I passed this information on to Eva, Charmaine, Monica, Jolene, and Candace, they said they would help me hold a couple of fundraisers and set up a GoFundMe account on Jill's behalf." With Maggie's assistance, Rip and I would utilize my iPad to donate $250 to this account a few days later.

Just as we were preparing to exit the Manfranz & Pine Funeral Home, the same facility where Dr. Moretti's services had been held, I spotted Terrence Smith, the president of the STAT Clinic's board of directors. I ran Jill's plight by him and he explained there was a position open for a receptionist at the clinic. The current receptionist was retiring at the end of the month and could spend her last two weeks of employment training Jill to take her position. The job paid twice what Jill had told me she was making at the bookstore and Terrence assured me he'd offer it to her before he left the funeral home.

On the way back to the campground, Rip and I discussed where we wanted to go next. I had never seen the giant sequoias in Calaveras Big Trees State Park, and Rip had always wanted to go to Las Vegas to try his luck at a craps table and take in a few of the shows on the infamous strip. We figured we could cross both locations off our bucket lists on our next excursion. We planned to head west as soon as our rent was up at the Autumn Woods RV Park. Our first stop would be Lazy Days RV Center in Denver, Colorado, where we'd look for a new fifth wheel. If we found one we liked in our preferred price range, we'd trade the Caboose in on it.

I had to laugh when Rip said, "I'm going to look for one of those models with a beautiful color design on the exterior so you won't feel compelled to paint it yourself."

When I spoke to Maggie Brown on the phone a month later from California, while basking in front of our new fifth wheel's gas fireplace, I asked her how things were going. She told me that Jill and her sister's three kids were getting along splendidly, despite the fact the twins still seemed to be struggling to come to grips with the loss of their mother, and their father at their mother's hands. But they were so young, Maggie had said, that they'd soon adapt. Jill was still debating on whether or not to take the girls to visit their mother in prison. She thought it might be easier on the toddlers if they weren't forced to visit the woman who murdered their father in cold blood. Maggie and I both agreed.

Maggie also told me Candace had been chosen as the operating room nurse for the surgeon who took Dr. Moretti's place and Jolene Sarcoxie had been relegated to the position Candace had vacated on the post-surgical floor. The demotion had humiliated Jolene to the point she'd resigned from the clinic and gone to work for a local dialysis center, much to the delight of Maggie and the rest of the nurses at STAT. I couldn't help but smile at the news. I was not surprised to hear Eva had decided to retire. Maggie said Eva now planned to move to Houston to live with her daughter Amy. I was happy for her.

With both Moretti and O'Ryan deceased, the board of directors had decided to promote the anesthesiologist, Mitch Murphy, as the new director of STAT Cardiac Clinic. "It's the first time an employee who wasn't a cardiologist had been picked for the prestigious position," Maggie said proudly.

"That's awesome," I replied. "How is your relationship with Mitch going?"

"As of two days ago, we are now engaged."

"That was fast. Are you sure you know each other well enough to make such an important commitment?"

"It became clear early on that Mitch and I are soulmates. I can't imagine spending the rest of my life with anyone else."

"Then I'm very pleased for you, sweetheart. I wish you both the best."

"Thanks, Rapella." Maggie was obviously over the moon about her recent engagement. "By the way, we hope to have a couple of children and Mitch wants me to be a stay-at-home mom, at least while the kids are young. We thought it'd be better if we didn't work together in the meantime, so next Monday's my last day at the clinic. Mitch thought that even though I'm already a good cook, I'd enjoy attending a local culinary arts school to hone my skills. I'm looking forward to beginning the course in three weeks."

"That should be a lot of fun for you." I thought back to her fiancé's comments about her atrocious cooking and had to refrain from laughing out loud. I was surprised by her next question.

"If I invite you and Rip to our June wedding, will you try to make it?"

"I can't promise, Maggie, but we will do our best to be there."

Rip and I were sitting in our lawn chairs under the fifth wheel's awning. We were watching the television mounted on the wall of the outdoor entertainment center and drinking our afternoon cock-tails when I told Rip about Maggie's invitation. He replied, "Maybe by then Billy and Bryce will be ready for us to visit for a few more days since we had to cut this last visit short."

I knew he was thinking about me when he made the remark, and I'd responded with a big hug. But I felt as though we'd spent enough time in Minnesota for the time being and told Rip so. There were so many other places on our personal bucket lists we wanted to visit while we were both healthy enough to do so. Rip's recent cardiac scare had made me realize we weren't getting any younger. The day may come when we'd be forced to stop galli-vanting across the country the way we'd been doing the past decade. The very idea was depressing so I changed the topic to the murder case that had consumed me in Rochester, Minnesota.

"I promise not to ever let something like that happen again, Rip, and I think you should promise me something just as impor-tant in return." I patted his arm as I spoke.

"And what might that be?"

"I want you to promise to make eating healthy a priority even if it isn't always what you'd prefer and to go on a walk with me every day, weather permitting. I'd like you to vow to do your best to make that the last time you have to have a cardiac procedure performed. It hurts *my* heart every time *yours* acts up, and I wouldn't be surprised if worrying about you doesn't take a few years off my own life."

"That's asking a lot, don't you think?" Rip asked with an ornery grin. "But I will agree to that deal. Like you just said, we have a lot of places we still want to see before we die, and I don't think either of us wants to visit them alone. We are better together. Always have been, always will be."

"I agree, with all of my heart."

Just then, Rip felt something touch his elbow and jumped to his feet in terror. I looked over to inspect his lawn chair, curious what had startled him so badly. I saw a walking stick inching its way along one of the aluminum armrests.

When Rip grabbed a large spatula off the grill to use as a weapon to thrash the threatening insect, I placed my hand over the harmless critter to protect it. "This walking stick can't hurt you, Rip. They aren't aggressive and they don't bite."

"I don't care," he grumbled. "It's freaky looking. I don't like bugs that pretend to be something they're not, like a twig off that mulberry bush behind our trailer."

"Oh, for goodness sake, Rip. I'll pick the poor thing up and move it over to the actual mulberry bush where it can't chew you up and spit you out like a wad of tobacco."

"Thank you," Rip said, too relieved to be embarrassed by his irrational fear of everything in the creepy, crawly department. "I love you, sweetheart."

His reaction to the harmless insect reminded me of how terrified he'd been of a garter snake when we'd first arrived in Rochester.

Laughing at my rough and tough husband, who was a former law enforcement officer, a veteran of the armed forces, and a first-class scaredy-cat, I replied, "I love you more, Grim Ripper."

RIP CHORD

A RIPPLE EFFECT COZY MYSTERY, BOOK 9

"Bringing in the sheaves, bringing in the sheaves.
  We will come rejoicing, bringing in the sheaves."

I listened to my husband, Clyde "Rip" Ripple's beautiful tenor tone as he sang along to the classic gospel hymn. We were sitting near the back of the sanctuary at the Pacific Light Church in Klamath, California. I was merely mouthing the words because the sound of me singing could make an owl purposely fly headfirst into a bridge abutment.

As full-time RVers for the last decade, we'd recently towed our brand new thirty-six-foot fifth-wheel trailer to the West Coast. Visiting the Redwood National Park had been on my bucket list for years. With no other plans in our immediate future, we'd decided to spend the entire spring in the Mystic Forest RV Park on Highway 101 in Klamath. The peaceful park, surrounded by gorgeous trees, was well-maintained, run by a delightful couple, and just a half mile from the historic Trees of Mystery nature attraction. It seemed the perfect place to spend the next three months enjoying the added space the longer trailer with three slide-outs provided. The thirty-foot travel trailer, affectionately nicknamed the Chartreuse Caboose, that we'd traveled in for nearly a decade had begun to feel cramped and outdated. We'd traded it off for the new, nicely-equipped fifth wheel in Denver, Colorado, on our way to California.

It was Easter Sunday and Rip and I had decided to attend services at Pacific Light, a nearby non-denominational church. It had been a good choice and we were both enjoying the sermon and hymns. I was no longer even pretending to be singing as I soaked in Rip's soothing voice as he sang along with the choir and most of the congregation.

"Sowing in the sunshine, sowing in the shadows
Fearing neither clouds nor winter's chilling breeze
By and by, the harvest, and the labor ended
We shall come rejoicing, bringing in the sheaves."

When the final chorus ended, a gentleman sitting in the row in front of us turned around and whispered softly. "Greetings, folks. I'm Charlie Short and this is my wife, Ferdinand, and our son, Jacob. Welcome to our fold here at Pacific Light."

"We're happy to be here," I responded. Short was an ironic last name for the couple because Charlie was so tall he nearly had to duck to enter the nave and his wife was so petite she was on eye level with her husband's navel. Jacob, who looked to be about ten or eleven, appeared to be of average height for a kid his age. "It's nice to meet you all. We are Rip and Rapella Ripple."

"It's nice to meet you two, as well," Charlie said. "My wife goes by Fern, by the way. We couldn't help admiring your lovely voice, Rip. The melodious nature of that last stanza you sang was music to my ears."

"Thank you," Rip said. By his expression, I could tell he wasn't sure what "melodious" meant but knew it was complimentary. "I sang in our church choir growing up and have always loved gospel music."

"I'm not surprised. I have a favor to ask of you. Will you meet us in the kitchen area when the services conclude? The Bible Study ladies always serve coffee and doughnuts afterward so we can all mingle and mix with the rest of the flock."

Rip looked mystified. He'd undoubtedly heard nothing after the word "doughnuts," and it had little to do with the fact that, as usual, he wasn't wearing his expensive hearing aids. I automatically replied to Charlie, "Of course."

"So you see, with Henry gone, we are in dire need of a fourth member of our group if we are to three-peat our championship in the upcoming Del Norte County Barbershop Quartet competition. Henry Hancock was a tenor with a very similar tone as yours," Charlie Short explained. "With the sudden loss of our tenor, it's going to be nearly impossible to win the competition for a third year in a row."

"When is this competition?" Rip asked, around a mouthful of chocolate long john. Doughnuts were not on the heart-healthy diet the STAT Cardiac Clinic in Rochester, Minnesota, had put him on following his recent coronary stent placement procedure. But I remained silent rather than chastise him in front of the Shorts. Rip had stated on more than one occasion that he'd rather be dead than be forced to give up every single pleasure in his life, so I decided one long john was not apt to kill him. I thought of the old adage, "death by a thousand cuts." In Rip's case, it would be more of a "death by a thousand doughnuts" kind of thing.

"The competition will be held on April fifteenth, which gives us almost exactly a month to prepare. We practice on Tuesday and Thursday evenings from seven to nine here in the church, where the acoustics are ideal. Occasionally, we practice at our house, when the church is unavailable."

"Well, I'm not sure if——"

"Listen," Charlie interrupted, sensing his reluctance, "I sing base, Buster sings soprano, and Stanley sings alto. With you singing tenor in place of Henry, Rip, the chords the four of us could create together would be magical. At least come to our practice this Tuesday to check it out before you make your decision. It will be held at our house because the Ladies Club meets at the church that night."

"Well, I don't know——"

"Rip!" This time I cut him off. As I spoke, I wiped a dusting of powdered sugar off Rip's upper lip. "Why not at least go to one practice before you turn down the opportunity? You love to sing and it's one of your greatest attributes. Besides, what have you got to lose?"

"I suppose it couldn't hurt me to give it a shot," Rip consented. Looking at Fern, he added, "Give Rapella your address and I'll be there at seven o'clock Tuesday night."

"Thank you." Charlie smiled and stuck his right hand out to shake Rip's. "I'm looking forward to harmonizing with you."

"What happened to Henry Hancock?" I asked. "Has he moved or fallen ill?"

"No," Charlie replied as Fern's eyes misted over. "He accidentally fell off the balcony of his thirteenth-floor apartment last Sunday. It was devastating to see such a healthy young man's life end so tragically. Especially immediately after Henry sang such a moving solo for the congregation at church: *I'll Fly Away* by Albert E. Brumley."

"I don't believe I've ever heard that song," I said.

Rip and I stood in silence as Charlie began to chant in a deep baritone voice.

I'll fly away, oh, Glory
I'll fly away
When I die, Hallelujah, by and by
I'll fly away."

As Charlie sang, I pictured a young man in his prime flying off of a thirteen-story balcony and wondered how one could topple over a balcony's railing accidentally. *Is it possible Mr. Hancock flung himself off the balcony intentionally?* I thought. *Or, worse yet, could someone else have been anxious for Henry to meet his maker?*

It was never a good omen when my thoughts drifted in that direction. I'd soon find out this time was no exception.

Available in Paperback and eBook from Your Favorite Bookstore or Online Retailer

ABOUT THE AUTHOR

Jeanne Glidewell lives with her husband, Bob, in the small coastal town of Rockport, Texas, on Salt Lake, just off Copano Bay.

Besides writing, Jeanne enjoys fishing, wildlife photography, and traveling both here and abroad. She and Bob visited Ireland in March 2022 with Jeanne's sister and brother-in-law, Sarah and Bruce Goodman. Among other things, they kissed the Blarney Stone, drank Guinness in Irish pubs, and marched in Killarney's annual parade on St. Patrick's Day.

As a 2006 pancreas and kidney transplant recipient, Jeanne is an avid advocate for organ and tissue donation. Please consider giving the gift of life by opting to be an organ donor should you no longer need them, and let your family know of your decision because marking "organ donor" on your driver's license is not enough to ensure your final wishes are met.

Jeanne is the author of a romance/suspense novel, Soul Survivor, seven novels and one novella in her NY Times best-selling Lexie Starr cozy mystery series, and seven novels in her Ripple Effect cozy mystery series. She's currently writing Ripple Effect book nine titled *Rip Chord* and expects to have it released in 2024.

www.JeanneGlidewell.com

www.ingramcontent.com/pod-product-compliance
Lightning Source LLC
Chambersburg PA
CBHW060344030726
47497CB00003B/596